D1602584

THE GUILD CODEX: DEMONIZED / ONE

TAMING DEMONS
FOR BEGINNERS

ANNETTE MARIE

dark owl
fantasy

Dark Owl Fantasy Inc.
PO Box 88106, Rabbit Hill Post Office
Edmonton, AB, Canada T6R 0M5
www.darkowlfantasy.com

Cover Copyright © 2019 by Annette Ahner
Cover and Book Interior by Midnight Whimsy Designs
www.midnightwhimsydesigns.com

Editing by Elizabeth Darkley
arrowheadediting.wordpress.com

ISBN 978-1-988153-36-0

BOOKS IN THE GUILD CODEX

DEMONIZED

Taming Demons for Beginners
Slaying Monsters for the Feeble

SPELLBOUND

Three Mages and a Margarita
Dark Arts and a Daiquiri
Two Witches and a Whiskey
Demon Magic and a Martini
The Alchemist and an Amaretto

MORE BOOKS BY ANNETTE MARIE

STEEL & STONE UNIVERSE

Steel & Stone Series

Chase the Dark

Bind the Soul

Yield the Night

Reap the Shadows

Unleash the Storm

Steel & Stone

Spell Weaver Trilogy

The Night Realm

The Shadow Weave

The Blood Curse

OTHER WORKS

Red Winter Trilogy

Red Winter

Dark Tempest

Immortal Fire

THE GUILD CODEX

CLASSES OF MAGIC

Spiritalis

Psychica

Arcana

Demonica

Elementaria

MYTHIC

A person with magical ability

MPD / MAGIPOL

The organization that regulates mythics and their activities

ROGUE

A mythic living in violation of MPD laws

TAMING DEMONS
FOR BEGINNERS

I

I **STARED** into the demon's obsidian eyes.

Wet blood cooled on my skin, but I felt no pain. Not yet. I was sure I would feel it before I died. Sprawled on my stomach, one arm pinned under me, I craned my neck to keep my gaze on the demon.

He crouched at the edge of the gleaming silver line set into the floor. That line had separated us since I'd first laid eyes on the summoning circle. It bound him to this realm—and protected the humans who had called him here.

The ethereal barrier rippled as he shifted closer, his black stare fixed on me.

Somewhere near my feet, the men who'd done this to me laughed. They *laughed*. If they'd been able to see the demon, bestial bloodlust rolling off him, they wouldn't have dared utter a sound. But swirling darkness filled the dome, and only I could see him.

A monster before me. Monsters of a different sort behind me. I had seconds to choose my executioner. One would probably kill me.

The other would definitely kill me.

My arm trembled as I slid my palm across the blood-splattered floor toward the silver line. The barrier shuddered more violently as the demon pressed against it. The jeering men fell silent.

My fingertips brushed the silver inlay.

Voices burst out in protest and footsteps thudded—the men scrambling toward me. Their hands grabbed my legs to tear me away.

I thrust my fingers through the barrier. The air shimmered but offered no resistance; it was an impenetrable wall only to the creature trapped within. My human flesh passed right through it, entering his space, his prison.

His gaze on mine didn't shift, didn't falter. His hand closed around my wrist, his skin cool and his grip like unforgiving steel.

The demon wrenched me into the circle.

2

Seventeen Days Earlier

LET'S GET ONE THING STRAIGHT: Magic is real. Cool, right?

Wrong.

Magic is trouble, turmoil, and life-threatening peril. Even when it's none of those things, it's still more hassle than it's worth. *Using* magic, I should say. All those fantastical sparks and glows and puffs of smoke come with never-ending inconveniences, but *studying* magic—that's different.

Magic has a way of attracting equal or greater mayhem, and my parents made it their lifelong mission to avoid all that nonsense. Stay away from magic, and it'll stay away from you. From early childhood straight through to my first year of college, I've strictly followed that policy. Until now.

Gripping the doorframe, I peered through a narrow gap into the room beyond. Sconce lights cast a soft yellow glow over the built-in bookshelves of the library, while the room's open center was split into three distinct areas.

On the right side, a dozen chairs hugged a long table stacked with leather-bound books and unmarred by a single speck of dust. On the room's left side, two leather sofas faced each other across a low coffee table, so polished its dark surface reflected the coffered ceiling and crystal chandelier above, while matching end tables supported Tiffany lamps. In the middle of the room, between the sofas and the table …

My fingers tightened on the jamb until my knuckles turned white.

Two men with their backs to me stood at a podium, an open book spilling over its edges. The shorter man slowly turned pages, his bald head gleaming in the dim light and his dress shirt stretching tight across a wide back pinched by the waist of his black slacks. The men murmured to each other, then the shorter one heaved the book shut. Turning, they started toward the door behind which I stood.

I froze like a mouse caught in the cat's shadow, panicking over which way to run.

"Time is money, Claude. How long do you expect us to wait?"

"As long as necessary. The creature will capitulate eventually, and if it doesn't, we'll try again."

Their voices were drawing closer. I broke out of my terrified trance and backpedaled down the hall on silent socked feet.

"We should try again *now*. The other one is ready. Let's clear that circle and—"

"Patience, Jack. Once we know what we have, this name could be worth—"

The library door swung open and Claude broke off, eyebrows rising at the sight of me. Pretending I'd just descended the stairs, I paused as though surprised to see them.

"Oh," I said breathily. My heart jammed itself between two of my ribs. "Uncle Jack, I didn't know you—"

"What are you doing?" His wide jaw tightened, his short, bristling white beard contrasting with his tanned bald head. "You aren't allowed down here."

I shrank back, my gaze fixed on the hardwood floor. How was I supposed to know that? It would've been nice if someone had mentioned it. *By the way, Robin, please stay out of the basement. We'd hate to implicate you in any crimes.*

After a second's thought, I revised my mental script. No one in this house would say "please" to me.

Uncle Jack murmured something to Claude, who chuckled dryly and replied, "I'll leave you to it, then."

As he walked past me toward the stairs, he offered a surprisingly kind smile. A thin white scar ran up his chin to his mouth, creating an odd pucker in his lower lip. With his tall, broad-shouldered frame and penchant for plaid-patterned tweed jackets, he blended the scholarly air of a college professor with the weathered fitness of a retired athlete.

"Robin." Uncle Jack's voice cracked like a riding crop. "Come here."

I slunk to his side and resumed my inspection of the floor, my glasses sliding down my nose. I pushed them back into place. Uncle Jack wasn't a tall man, but I was the opposite of a tall woman and his cold attention beat down on my shoulders, which were half the width of his.

He cleared his throat. "How are you settling in?"

My brow wrinkled at the odd high note in his voice and I snuck a quick appraisal of his face. His lips were turned up in a grimacing smile. It looked painful.

"You've been here … a day now, haven't you?"

"Two days," I mumbled. Forty-five hours and twenty minutes, if I were counting. Which I wasn't. Not constantly, at least.

Okay, it was constantly.

"And how are you doing?" he asked with forced friendliness.

"I'm fine."

"Has Kathy shown you the ropes?"

"Yes." Minus the *Stay Out of the Basement So You Don't Discover Our Illegal Activities* rule.

He brushed his hands together like I was trash he was preparing to haul to the curb. "Well, it's time to give you your final introduction. I'd planned to wait, but since you're already down here …"

I wilted. "Kathy had mentioned a library and I just wanted to …"

"Ah, yes, you like books, don't you?"

Had he phrased that so patronizingly on purpose? "I don't need to see—"

Deaf to my quiet protest, he waved at me to follow him into the library. I minced in his shadow, boring holes into the floor. I didn't want to know what was going on in this room. I didn't want to know about the magic.

Stay away from magic and it'll stay away from you.

Uncle Jack stopped in front of the podium. "Do you know what this is?"

Reluctantly, I lifted my eyes to the glaringly out-of-place feature in the elegant library.

A flawless circle, ten feet across, had been carved into the beautiful hardwood floor and filled with silver inlay. Straight lines, sharp angles, and perfect curves intersected along the circle's outer edge, but runes, sigils, and disturbing marks that twisted into unpleasant shapes interrupted the precise geometry.

Inside the circle, darkness formed a perfect dome that seamlessly matched its circumference. The half-orb sat on the library floor like a black igloo from hell, sucking light into its inky depths.

"Do you know what this is?" he repeated with an impatient bite.

I worked my tongue, wetting it enough to speak. "A summoning circle."

"Have you seen one before?"

"No," I whispered.

He gave me an odd look, as though surprised I'd recognized a summoning circle with no prior exposure. But what else could it be? The circle on its own I might not have identified, but that dome of nothingness was not of this world.

Gooseflesh prickled on my bare arms and I wished for a sweater. The library was uncomfortably cool, the leather-scented air chilling my nose, and shadows lurked in the room's farthest corners.

"Why is it so black?" I asked before I could stop myself.

"The demon is hiding itself," Uncle Jack answered irritably. "Thus far, it hasn't been interested in negotiation."

Demon.

The word thudded into my skull. Each syllable, each sound, struck like a mallet against a gong. A demon in the circle. In the library. In the basement of the house I was now living in.

I never should've come here.

"Your parents weren't interested in the family business," Uncle Jack went on, "but summoning is lucrative. It's also ... sensitive. A delicate process. We don't need distractions."

I counted the floorboards between my sock-clad toes. Distractions like ... an MPD investigation into their illegal activities?

"I expect your full support, Robin."

He didn't need to say, "Or else."

"Yes, Uncle Jack."

"For obvious reasons, this room is off-limits, but you should know the rules either way."

He grasped my elbow and pulled me toward the circle. My socks slid across the polished hardwood as I tried to stop. I didn't want to go any closer.

"The circle is a barrier. It's impenetrable to the demon, but *only* to the demon." He gestured at the black dome. "You can pass through it just fine. You wouldn't even feel it. One slip ..."

His hand tightened on my arm, then he shoved me toward the flimsy silver line. A terrified gasp seized my lungs and I flailed backward, even though I was several steps away.

He laughed. "So don't get close. One toe over that line and the demon will haul you in and rip you apart. Don't drop anything in there either. Even a coin can be deadly in a demon's hands. It can't get its magic through the barrier, so make sure you don't hand it weapons."

I automatically checked my jeans pockets for change. I never carried change.

"If it tries to get your attention or calls you over, don't listen. And don't *ever* speak to the demon. If it shows itself, get me or Claude immediately." He glowered at the impenetrable darkness. "Not that I expect it to. The most obstinate demon I've ever encountered. If it doesn't respond soon …" He abruptly refocused on me. "You're to stay out of this room, understood? I don't want you in here alone."

"All right."

"Good." Then, contradicting his words, he swept right past me and out of the library.

Rooted to the spot, I mentally floundered. The open doorway beckoned, safety only steps away, but the inky dome drew my gaze. Shivers rippled down my spine. It was so cold in here.

A soft sound whispered on the edge of my senses and I sucked in a breath. In the silence, I could almost hear something. Something like …

A low, husky laugh crawled out of the darkness inside the circle.

My blood turned to ice and I bolted out of the library.

3

FACING THE CLOSED DOOR, I took slow, controlled breaths. This wasn't the library door in the basement and no demons waited on the other side, but I was almost as nervous.

Deep, deliberate breaths. I summoned a mental image of the book I was reading: Chapter Six, "Confidence in Confrontation." I visualized the coming conversation and how I wanted it to go, then pushed my shoulders back and straightened my spine, giving myself a precious inch of additional height. I rapped on the door.

"Who is it?" Uncle Jack barked from within.

"Robin." My voice didn't tremble. A good start.

"Get in here, then."

I opened the door and stepped into his office. The room had started as a den, and a cushy sofa in the corner invited visitors to sit down, maybe have a snooze. Ugly filing cabinets ruined the elegance of the solid wood desk, its top blanketed with papers. Two leather chairs sat in front of it, waiting for Uncle Jack's next "clients."

As he hammered furiously on his keyboard, I inched into the room, then remembered I needed to project confidence. I took three long steps to a chair and perched on the edge. The dusty odor of printer toner mixed with his spicy cologne.

He continued typing, his stubby fingers stabbing the keys. I waited, counting in my head. When I got to thirty, I cleared my throat.

He kept typing.

"Uncle Jack?"

"What do you want, Robin?"

I fought the urge to shrink. Chapter Six, Part Three. "Visualize your results. Remember your goal."

"I'd like to discuss my parents' will."

Saying the words stirred my grief into a fresh spiral, and my hands twitched against my thighs.

His gaze snapped to me, then back to his monitor. His typing didn't stutter. "I don't like repeating myself, Robin. These things take *time*. There are lawyers and paperwork, and the insurance company requires ten forms for every little thing."

"It's been six months." Plus three days, but I wasn't counting. "It shouldn't take this long to—"

"Not every estate is easy to settle." His hands stilled and he swiveled to face me, his bald head shining grossly. "I'm sure you're anxious to get your inheritance, and I'm doing everything I can to make that happen. Is it that painful to live here for a few weeks? I'm not charging you rent, am I?"

My gaze dipped toward the nice, safe floor, which neither glared at me nor casually dismissed my parents' early demise, but I caught myself and forced my eyes back up. Living here hadn't been my first choice. I'd have preferred to stay in my parents' home, where I'd lived my whole life, but as the executor of their estate, Uncle Jack had sold it. Against my wishes. I'd handed the keys over to its new owners last week.

"I understand if there are delays with the life insurance," I said, "but what about their belongings? They left me several heirlooms, which I would like to get from—"

"Your parents left you their house and everything in it," he interrupted. "Everything you inherited was in the house. Didn't you put it all in storage?"

Every time he interrupted me, my thoughts scattered. I pulled them back together. I'd *had* to put all of my and my parents' belongings in storage because he'd sold our house. And no, I hadn't gotten anything from the sale, even though the money was mine. The fees for storing an entire house's worth of furniture and belongings was bleeding my savings dry.

"I'm talking about the heirlooms they placed in a special facility," I clarified. "I spoke to the estate lawyer and he said—"

"You spoke to the lawyer? *I'm* the executor. Why didn't you ask me?"

Because he ignored me, dismissed me, and interrupted me, that's why. "The lawyer said accessing items in storage should be simple, and—"

"It's not *simple*, whatever that fool of a lawyer told you. I'm working on it, but I don't have access yet." He tapped a stack of papers on the desk to straighten them. "I have work to do, Robin. I'll let you know when I have an update."

Dismissed, again. Mumbling a farewell, I speed-walked into the hallway. Out of petty revenge, I left the door open a crack. He'd have to get up and close it himself.

Oh yeah, I was so bad. Look at me, the rebel niece.

Disgusted with my latest failure to get anywhere with my uncle, I stumped along a hall lined with oil paintings and ten-foot-tall windows with heavy drapes, then passed a parlor, a formal living room, and a dining … hall. Not room. "Room" was too plebian, too small and contained. The dining hall cradled a table long enough to seat eighteen.

Uncle Jack hadn't been kidding about demon summoning being "lucrative." This house had so many rooms that I was still getting lost on my third day.

Stopping at a window, I glared at the sprawling lawn, bathed in an orange sunset. Despite my uncle's assumptions, I hadn't moved in here because I needed somewhere to live—though I did. I was here because he hadn't given me *anything* I was supposed to inherit from my parents. Money, even though I desperately needed it, wasn't my main concern.

I wanted the heirlooms too precious to keep at home—specifically one keepsake that meant more to me than anything—and I was staying right here in this house until I got it.

I squinted at my reflection in the glass—my blue eyes narrowed ferociously behind black-rimmed glasses, my shoulder-length hair wild and dark around my pale face, my small mouth pressed into an angry line. Why couldn't I give Uncle Jack a look like that? Instead, I crept around him like a scared mouse, flinching every time he interrupted me.

Shoulders slumping, I headed toward the kitchen. Voices trickled out, followed by a cheerful laugh. The scent of tomato sauce and melted cheese reached my nose.

The chef's kitchen dominated the house's back corner: a high breakfast bar with beautiful marble counters contrasted with a monster-sized, stainless steel island with a double gas range, two ovens, and a massive range hood that descended from the ceiling.

Uncle Jack's daughter, Amalia, and stepson, Travis, were bent over something on the stovetop that steamed in the way only delicious food could steam. Amalia was twenty like me, while Travis was a couple of years older. Unaware of my arrival, they dished food onto plates while Travis joked about something and Amalia laughed.

I hovered awkwardly, debating what to do. Telling my social-interaction jitters to take a hike, I got up the nerve to speak. "Hey guys."

They didn't react.

Too quiet. I tried again. "Hey guys. What are you making?"

Holding plates heaped with spaghetti noodles and thick red sauce, they turned around. Amalia's gray eyes, edged in heavy eyeliner, went flat and the laughter on her face died. She swept her messy blond waves over one shoulder, grabbed a fork, and exited the kitchen without a word.

My innards shriveled like seaweed drying in the sun.

Travis shifted his weight from foot to foot. "Hey Robin. How's it going?"

"Good," I muttered. Nothing was good. Everything was crap.

"We made spaghetti," he said after a moment. "There's a bit left, if you want it."

"Sure," I told the floor.

A painful silence, then he carried his plate out of the kitchen. I looked up in time to see his back disappear, his tight t-shirt showing his muscular arms and broad shoulders.

I stood alone in the kitchen, furious and embarrassed by my inability to act like a socially capable human being, then approached the gas range. A pot and a saucepan held a few dregs of food. Sighing, I scooped the child-sized portion onto a plate. Maybe they thought that was all the food I needed. Short people didn't require nourishment or something.

Leaning against the counter, I ate my inadequate meal as my thoughts jumped from my failed attempt to confront Uncle Jack, to my missing inheritance, to this stupid house and the demon in the basement. I didn't want to be here.

I wanted to be home, tucked in my favorite reading chair with an old book, listening to my parents' voices as they prepared dinner in the kitchen. We would've sat together at the table to eat, and Mom would've told me about the three-hundred-year-old book she was restoring for a client. Dad would've complained about his boss at the bank. I would've told them about the paper I was researching for my Roman history class.

Scooping the last noodle into my mouth, I set my plate in the sink and dried my tears on my shirt. Grief weighed on my chest, and I was desperate for something familiar—but what in this cold, sprawling mansion could possibly bring me comfort?

My gaze drifted to the pantry.

Five minutes later, I'd stacked the island with flour, butter, baking powder, baking soda, salt, shortening, white sugar, brown sugar, two eggs, vanilla extract, semi-sweet chocolate chips, and a surprising find—a bulk bag of pecans.

I searched the cupboards for mixing bowls, measuring cups, and utensils, and in no time at all, I was mixing dry ingredients in a bowl. As I worked, my worries faded. The unfamiliar kitchen didn't matter. With each precise measurement and carefully followed step, I slid backward in time. I was baking in my parents' kitchen, testing a new iteration of my chocolate-pecan cookie recipe.

The kitchen filled with the mouthwatering aroma of melted chocolate, and I tidied up while the cookies baked. When I pulled them from the oven, their centers fluffed with heat and edges golden brown, I could almost hear my mom exclaiming in delight. Leaving the cookies to cool, I finished cleaning, then stacked them on a plate.

It was a long walk to the bedrooms on the second level. I stopped in front of Amalia's door, practiced breathing, then knocked. A moment passed.

The door cracked open and a gray eye glared at me. "What do you want?"

I held up the plate. "I made cookies. Would you like—"

"I'm on a diet."

The door slammed shut.

I blinked rapidly, then exhaled. A dozen paces down the hall, I stopped in front of Travis's door. Electronic music throbbed through the wood. I knocked. No answer. I knocked louder. The music pounded on. I couldn't bring myself to shout for his attention. He was probably busy anyway.

Cradling the full plate, I continued down the never-ending hall and stopped in front of a third closed door. I didn't need to knock on this one. Inside was a bed that wasn't mine, with a gray-striped comforter I didn't like. My suitcase sat on the floor in the walk-in closet, filled with socks and underwear, and six shirts hung on hangers above it. Ten of my favorite books lined the dresser, the only ones I'd brought with me. The rest of my belongings were in storage with my parents' things.

I stared at the cookies, knowing what my evening would involve: sitting alone on the unfamiliar bed, reading old books, and trying not to cry. This time, I could weep into my giant plate of cookies. I'd be sad *and* sick to my stomach. Extra fun.

I needed a better distraction. When was the last time I'd gone this long without a new book to read? I used to spend half my free time browsing library shelves at my college campus—

Library shelves.

My gaze dropped to the floor as though I could see through it. There was a library right in this house—a big, private library full of fascinating leather-bound books.

Books … and a demon.

Uncle Jack had told me to stay out of the basement—but did I care what he wanted? Reckless daring swept through me. Turning on my heel, I strode toward the stairs.

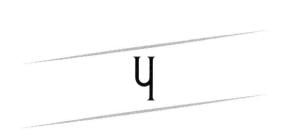

4

BALANCING THE PLATE of cookies on my palm, I cracked the library door open and peeked inside. In the sconce lights' soft glow, shadows swathed the room. The demonic dome sat in the center, bizarre and disturbing.

I hovered in the doorway, remembering the quiet laughter from my first and only visit.

Slipping through the door, I found a sliding switch on the wall and pushed it up. The lights brightened, banishing the dimness to the corners. The dome of unnatural night looked even stranger. I edged along a wall of shelves, clutching my plate as though to hurl it at the first sign of movement.

The circle was black and silent. No sign of life.

Prickles ran over my arms. Concealed inside that darkness was a demon. A creature from … well, not theological Hell. A hellish dimension, though. That was all I knew; I'd only read passing descriptions of demon summoning. Unsurprisingly, it wasn't an interest of mine.

I contemplated retreating but the lure of books was stronger. The demon was stuck in that circle. The worst it could do was laugh at me. I deposited my cookie plate on the end table beside a leather sofa, selected two cookies, then set out to explore.

Most people couldn't have ignored a demon sharing the library with them, but most people didn't love books as much as I did.

Thirty minutes slipped away as I browsed the shelves, finding encyclopedias, histories of every culture and country I could think of, geography and nature studies, copies of ancient classics, some modern classics, travel books, and, oddly, a single shelf in the back corner stacked with outdated romance novels, their paper covers boasting faded men with long hair and open shirts billowing in the wind.

Returning to the cookies, I grabbed a morsel and bit into the chocolaty goodness. I was itching to pick a book and get reading, but one section of the library remained unexplored: the shelves across from the door, right behind the demon circle. Those books differed from the rest—more sizes, more colors, and disorganized like someone had been shifting them around.

I studied the six feet of space between the circle's silver inlay and the shelves. Six feet was plenty. As long as I didn't trip and fall over, I'd be fine.

Heart thudding in my chest, I slipped in front of the shelves and scanned the spines. My racing pulse kicked up a notch. Everything I'd seen so far were histories, texts, and novels I could find in most well-stocked libraries, but these—these books were about magic.

Magic textbooks. Magic studies. Magic histories. Arcana, Elementaria, Spiritalis, Psychica, and Demonica—all five classes of magic were represented on the shelves.

Studying magic was my greatest passion. Technically, I was a sorceress—a mythic of the Arcana class—but I'd never begun an apprenticeship. *Stay away from magic.* That was our family motto, and studying the supernatural phenomena of the world was as close as I was willing to get to real power. I was an academic spectator to the most dangerous game in the world—and perfectly happy to stay out of the arena.

Eyes sweeping across the titles, I excitedly pulled out a book: *An Examination of Astral Constructions in Arcana.* The next one: *The Unique Physiology of Elementaria.* Then, *Infamous Psychics of the 21st Century* and *The Witch's Mission: Balancing Modernity, Nature, and Fae.*

I stacked the books in my arms, then crouched to read the titles at the bottom—but the spines were blank. Curious, I chose a thick tome at random and slid it out. The leather cover wasn't old and peeling as I'd expected, but shiny and stiff. I flipped it open. The title page stuck to the cover, and my eyes fell on the table of contents instead.

1. An Introduction to Demon Summoning
2. MPD Regulations and Requirements
    2.1 Legal Practices & Penalties
    2.2 Permit Paperwork
    2.3 Inspection Timelines
    2.4 Contractor Registration
3. Summoning Rituals
    3.1 Standard Variations
    3.2 Greek vs. Latin Incantations
    3.3 Location Requirements

3.4 Constructing the Ritual
3.5 Common Execution Errors
3.6 Containment Failure
4. Contract Basics
4.1 MPD-Approved Templates
4.2 Common Mistakes
4.3 Contract Length: Brevity vs. Diligence
4.4 Language to Avoid
4.5 The Banishment Clause
4.6 Recommended Advance Preparations

It went on like that for thirty-two chapters and countless more subheadings, covering everything from selecting contractors to negotiation techniques to demon names. I thumbed through a few more pages, then unstuck the title page.

Legal Demonica: The Summoner's Handbook
Presented by the Magicae Politiae Denuntiatores

Magicae Politiae Denuntiatores—a semi-secret international organization commonly known as the MPD or MagiPol. Not only did the MPD conceal the existence of magic from the public, but they also policed anything and everything that used or abused preternatural power. If this summoning guide was their literal rulebook, why not learn exactly how Uncle Jack was breaking the law? I was betting Chapter 3.3, "Location Requirements," didn't include residential basements as a legal option.

I carried my book selections to the leather sofa and curled up beside my plate of cookies. As I flipped *The Summoner's Handbook* to the first page of text—"Foreword by Arnaldo

Banderas, MPD Special Agent"—and lifted a cookie to my mouth, I remembered I wasn't alone in the library.

My gaze shot to the inky dome. How had I forgotten about the demon? I briefly considered sneaking the books up to my room, but stealth wasn't a strength of mine. Besides, all was quiet—no creepy laughter, no sounds of movement.

I took a big bite of my cookie and began reading. The minutes slipped past as I breezed through the book's foreword and introduction. It wasn't until the end of the second chapter that I noticed my eyes were tired.

Closing the cover, I mused about what I'd learned. Uncle Jack was *definitely* breaking laws, and if the MPD caught him, he'd face jail time or even the death penalty. The MPD didn't mess around when it came to illegal summoners. My impression so far was that they'd rather people didn't summon demons at all.

My gaze drifted to the dark circle again. The creature hidden inside was a killing machine; its primary function was murder, and if it ever escaped, it would slaughter every person it encountered until someone killed it.

I decided I didn't want to be in this room any longer.

With numb fingers—why was it so cold in here?—I set my chosen books on the floor and, one by one, slid them under the coffee table. Unless someone decided to rearrange the furniture, they'd never know the books were there.

Satisfied, I got to my feet and took two steps, then remembered my half-eaten plate of cookies. I grabbed the plate, accidentally jarring it in my haste. The stack of cookies slid across the sleek ceramic surface and tumbled off. They hit the floor in a spray of crumbs, bouncing everywhere. One, rolling like a perfect little wheel, trundled across the hardwood floor.

It rolled, wobbled, curved—and disappeared across the silver line.

I gawked at the spot where the cookie had vanished into the black dome. Panic screeched in my head, and I jerked backward, expecting the cookie to come flying out, hurled like a doughy bullet into my eye socket. Could a demon throw a cookie hard enough to kill?

At that last thought, my panic waned. A cookie would hurt, should it be whipped with inhuman force into my soft flesh, but I doubted it could do serious damage. Maybe the demon realized that too.

Unmoving, I waited a full minute, but no sound came from the circle. The cookie did not reappear.

Breathing out, I cautiously scooped the fallen cookies off the floor and restacked them on the plate. I pondered the crumb-strewn hardwood, then used my socked foot to sweep the crumbs under the side table. Did I care that I was befouling Uncle Jack's mansion? Not one bit. If I was contributing to a vermin problem, all the better.

Plate in hand, I crossed to the door, then looked back at the circle. Had the demon noticed the cookie enter its prison?

Curiosity sparked through me. Impulsively, I picked up a cookie, took aim, and lobbed it. It flew in a beautiful arc and dropped into the black dome.

I listened. No crunch or patter. No sound at all. Weird. I threw a second cookie. It too fell into the unnatural darkness, and again, nothing but silence. Either the interior of the circle was a gravity-free pocket dimension with no solid surfaces, or …

… or the demon had caught the cookies before they hit the floor?

I squinted at the circle, imagining what a demon might look like. Warily, I inched closer. Silence from the circle. I clutched my plate with the last five cookies and an assortment of largish pieces. Did I dare?

Before I could talk myself out of it, I flipped the plate toward the dome.

The cookies soared in a shower of chocolate, pecans, and crumbs that disappeared into the black dome. A distinct patter sounded as they hit the floor. Aha! So the demon *had* caught the first two cookies. Did that mean—

A soft scraping sound, then something flew out of the circle at warp speed.

The cookie hit me smack between the eyes.

I yelped, staggering and almost dropping the plate. Tears of pain sprang into my eyes. Whirling, I ran for the door, then skidded to a stop and ran back to grab the cookie off the hardwood. Didn't want Uncle Jack to see that—

Oh crap. What if the demon hoarded the cookies to throw at Uncle Jack next time he came down here?

Cursing my stupidity, I raced up the stairs and stumbled into the dark, empty kitchen. I gingerly prodded my throbbing, burning forehead. A tender welt was forming between my eyes, and crumbs peppered my glasses. *Ow.*

If not for the pain, I might've doubted my memory. A *demon* had thrown a cookie at my face? Hands down the strangest thing that had ever happened to me.

I looked at the chunk of cookie between my finger and thumb. The demon had *touched* it. Held it. Taken aim and thrown it. Nose wrinkling, I pitched it into the garbage and scrubbed my hands until my skin was pink and raw.

5

WITH ONE EAR tuned for sounds from the upper floor, I pried the lid off a plastic tote and shone my phone's flashlight inside.

The storage room, like the rest of the house, was so oversized it practically echoed, with endless boxes and plastic totes neatly stacked on simple wooden shelves. So far, I'd uncovered winter clothing and skiing gear, Christmas and Halloween decorations—weird, because Halloween was only a couple of weeks away, so why not put them out?—dated décor, toys from Amalia's and Travis's childhood, and three boxes filled with the same old romance novels I'd found in the library.

I rummaged around in the tote, filled with barely worn women's shoes, then returned it to the shelf. Sitting back on my heels, I swept my bangs out of my eyes.

Was I snooping around my uncle's house? Yes, I was.

Seeing as Uncle Jack was an illegal demon summoner, morals clearly didn't concern him. Even without that mark of character to consider, I had more than enough reasons to distrust him. I wasn't sure what I was searching for, but there was a chance Uncle Jack had already claimed other parts of my inheritance besides my rightful money.

Jaw tight with determination, I switched off my phone's flashlight and cracked open the storage room door. The hall was dark and empty. I slipped out and tiptoed across the cold hardwood. When I drew level with the library, I paused.

Two days had passed since my … adventure … in the library, and Uncle Jack hadn't stormed into my room to demand how his demon had gotten hold of freshly baked projectiles. He also hadn't offered any updates on my inheritance or heirlooms. Amalia and Travis continued to ignore my every awkward attempt to instigate conversation. Oh, and the estate lawyer had stopped responding to my emails, meaning Uncle Jack had warned him off communicating with me.

I was losing hope that I would ever get my inheritance. Uncle Jack wasn't playing fair, but what could I do? I had no power and no advantages. I was probably wasting my time. At this rate, I would need to sue him to get anything.

Right, yeah. Hire a bargain-bin lawyer with the pennies in my bank account and take my rich uncle to court. That would go well.

I had most of my treasured keepsakes already, and money was a convenience, not a requirement. Some heirlooms, however, were more precious than a check from the insurance company, and that's why I was here. And why I wasn't about to give up.

I wasn't leaving until I had my mother's grimoire in my hands.

All grimoires—the handwritten journals of sorcerers that documented their magical experiences—were valuable, but my mother's was even more special. Passed from mother to daughter for countless generations, it dated back centuries. The grimoire was my mother's—and my family's—legacy, and it was *mine*.

My mother had kept it in special storage to protect the aging paper from degradation. I didn't know where it was or how to access it, and I was afraid to mention it to Uncle Jack. He might not know it existed—or that I wanted it—and if I tipped him off, the grimoire could disappear forever. He'd auction it off for extra cash or bequeath it to his own daughter instead of me.

The timer on my phone beeped. I hurried away from the library door and trotted up the stairs.

The kitchen lights were already on when I walked in. Kathy stood at the sink, a pink apron tied over her floral-patterned dress as she scrubbed dishes. Her black pumps clacked against the floor with each shift of her feet.

I stopped at the counter, confused. The cooling rack was gone. No, not gone. I spotted it in the draining rack beside the sink of soapy water.

"Aunt Kathy? Did you move my muffins?"

She smiled at me with her overly red lips. "Did you make them?"

Who else would've? "Yes, I—"

"Travis is allergic to peanuts. Didn't I tell you? I threw the muffins out."

My mouth hung open. "You threw them out? But—"

"Just because Travis has an epi-pen doesn't mean—"

"They didn't have peanuts!" I interrupted shrilly.

"There were nuts on top."

"*Pecans!*" I exclaimed, my hands curling around the hem of my sweater and squeezing. "Those were pumpkin muffins with cream-cheese filling and cinnamon-pecan streusel topping."

"Oh." She shrugged. "I didn't realize. Can't be too safe with a peanut allergy."

"You could've asked me!"

Her black-lined eyes squinched. "Don't take that tone with me, young lady."

I glared into her foundation-coated face, her pouchy cheeks quivering above her wide shoulders, then my gaze fell to the floor. I walked out of the kitchen.

Earlier this afternoon, I'd bussed to the store to get ingredients. I'd prepared the cream-cheese filling before dinner so it could harden in the freezer, then made the batter and streusel after the kitchen was free again. Just because I was using baking as an alibi while I searched the house didn't mean I'd committed minimal effort to the task. The muffins had come out of the oven perfect. The pumpkin aroma still lingered in the hall.

Tears stung my eyes. I hated this house and everyone in it.

* * *

I'D SEARCHED the storage room in the basement. The garages—both of them. The spare bedrooms. Every closet in the house, except the ones in Uncle Jack's, Amalia's, and Travis's rooms. There was nowhere else to look for evidence of Uncle Jack's lies or my parents' belongings.

Well, there was Uncle Jack's office, but he was always in there and I wasn't brave enough to risk him catching me. The library, however … *If* Uncle Jack had somehow gotten his greedy hands on my mother's grimoire, the library would be an ideal place to store—or hide—a book. Yeah, it was a long shot, but what else could I do?

I squinted at the library door, a foot in front of my nose. I hadn't been back since the cookie-throwing incident.

At the reminder, I lifted the paper towel I held. Stacked on it were half a dozen dark brown cookies, their crispy surfaces deliciously cracked to reveal the fluffy, cake-like insides mixed with chocolate chunks. White sea salt sprinkled the tops.

When I was stressed, I overindulged in my two favorite hobbies—reading and baking. I bit into a cookie and almost moaned. Perfect. Melty, chocolaty, sweet and rich, and a touch salty. Absolute perfection.

Fortified by sugar, I cracked the library door open and peered inside. Abandoned. Jack and his partner, Claude, usually visited in the afternoons, and it was almost nine o'clock now. I turned the lights up, then waited, staring at the black dome where the cookie-hurling demon hid. Had it saved any crumbling missiles for my inevitable return?

It seemed not, because nothing happened. I scooted the long way around the room to the sofas, set my snack on the end table—the one farthest from the circle—then surveyed the room. I'd already given the shelves one pass, but I hadn't been looking for grimoires.

Keeping an eye on the inky dome, I started with the section on magic. I pulled out each book, checked it, then slid it back. Slow work, but I didn't want to miss anything. The always-ravenous bookworm in me filed away each title, compiling a reading list so long it'd take me all year to finish.

Something scuffed against the floor.

With my hand raised to slide *The History of Celtic Druidry* onto a shelf, I froze, my senses stretching toward the summoning circle four feet behind me. Another soft scuff—like a body shifting position, limbs brushing the floor.

Silence thrummed in my ears. After a minute, my spine relaxed and I released the breath I was holding.

"*Hh'ainun.*"

I gasped in air to scream and choked on saliva. I started to lurch backward but realized the circle was right behind me, and as I spasmed in place, *Celtic Druidry* fell out of my hand and the spine hit me in the forehead. The thick tome tumbled to the floor and landed with a loud *thwack*.

Gasping and hacking, my eyes watering, I spun around and pressed my back against the bookshelf. The black dome loomed too close. I blinked away tears, my nose throbbing and knees trembling. My glasses hung crookedly off one ear.

"*Hh'ainun.*" The quiet, growling voice rolled out of the black dome. "Will you answer a question?"

Panic squealed incoherently in my ears. My limbs had gone numb and I couldn't remember how to run for the door. The demon was talking. *Talking*. To *me*. It had … asked me to … "Huh?"

The demon didn't respond. Maybe it didn't know what "huh" meant.

Gulping, I sidled along the bookshelf until I was a safe distance from the circle, then took a wobbling step toward the door. I needed to leave. Uncle Jack had been very clear—if the demon ever spoke, fetch him or Claude immediately. Whether I reported the demon's behavior or not, I should get the hell out of the library.

And yet …

From out of the circle's inky nothingness, a creature from another world had spoken to me. Call me insane, but I kind of wanted to hear what it had to say. It was contained in the circle. It couldn't reach me, couldn't hurt me.

Pulse thundering in my ears, I backed toward the sofa and dropped onto the cool leather, relieved my weak knees hadn't given out. I straightened my glasses, taking deep breaths. Inhale, exhale. I was okay. I was safe.

"Why should I answer a question?" I whispered cautiously. Then, since I'd already hitched a ride on the crazy train, I added, "You threw a cookie at me."

"You threw it at me first."

I stared at the black dome, even though there was nothing to see. That was … true, I supposed. "What's your question?"

A long pause, as though the creature were second-guessing its words. "What is it you threw into the *kaīrtis vīsh* before?"

My brow wrinkled. Its English was heavily accented, but part of its query hadn't been in English at all. "Threw into the … what?"

"The … *vīsh* … the magic."

The magic? Threw into the … oh. "You mean the summoning circle? You're asking what I threw at you?" Mad laughter bubbled in my throat but I swallowed it down. "Cookies. I threw cookies."

"This is … food?"

"Yes." I blinked bemusedly. "Did you eat them?"

Silence. Did that mean … yes? I had no idea how to interpret its lack of response. Who knew what long silences meant in demon conversation?

Oh god. I was having a *conversation* with a *demon*. I'd lost my mind. Stress-induced insanity. That had to be it.

The door called to me, but I felt tethered in place. It wasn't fear that held my butt to the leather cushion and my socked feet to the hardwood floor. A new feeling had awoken inside me.

My archnemesis: curiosity.

A painfully familiar voice murmured in my memory.

"Oh, Robin," my mother had laughed as she'd bandaged my scraped knees. I'd climbed a tree to look in a bird's nest after reading about how sparrows care for their young, but had fallen on my way back down. *"Curious and impulsive—it's a volatile combination. You need to remember to think through your decisions."*

I thought I'd learned that lesson years ago, but even as I told myself I needed to leave, the demon's quiet voice fed my thirst for knowledge, its words tinged with an alien accent—vowels sharp and crisp, consonants heavy and deep. A bit of throaty German and lilting Arabic, and a touch of rolling Greek.

A hundred questions crowded into my head. Where and how had the demon learned English? Why had it spoken to me? What was Uncle Jack trying to negotiate and why wasn't the demon responding?

Or, even better, where had the demon come from? What was it like to be summoned to Earth? What sort of life had it led before this?

Don't ever speak to the demon. Though Uncle Jack's warning was easy to dismiss, I wasn't about to forget my parents' most important lesson: *Stay away from magic.* But my curiosity burned, and really, what was the harm?

"Um, demon?" I began tentatively.

Silence.

"Are you listening?"

Nothing.

"Helloooo? Demon?"

Not even a peep.

I slumped into the sofa, disappointed that the demon had no further desire to communicate. Well, if it didn't want to answer my questions, I'd get the information myself. Bending forward, I slid *The Summoner's Handbook* from under the coffee table. As I settled back, I remembered my waiting snack.

Biting into a chocolate morsel, I opened the book to Chapter Three, "Summoning Rituals," but the introduction was painfully dry. Craving something as intriguing as the demon's voice, I began flipping the pages.

Chapter Twelve, "Negotiation and the Demonic Psyche." I read the first page.

"Profoundly immoral and wicked." The definition of *evil* is an apt description of the demonic psyche and should be kept at the forefront of a summoner's mind throughout contract negotiation. A demon does not conceive of morality or integrity—though they can imitate those qualities to manipulate a summoner.

Remember, a demon's ultimate goal is, always, your death.

The debate of inherent truthfulness has consumed the summoner community for centuries, but it has yet to be proven that demons are incapable of lying. It is safer to expect demons to lie, though they may avoid outright falsehoods. Do not assume a demon's aversion to verbal fabrications means it is incapable of deception. Assume, instead, that the demon is both more cunning and more manipulative than you.

For these reasons and more, we recommend negotiations be brief and aggressive. The MPD's recommended approach is outlined in detail in this chapter, and in later sections, we will address the best techniques for handling uncooperative

The text cut off at the bottom of the page, but I didn't turn it. My eyes lingered on the introduction. *A demon does not conceive of morality or integrity ... A demon's ultimate goal is, always, your death ... Assume, instead, that the demon is both more cunning and more manipulative than you.*

"'It has yet to be proven that demons are incapable of lying,'" I read in a mutter, tracing the line with one finger. "That's interesting. Why would a demon with no concept of morality *not* lie?"

Absently nibbling another cookie, I skimmed the next page. More of the same—demons were wicked and bloodthirsty, demons enjoyed violence and death, demons were intelligent and calculating, and all the reasons those qualities needed to be considered during negotiations.

My brow wrinkled. I shouldn't have skipped ahead. I still didn't know what the summoners were so keen to negotiate.

I ran my finger down the page to a new paragraph.

> A concept that demons and humans both grasp with ease, and upon which our recommended negotiation strategy heavily relies, is that of fair exchange. A demon is more likely to agree to a contract that is presented as the demon's surrender in exchange for its life. Leveraging the Banishment Clause is a crucial element of this approach.

"That's a crappy deal," I mumbled. "Surrender or die? Lame."

I nudged my glasses up my nose and read on, but my attention drifted disobediently to the summoning circle.

After what I'd read, I should have been terrified of the demon, yet I couldn't work up more than fluttery anxiety.

Maybe it was because the creature was hidden in that darkness and unable to reach me. How scary was a voice, really?

It wasn't a monster. It was a fascinating curiosity. Another bird's nest high in a tree.

I snapped the Demonica guide shut and replaced it under the table, then scooped up my remaining cookies and walked across the hardwood floor. I stopped two long steps from the circle. My heart lurched, just as it had in that long-ago tree when I'd realized the branches had gotten dangerously thin.

I held up a cookie.

"This," I announced, "is a double-chocolate brownie cookie. It's delicious, and I'll give it to you if you answer a question for me."

Silence.

"I answered your question," I added accusingly.

Quiet lay upon the room—then a soft, husky laugh.

"A question, *hh'ainun?*" the demon crooned. "What would you ask?"

Doubts trickled through me. This was a bad idea, but I plowed on. "Do demons lie?"

"*Ch,*" it replied, a sound of cold amusement. "*Zh'ūltis* question. Ask another."

I frowned. "What does *zhuh-ool* ... what does that word mean?"

"Stupid. Stupid question."

My frown deepened into a scowl. I rephrased. "*If* it's true that demons don't lie, why is that?"

A long pause, but it wasn't the same silence as before. My skin prickled, instinct warning that a predator's attention was locked on me.

"Tell me truths and lies, *hh'ainun.*"

"What?" I asked blankly.

The demon said nothing, waiting.

Brow furrowed, I searched for harmless things to say. "I moved here six days ago. I miss my college classes. My favorite class was biology. I enjoy baking for my family."

"Moved here," the demon repeated in its swirling accent. "True. Miss your ... *college*," it enunciated carefully, as though unfamiliar with the word, "true. Biology ... lie."

My eyes widened.

"Your *family*." It rolled the last word as though tasting it. "Lie."

"No," I said. "That one is true."

"Lie," the demon repeated with certainty.

"You're wrong. I love baking for my family."

"*Zh'ūltis.*"

"Did you just call me stupid?" I clenched my jaw, then relaxed. "You didn't answer my question."

"I did."

"No, you didn't." Glaring, I took a deep breath. "Fine. Whatever. If that's your idea of answering a question, I won't bother asking any more."

I stepped closer to the circle, knelt, and carefully set the paper towel of cookies on the floor. Keeping my body as far away as possible, I nudged a corner of the paper across the silver inlay, then snatched my hand back. This was the closest I'd ever come to the circle.

A soft scuff against the hardwood. The paper towel twitched, then slid into the black dome.

Icy blades of fear cut through me. Suddenly, the demon was no longer a voice—it was a physical being. Something alive and solid and real that could pull the cookies into its prison cell. My gaze rose from the floor where the treats had disappeared to the curved black wall.

A spark of red in the darkness.

Flames burst to life and shot upward in a hungry blaze. I flung myself back. As I landed on my butt, the brief flare lit a shape within the black—the dark outline of shoulders, the edge of a jaw, the plane of a cheekbone.

Burning crimson eyes caught the light and glowed.

The fire died as quickly as it had appeared, and the dome was once again filled with impenetrable darkness, the demon hidden within. Gray fluff fluttered out of the circle—ash. Flakes of ash. The demon had burned the paper towel.

I scooted across the floor, then pushed onto trembling legs. Without a word or a backward glance, I ran through the door and pushed it shut behind me, swearing never to return.

An hour later, as I lay in bed, trying to sleep, all I could see was the demon's dim outline—and those eyes that had glowed like hot coals, like magma erupting from a volcano's heart. I realized two things.

First, the demon *had* answered my question, if indirectly. I'd asked why demons wouldn't lie, and the creature had shown me the reason: it could easily identify the fabrications among my simple statements. If all demons had a similar ability, lying was a useless endeavor.

Second, the demon hadn't been wrong about my last "truth." *I enjoy baking for my family* … It had once been true, but my family was dead. Baking nowadays was comfort and torture wrapped into one, and the satisfaction it brought me was saturated with grief.

Even that, the demon had detected, and I shivered under the blankets for a long time before falling into a fitful slumber.

6

I READ my carefully scribed notes for the eighteenth time. After reaching the end of the page, I started from the top again. Twenty was a nice round number. I should read it twenty times.

No, I shouldn't. Sitting in my room reading my notes wouldn't bring me any closer to my goals—namely, getting my mother's grimoire and my inheritance, then leaving this awful house forever. Besides, I'd memorized the whole page by my third read-through.

I folded the paper and tucked it in my pocket, ready to reference in case I lost my nerve partway through the conversation. My search of the house had produced zero results, so I was back to my least favorite thing in the entire world: confrontation.

Honestly, I'd rather talk to the red-eyed demon than confront my uncle.

Why was I so lame? Why couldn't I be more like the famous mythics from my history readings? If I were cunning like the famous druidess Branwen, who'd saved a fourteenth-century town from a powerful wyldfae, I could easily outwit Uncle Jack. Or if I were an insanely powerful tempemage like Clementine Abram, who'd singlehandedly flooded a British town in 1952—a disaster blamed on military experiments—I could intimidate my uncle into cooperating. Or if I were a genius inventor like the sorceress Aurelia Metellus, the true creator of Archimedes's infamous death ray, I could ... um ... actually, a death ray would be overkill in this situation.

The point was, I couldn't even work up the nerve to tell a store clerk if they scanned an item twice. How was I supposed to strong-arm my uncle into cooperating? I didn't know, but I had to try anyway.

Ducking into the Jack-and-Jill bathroom attached to my bedroom, I checked myself in the mirror. My dark brown hair fell almost to my shoulders in untidy waves, but it looked respectable enough. I adjusted my glasses, straightened my baby blue sweater, and tugged my snug jeans over my socks. Was baby blue too soft a color? Maybe I should change into something red. My current self-help book claimed red was a "power color." Did I even own a red top?

Since I only had six shirts to choose from anyway, I discarded the idea of a wardrobe adjustment. Outside the bathroom, I hurried past Travis's rattling door—did he ever turn his music off?—and down the stairs. The late afternoon sun blazed through the windows as I cut across the formal living room toward my uncle's office.

"... get you anything to drink?"

I slid to a stop as Uncle Jack's voice reached me.

"Coffee? Wine? I have an exceptionally fine brandy—"

"We aren't here to socialize, Mr. Harper," a male voice cut in.

I smiled. Hearing someone else interrupt my uncle was so gratifying. I poked my head around the corner.

Uncle Jack was ushering three men across the grand front entrance and into the hall that led to his office. Claude, his business partner, walked beside him, but the other two were strangers. One man was tall and bulky like a WWE wrestler, while the other was shorter than Uncle Jack and moved with jerky, bird-like movements.

"Our patience for delays is dwindling," the short man continued with distinct hostility. "We're reconsidering the wisdom of our generous down payment."

Uncle Jack muttered a response as they disappeared down the hall. A door clacked shut and the sound of their voices quieted. Heart galloping across my ribs, I crept to the office door and pressed my ear against it.

"… demon has proved exceptionally willful," Uncle Jack was saying in a greasy, soothing tone, "but we're confident we can bring it under control in time for a contract. And, as I mentioned, the other demon is ready. We can complete the ritual as soon as you select a contractor."

"Our top contractor is waiting to see the new demon before deciding," Birdman replied, his words fast and clipped. "You've told us nothing about it."

"The new demon is an unknown entity." That was Claude's voice. Instead of cringey persuasiveness, he sounded mild-mannered and confident. "It could be the most powerful demon ever summoned, or it could be the weakest. We're just as eager to uncover its secrets, but we can't rush the delicate negotiation process."

No one spoke for a long moment.

"Demon contracts are expensive," Birdman said. "Demon names are even more valuable. If you've discovered an unknown name—well, I've already made my offer. All you need to do is prove the name is worth it."

"We will," Uncle Jack assured him. "We'll have the demon ready for a contract in two weeks or less."

"I should hope, or you will begin again—without our funding."

"Of—of course," Uncle Jack stammered. "But would you like to proceed with the other demon?"

"We'll determine that in two weeks, Mr. Harper." An ominous pause, then Birdman continued in a more normal tone. "What of the paperwork? I want this contractor to be fully registered."

"We have a secure system in place." A clatter, like a drawer opening, followed by the rustle of paper. "When you're ready, you can add your contractor's registration information to this form and I'll forward it to my contact at the MPD, who will insert the documents into their database without—"

High heels clacked against the hardwood, and I jerked back from the door. I got three hasty steps away before Kathy rounded the corner, the skirt of her striped A-line dress fluttering around her calves.

"What are you doing?" she asked sharply, tucking a strand of perfectly curled, fake-red hair behind her ear.

Shriveling with apprehension, I counted the knots in the hardwood between my toes. "I want to speak with Uncle Jack, but he has people in his office."

"He's entertaining clients tonight. Don't bother him."

"Okay."

"And don't pester him about your parents' will. He's got enough to work on already."

"Yes, Aunt Kathy."

"Get moving, then."

I hurried back into the formal sitting room, then sank onto the nearest chintz armchair. This counted as leaving him alone, didn't it? I whiled away ten minutes in the sterile room, rereading my notes—forty-six reads now—until a door creaked open and voices spilled into the hall.

"Thank you for your patience," Uncle Jack babbled, trotting behind Birdman and his hulking counterpart. "We'll keep you updated—"

"Don't contact me until the new demon is ready," Birdman snapped. "Your time is almost up. Don't waste it. I—and my superiors—do not enjoy disappointment."

They hastened past the formal sitting room, and Claude came last, hands in his pockets and his lined face calm. He glanced into the sitting room as he passed, his expression unchanging though he must've seen me, then disappeared after the other three. Male voices rumbled terse farewells, then the front door opened and closed.

"We shouldn't have lied to Karlson," Uncle Jack fretted, his voice echoing off the entrance hall's twelve-foot windows. "If they realize we're no closer to negotiating with that demon than we were on day one—"

"Negotiations sometimes fail," Claude replied evenly. "It's a fact of summoning. Some demons aren't willing to subjugate themselves."

ANNETTE MARIE

"Maybe you haven't troubled yourself with the numbers, Claude, but we have a demon that's *never been summoned before*. Karlson has already offered ten million for its name—but unless we can prove the demon has value, it's worthless."

"If this one won't submit, we'll summon another."

Uncle Jack grunted angrily. Footsteps thudded, then he and Claude passed the sitting room on their way back to the office. A moment later, the door banged shut.

I listened to see if they'd return, then hurried away. Kathy was in the kitchen, and Amalia and Travis were in their bedrooms, meaning I didn't have to worry about witnesses. I zipped down the stairs and, throwing the library door open with no caution whatsoever, strode into the sitting area. Pulling the Demonica guide out of its hiding spot, I turned on a Tiffany lamp and checked the table of contents, then flipped to page 212: the section on demon names.

Before summoning can commence, a demon name is required. These rare appellations are akin to lineages and correspond to demonic archetypes; demons of the same name share distinct size, form, and strength attributes.

Demon names are typically passed from summoner to apprentice but can also be purchased, though even the most commonly known names sell for prohibitively large sums. The rarest are carefully guarded by unbroken lines of summoners and cannot be purchased. With such a small number of names available—believed to be between nine and eleven—procuring one is among the greatest challenges a new summoner will face.

Wow. So that's why Uncle Jack was so frantic over this demon. Karlson—his bird-like client, I was assuming—was offering *ten million dollars* for a new demon name, but unless Uncle Jack and Claude could prove it was valuable, they'd never see a penny.

Shadows, wild and alive, drifted around the ebony dome in the library's center. The creature hidden in that circle was worth a sum of money that people would kill for, but it was refusing to negotiate or show itself. Uncle Jack had no idea what sort of beast they'd called into this world or how valuable this new "lineage" might be.

I carried the book to the circle and crouched two paces away. Balancing the open cover on my knees, I peered into the darkness for a glimpse of those crimson eyes.

"How long have you been here?" I asked. "In this circle?"

Like usual, the creature made me wait before responding. "Ask the other *hh'ainun*."

"I'm asking you."

"What did you bring?"

Nothing. I hadn't baked today, nor had I thought to bring a treat to exchange for answers.

"I'll bring you something tomorrow night," I offered.

A long pause. "*Ch.* I see nothing except this room."

Its statement confused me before I realized that was an answer. The library was windowless, meaning the demon had no way to gauge the passage of time. It didn't know how long it'd been in the circle.

Did it even matter? Uncle Jack's business dealings—*illegal* business dealings—were trouble I wanted no part in, yet a nagging prickle in the back of my head had me running through the men's various remarks, searching for … something.

"The room warms and colds," the demon said abruptly. "The other *hh'ainun* come in the warm. You come in the cold. Sixty-one cycles since the first."

"Warms and *cools*," I corrected automatically. The basement was warmer during the day, and the demon had counted the temperature fluctuations. Sixty-one days, which was … "Eight weeks and five days. You've been here for *eight weeks* and five days."

Eight weeks in a ten-foot diameter dome in an empty room. An unpleasant twitch in my stomach made me swallow, but I caught myself. Did cruelty toward a *demon* really disturb me? The creature in that circle was a brutal, evil killer. Given the slightest chance, it would tear me apart. Then again, if someone had locked me in a tiny circle for weeks and weeks, I'd probably feel murderous too.

According to Uncle Jack, he had two weeks to get this demon to agree to a contract. Why the time limit? Why two weeks? I looked down at *The Summoner's Handbook*. Demon names. Lineages. Secrets passed from summoner to summoner.

My gaze rose to the dark circle. "Do you have a name? Your own name, not a lineage name."

"Yes."

"What is it?"

The unseen demon laughed, and its next words were a silky croon. "What will you give me for my name, *payilas*?"

Oh, a new nickname. Its *huh-aye-none* one seemed to mean "human," but I couldn't guess this one's meaning.

I sat back on my heels. "In exchange for your name, I'll bake something for you—*specifically* for you."

"Why would I want this?"

Embarrassment pulled at my mouth, which only annoyed me. I would not feel embarrassed that a *demon* didn't want my baking. "That's my offer, so take it or leave it."

I pushed to my feet, returned the handbook to its hiding spot, and stalked toward the door. As I placed my hand on the knob, a low call stopped me.

"*Payilas.*"

I looked over my shoulder.

"Bring your *something* to me," the demon said, "and I will tell you my name."

I regarded the black dome, then slipped through the door and closed it without answering. Curious and impulsive, my mom had called me. A volatile combination.

Clearly, I *still* hadn't learned my lesson.

7

I STOOD IN FRONT of the kitchen island, its surface stacked with raw ingredients, and dabbed the tears from my eyes.

After missing my chance yesterday to confront Uncle Jack about my inheritance, I'd cornered him this afternoon. Cue another round of interruptions, dismissals, and glares that sent my gaze skittering to the floor. I was as angry with myself and my cowardice as I was with his deceit and greed.

Sniffling, I began sorting the ingredients. Did I have any reason to doubt that Uncle Jack intended to cheat me out of my inheritance? Taking him to court might be my only option, but the thought made my skin tingle with anxiety. Calling lawyers' offices ... finding someone who would work for cheap until I won my case ... *going* to court ...

I took deep breaths.

Suing him would probably win me my money, but it would forever lose me the grimoire. How could I sue Uncle Jack for a book I couldn't describe? I'd only seen it a few times. I'd never opened it and had no idea what it contained.

Pulling myself together, I measured flour into a bowl. Tonight, I would resume combing the library shelves for any sign of my mother's grimoire or other books from her collection. And while I was down there ... why not learn the demon's name? There was something perversely satisfying in not only defying Uncle Jack, but also in succeeding to communicate with the otherwise silent demon where he'd failed for weeks.

As I sifted flour from one bowl to another, Amalia breezed into the kitchen, her long blond waves fluttering around her. She spotted me and stopped.

I glanced at her, then returned to sifting. What was the point in saying hello?

Stomping to the fridge, she pulled it open, rooted around, then carried an armload of food to the breakfast bar across from me. She dumped it on the counter and went back for more. I watched bemusedly as she collected three kinds of cheese, crackers, pickles, smoked meat, an apple, peanut butter, and a croissant before sliding onto the stool.

Her gray-eyed glower dared me to comment.

Staying silent, I opened a carton of eggs and cracked the first one, separating the whites from the yolks. As I worked, Amalia opened the cheese and started slicing cubes, popping every third or fourth one into her mouth. We ignored each other, me working diligently while she grazed on her selection of snacks.

Switching on the mixer, I beat the eggs into a foam, then sprinkled in powdered sugar one tablespoon at a time. When the egg mixture had formed stiff peaks under the beaters, I switched it off. Shooting me irritated looks in between reading on her phone, Amalia tore bites out of her apple.

"Why do you hate me?" The question popped out of my mouth against my better judgement.

Her head came up, disbelief on her face as she chewed her mouthful of apple. Flushing, I pretended I hadn't spoken and added a dollop of flour to the egg mixture.

She swallowed. "Isn't it obvious?"

I winced at her dismissive tone, then stiffened my shoulders. "Not to me."

"Give it up, Robin," she suggested nastily. "I'm not buying your girl-next-door act. We all know why you're here."

Folding more flour into the batter, I breathed through my panicky need to flee her hostility. "What are you talking about?"

She shoved a block of smoked gouda into a baggie. "Don't think I haven't noticed you snooping all over our house, but you won't find anything. We don't leave our summoning secrets lying around."

My mouth dropped open. *Summoning secrets?*

She pushed to her feet. "Just take your inheritance and get lost, Robin. Your parents already hoarded the family's knowledge instead of sharing it with my dad. If the names they gave you weren't enough, you can put yourself in horrible debt to buy some—like my father did."

Her casual mention of my parents punched the air out of me. As emotions ricocheted through my head, I whispered hoarsely, "The … names?"

"The demon names," she snapped.

"My parents didn't have any demon names."

"Seriously? How stupid do you think I am?"

"They didn't," I insisted, blinking rapidly. "They weren't summoners."

She shot me a scathing look. "We're *all* summoners."

"My parents weren't." I resumed stirring the batter with jerky movements. "They didn't practice magic at all. Neither do I. I've never even seen a demon." That brief glimpse in the library didn't count.

I finished folding the batter and shakily poured it into a tube pan. My eyes were stinging—typical Robin, tearing up at the first sign of scary, scary confrontation. As I smoothed the batter into the pan, Amalia stepped back from the counter.

"Come with me," she said.

"Come … where?"

"You'll see."

I slid the pan into the oven, set a timer on my phone, then followed her across the kitchen. She pulled on a pair of sandals and pushed through the French doors. Her long legs carried her across the sprawling deck and onto the lawn. I stuck my feet into someone's oversized flipflops and trotted after her on my much shorter legs, shivering in the October air, its chill resisting the afternoon sun's warmth.

A large greenhouse was nestled among shrubbery near a high white fence, and Amalia swept into the humid interior. Confused, I peered at the rows of plants as she opened a storage cupboard dominated by a rack of gardening tools.

Then she swung *that* open, revealing a hidden staircase leading underground.

My pulse throbbed in my ears as I cautiously followed her down the dim stairs. She wouldn't hurt me, would she? Hostile or not, she didn't seem like the type who'd chop me up and use my decomposing bones to fertilize the greenhouse.

She halted at the closed door at the bottom and checked I was right behind her. With a cold smirk, she shoved the door open and stepped aside to give me an unobstructed view of what lay beyond.

Dimly lit by a single bare bulb in the ceiling, the forty-square-foot room was windowless and damp. Water stains streaked the cinderblock walls and unfinished concrete floor, and in the center of the cold, ugly square, a ten-foot-diameter circle shone silver. Lines, arches, intersecting shapes, and hundreds of runes spiraled over the ring, weaving in and out of its interior. I knew exactly what it was.

A summoning circle. A *second* one. Unlike the library's circle, this one held no darkness ... but it wasn't empty.

A demon crouched inside it. Four long horns rose off its head, a pair protruding from each temple. Enormous wings were folded against its back, and a thick tail lay on the concrete behind it, ending in a mace-like scale plate. Heavily muscled shoulders supported its large head and those huge horns.

Even crouched, it was massive. Standing, it would be seven feet tall and built like a linebacker. Dark, reddish-brown skin stretched across bulging muscle.

Deep-set eyes fixed on me. They glowed like lava, but instead of heat, they radiated primal hatred and zealous bloodlust. Its need to kill, to rip and tear and spill my blood across the floor, hung in the air like a poisonous miasma.

I didn't realize I'd moved until my heel caught on something. I fell back into the stairs, slamming my elbows into the concrete.

Amalia swung the door shut, concealing the circle and beast behind it. She stood over me, a dark shadow under the weak light of the bare bulb overhead.

"You weren't lying," she murmured. "You've never seen a demon before."

I sat up. My limbs were shaking, my teeth chattering. My stomach twisted, threatening to jump out of my body, and air whistled through my teeth. Fear more intense than I'd ever felt before coursed inside me.

The definition of evil is an apt description of the demonic psyche. Now I understood. I no longer doubted those words in the slightest. The winged beast in that circle wanted to kill me— me and every other human it could lay its hands on. If not for the invisible barrier holding it in that circle, it would've already murdered us.

"If you aren't a summoner, why are you here?" Amalia asked.

"M-m-my p-parents' will," I chattered as I wrapped my arms around myself to stop their shaking. "Uncle Jack is the executor."

"Yeah, so?"

"I h-haven't gotten my inheritance yet." I peered up into her shadowed face. "It's been six months, but Uncle Jack keeps making excuses. Then he sold my house and kept the money, so I came here to … to try to …" I trailed off hopelessly.

"Aw shit," she muttered. She held out her hand.

I stared, shocked, then reached up. She pulled me to my feet and ascended the stairs.

"You really aren't training as a summoner?" she asked over her shoulder. "But your parents were summoners. Why didn't they teach you?"

"My parents aren't—weren't—" Pain slashed me as I corrected my error in verb tense. "They weren't summoners."

"I thought they were. Dad used to complain about how your mom sabotaged his career and forced him to start summoning from scratch."

We exited the greenhouse, but the golden sunlight did little to warm the shivery cold inside me.

"My parents never mentioned demon summoning," I said quietly. "Not once. I didn't know Uncle Jack was a summoner until I got here."

Facing me, Amalia brushed her hair off one shoulder. "Summoning is the family business. We've been summoners for generations."

"But that … that can't be. My parents would have …"

Stay away from magic and it'll stay away from you. That was the lesson my parents had taught me. Pursue a career in the human world, not the mythic one. Study mythic history if you want, but don't get involved in magic. And ignore the mysterious, ancient grimoire your mother diligently protects.

What had my parents been hiding from me?

I SAT ON THE KITCHEN STOOL Amalia had vacated, my elbows propped on the counter and chin on my palms. A plate sat in front of me, and on it was a perfect slice of fluffy white cake, frosted with whipped cream and topped with artfully arranged strawberry slices, a sprinkle of plump blueberries, and a drizzle of dark chocolate ganache.

Angel food cake. The most perfectly ironic bribe for a demon.

A memory, laced with terror, rose in my mind: the winged, horned monster with dark reddish skin crouched in the underground circle, radiating its desire to kill. I imagined the husky laugh of the library demon coming from its thin lips.

Picking up the fork beside my elbow, I poised it over the whipped-cream-and-ganache topping. I should eat this beautiful piece of cake. Scarf it right down, then head up to my room and plot my next move in the battle against Uncle Jack. I had nothing to gain from interacting with the demon.

But I was going to the library anyway, because reading *The Summoner's Handbook* was no longer a passing curiosity. With one conversation, Amalia had rocked the foundation of my world.

Summoning is the family business.

The fork wobbled and I set it down. Chewing my lip fretfully, I opened the breadbox and loaded a napkin with the cookies I'd baked early this morning, then picked up the plate of angel food cake. Lost in new worries that had joined the ever-present ache of my parents' loss, I headed into the basement.

The library lights were dimmed, the obsidian dome almost invisible. I nudged the slider up with my elbow and a soft glow pushed the shadows away. Cautiously, I approached the circle and knelt on the floor, then skooched close enough to slide the napkin of cookies over the silver inlay.

"That's for answering my question last time," I said.

Quiet was the only response, then …

"Keeping your word, *payilas*," the demon whispered, its voice only feet away.

I couldn't look at the darkness. Was there a monster concealed inside it—a seven- or eight-foot beast with giant horns, wings, and a tail made for crushing enemies? The crimson eyes I'd glimpsed—did they too burn with murderous hatred and insatiable bloodlust? Uncle Jack and Claude thought this demon could be the most powerful of all.

And yet … no matter what version of that winged demon I imagined, it didn't match the quiet voice that slid from the darkness of this circle.

I peered down at the plate. A strawberry was slowly slipping off the cake. "I made this for you. In exchange for your name. But … but I want to ask for something else instead."

The demon waited. A patient hunter.

"I want to … would you … can I see what you look like?"

"No."

"Oh." I deflated, but I wasn't sure if it was from relief or disappointment. "Okay."

I set the plate down and slid the cake, resting on a napkin, onto the floor. Wary as always of getting too close to the protective barrier, I prodded a corner of the napkin into the darkness. It was probably better I didn't see the demon. Did I really want to add more fuel to my nightmares?

Sitting back on my heels, I squinted toward the coffee table where the Demonica book waited. Demon summoning. My family's legacy. An ancient grimoire. Secrets. So many secrets. Had my parents been summoners like Uncle Jack or had they eschewed magic as they'd taught me to do? What had they been hiding from me? Could Amalia be wrong?

If demon summoning *did* run in the family, and the ancient grimoire had been passed from summoner to summoner for generations, Uncle Jack would never, ever let me have it. I had to get it first.

"*Payilas.*"

I glanced at the dark dome. Both napkins sat untouched on the silver inlay.

"What do you want?" the demon asked.

The grimoire. The truth. My parents alive again. "I want to see your face."

"*Ch.* Stubborn *payilas.*"

I assumed that was a refusal. I was already turning away when the darkness inside the circle swirled—then disappeared.

He sat at the edge of the circle, with one arm propped behind him, a knee raised, and his forearm resting on it. At my shocked gasp, he canted his head, the motion cocky and challenging, and his crimson eyes locked on mine. A faint magma glow emanated from his stare.

He was definitely a demon, but he was so different from the one under the greenhouse that they could've been different species. He had no wings, for starters. In fact, he looked … he looked …

He looked almost human.

His smooth skin was the color of toffee with a reddish undertone. Black hair, short in the back but longer in the front, was rumpled above his dark eyebrows and wild as though a brush had never touched it. The sharp line of his jaw smoothed to softer cheekbones, and his ears had pointed tips. Like the other demon, four dark horns poked out of his hair, two rising above each temple, but they were minuscule—only a couple of inches long.

My pulse thundered in my ears. I realized I was leaning forward where I sat, straining to get a closer look without actually moving.

"Satisfied?" he asked.

Those husky, swirling tones. Seeing his mouth move and hearing the sounds falling from his lips … how could I have imagined that winged monster speaking in his voice?

If I'd heard his remark from out of the darkness, I would've detected only a flat question, but now, watching his face, the angle of his head, the slight narrowing of his crimson eyes—dry sarcasm, irritation, and perhaps a hint of displeasure at my ogling him.

"I—I—" I couldn't speak. I was too stunned. "Try the cake."

His gaze dropped to the angel food cake. He sat forward, movements smooth and swift, and pinched the napkin sticking into the circle. He dragged the slice across the inlay, then scooped it onto one palm.

As he lifted it, his gleaming crimson eyes turned to mine. "*Payilas mailēshta.* Stop staring."

My mouth fell open. I forced it closed. "Sorry."

He waited a moment. "Still staring."

I forced my gaze to the floor. For about ten seconds, I resisted looking, then like a magnet drawn to steel, my eyes rose again—in time to catch him stuffing the final bite of cake into his mouth.

"You ate it already?" I gasped.

He swallowed, then licked a dollop of whipped cream off his thumb. Had he even *chewed* it?

I scanned his alien face, trying to read his expression. "Did … did you like it?"

He ignored my question and slid the cookies—classic chocolate chip—into the circle. He snapped one in half and shoved both pieces into his mouth. Swallowed. Picked up the next cookie.

"You should chew," I said faintly. "It's … better …"

He shot me an annoyed look, then rammed the next cookie into his mouth like he hadn't eaten in weeks.

Which, I realized, he hadn't. Aside from the few cookies I'd given him, I'd never seen anyone bring food down here. Did he need food? He was obviously capable of eating.

I unabashedly watched him devour the cookies in record time, my gaze darting from detail to fascinating detail. I hadn't noticed anything about the other demon's clothing, but now I studied this one's garments.

The most familiar shape was his dark fabric shorts, topped with a thick leather belt. Worn leather straps crisscrossed his right shoulder and side, holding a metal armor plate over the left side of his chest. Two overlapping plates shielded his left shoulder, and a shining armguard covered his left forearm, strapped over a fitted sleeve that ran up to his bicep. Matching greaves protected his shins atop ... leggings? I didn't know what else to call the tight black fabric that ran from his ankles up over his knees. Strips of fabric wrapped around the arches of his feet, leaving the rest of his soles bare.

Aside from the shorts, the other fabric he wore seemed only for the purpose of protecting his skin from the metal armor and its leather straps. That left ... a lot of bare skin.

He swallowed his final mouthful, then pinched the napkins between two fingers and his thumb. Red glowed over his fingertips. The paper smoldered, then erupted into flame. I jolted backward, but the fire consumed the flammable napkins in seconds. Ash fluttered to the hardwood, and I gulped.

His eyes, glowing as brightly as the other demon's had, turned back to me. His lips curved into a wolfish smile that exposed a hint of white teeth—a smile that mocked me, taunted me. A savage, hungry smile.

Then darkness swept over the circle and it was an impenetrable black dome once more.

8

I FLIPPED THE LIGHTS ON. "All right!"

A yellow glow swept across the library. Balancing a plate on one hand, I crossed to the dark dome and dropped down to sit crossed-legged.

Last night, after giving the demon his slice of cake, I'd spent three hours on the sofa reading *The Summoner's Handbook*. Determined to gain a proper understanding of Demonica, I'd returned to Chapter Three and slogged through endless pages about summoning rituals. Even with my college-level fluency in Latin and Ancient Greek, the technical instructions were over my head.

While reading, I'd felt the demon's gaze on me. He hadn't spoken again and I hadn't tried to engage him, but hidden in that darkness, he'd watched me read. It'd been ... weird.

"Are you paying attention?" I asked. "Tonight, I brought you the *entire* cake—minus the piece you ate yesterday."

I set the plate on the floor. Four thick white slices were buried beneath whipped cream, strawberries, blueberries, and chocolate drizzle. Technically, it wasn't the rest of the cake— I'd eaten a piece too—but I saw no need to mention that.

A quiet snort from within the circle. "Should I be flattered, *payilas?*"

My cheeks heated with embarrassment. "If you don't want it, I'll just take my cake and leave."

Like smoke caught in a breeze, the darkness in the circle swirled away. The demon cast me a sideways look, his lava-red eyes glowing dimly. He lay on his back in the middle of the circle, one leg bent at the knee, the other ankle propped on it, foot in the air. With an arm tucked behind his head like a pillow, he looked surprisingly comfortable lying on the hard, cold floor.

I drank in the sight, tracing the strange lines of his clothes, the shine of his armor, and his reddish-toffee skin. I should've been afraid, but his danger had been stripped, his weapons disarmed. He was a tiger at the zoo, a wild specimen safely behind bars, exotic and mesmerizing.

His gaze slid to the dessert. "What do you want this time?"

"I want your name."

"Which one?"

I waved my hand. "Not your summoning name. Your personal name."

A corner of his mouth curled—that mocking smile—and he swung into a sitting position. As he faced me, a flick of motion drew my eyes—something long and thin sweeping across the floor behind him.

My expression froze. "You—you have *a tail?*"

He looked over his shoulder. The long, whip-like appendage swept across the floor again, and as it stilled, I spotted two curved barbs on the end.

"You do not?" he retorted, facing me again. "How do you balance?"

"I balance just fine."

"Because *hh'ainun* are slow."

I lifted the first piece of cake off the plate and set it beside the silver inlay. I'd prepared each one on a napkin so I could move them easily. "Your name."

"*Ch.*"

I leveled him with a stare, shocked by my own boldness. Where had my shy timidity disappeared to? Maybe the key to my confidence issues was conducting all interactions through an impenetrable barrier.

He considered me. "Zylas."

"That's your name? Zylas?"

"Not *zeeeellahhs.*" He mimicked my attempt in an exaggerated tone. "Zuh-*yee*-las. Try again."

"Zee-las."

"Zuh-*yee*-las. Three sounds, not two."

"*Zyee-las.*"

"Close enough," he muttered.

"I'm trying my best here," I complained. "*My* name is much easier to say. Robin."

"Robin?"

Surprise fluttered through me. In his strange accent, my name sounded almost as exotic as his. Grinning, I pushed the napkin's corner across the circle. He pulled it in, scooped the cake up, and devoured it in three bites. Still no chewing.

"You never said if you like it," I prompted.

"Your name?"

"The cake." But now I was wondering what he thought of my name.

He eyed the remaining pieces. "What else do you want?"

I thought for a moment. "How old are you?"

"*Ih?*"

"Huh?"

We stared at each other, stymied by the language breakdown. His age was hard to judge. If he'd been human, I would've pegged him as early twenties—but who knew how aging and maturity worked for demons?

I tried again. "How many years have you been alive?"

His face scrunched in bewilderment. "You count this?"

"Yes, of course. I'm twenty."

"Twenty?" He scanned me from the top of my head down to my jeans-clad knees. "I learned your numbers wrong. Twenty is wrong."

I held up one finger. "One." I spread my fingers and thumb. "Five." I added my other hand. "Ten." I opened and closed my fingers twice. "Twenty."

"How long is a year?"

"Uh ... three hundred and sixty-five days, so ..."

He rubbed his hand over his face in a gesture so human I did a double take. "*Dilēran.* I do not know this. I have no numbers."

Disappointed, I slid him another slice of cake.

He shoveled it down. "What else?"

"What do you keep calling me? *Payilas?*"

"*Pah-yil-las,*" he sounded out bossily. "It means small female."

So ... "girl." I scrunched my nose.

He flicked his fingers at the cake in a "give me that" gesture, but I scoffed.

"You don't get a piece for that little answer. Hmm, what else …" I studied his irritated scowl. Black hair tangled across his forehead. If not for the crimson eyes and small horns, his face could've belonged to a human. It was disconcerting. "Why did you show yourself to me this time? You didn't have to."

"To see you properly. Wasted question, *payilas*."

"See me? You mean you can't see me through the darkness in there?"

"No eyes can see without light," he replied dismissively. "I can see in a different way but it is … not details."

I leaned forward curiously. "What sort of different way?"

"I can see … hot and cold. Shapes of heat."

"No way! You have infrared vision? Like a snake?"

He frowned. "I do not know those words."

"Infrared is a spectrum of light and a snake is an animal. A reptile—long and skinny with scales and—wait." I pushed to my feet. "Hold on."

I hastened toward the encyclopedias I'd examined on my first late-night visit. A set of handsome zoology texts with matching spines sat on a high shelf. I pulled one down and flipped through it.

"Here!" Rushing back to the circle, I dropped to my knees and held the open book up, the right-hand page filled with a glossy full-color photo of a viper. "This is a snake."

He leaned in for a closer look at the page—and his head jolted. A shimmer distorted the air as the barrier rippled from the contact. Hunching to avoid the invisible force, he studied the encyclopedia page, then looked up.

My heart leaped with something approaching terror. I was kneeling close to the circle's edge—closer than I'd ever gotten before. I could see the smooth texture of his skin and the dark, narrow pupils almost lost in the unbroken glow of his crimson eyes. I could've stretched my arm out and touched him.

"How am I like this animal?" he asked, snapping me out of my daze. "It is nothing like me."

"Snakes can see heat too." I pulled the book away and shifted backward, distancing myself from that dangerous line, then scanned the page. "It's called 'infrared thermal radiation sensing.' Humans don't have that ability."

His attention had returned to the waiting cake. I slid him the next slice and watched him eat it with renewed curiosity.

"You said you wanted to see me properly. Why?"

"Why not?" he retorted. "Only three *hh'ainun* come here— you and two males. I see *them* only with … *infrared thermal radiation sensing*." He pulled a face as though the term disgusted him.

I pursed my lips, surprised and a touch uncomfortable. He picked up new words very easily. How much was he learning from our interactions?

"I've seen two demons," I remarked absently, distracted by my worries. "Including you."

Interest sparked in his face. "Two?"

I recoiled under his gaze, but I saw no harm in revealing the nearby demon. Trapped in his dome-shaped prison cell, Zylas could do nothing with that information. "There's a second summoning circle here with a demon in it."

"Who is the other? His name?"

"I don't know."

"Describe him."

"Um … very large. Long horns, big wings, a thick tail with a bony plate on the end."

Zylas's eyes gleamed. "*Na?* Him?" His head tipped backward and he laughed, the husky sound rolling through the room.

I inched away, my stomach dancing with fearful butterflies. Cruel delight lit Zylas's face.

"To see his arrogance ground under a *hh'ainun*'s foot …" He sighed wistfully. "I would like to watch that."

"You … you know that demon?"

He pointed at the last piece of cake. "Ask."

Disturbed and no longer sure I was enjoying this conversation, I thought of Uncle Jack and Claude, of the other demon "ready" for a contract, and of Zylas's refusal to negotiate or interact with them.

"Okay," I said slowly. "My final question … why won't you talk to the summoners? The other demon—"

His hand whipped out so fast it was a blur. I lurched back as his fist hit the barrier and ripples erupted across its transparent surface.

"*Kanish!*" The guttural word snarled from his throat, his eyes blazing red and face twisting with fury. "They sent you, didn't they? A meek *payilas* to disarm me, *na?* Make me pliant? *Satūsa dilittā hh'ainun eshanā zh'ūltis!*"

Gaping, I shoved backward across the floor on trembling limbs.

He slammed his fist against the barrier again. Scarlet light burst over his fingers and snaked up his wrist. "*Kanish!* Get out of my sight!"

"Th-they didn't send me," I whispered, stumbling over the words. "They didn't—"

"Get out!"

"Please listen to me—"

He bared his teeth—revealing pointed, predatory incisors. My mind blanked with terror. Tears stung my eyes, my hands shook, and my lungs quivered. Confrontation always undid me, even without murderous intent behind it. If Zylas could have reached me, he would've torn out my throat.

Actually, I corrected, he'd always wanted to kill me. He was a demon. Killing me would be the highlight of his imprisonment.

Gulping painfully, I forced my eyes up from the floor. Zylas's burning glower sent my gaze skittering away, but I forced it back and focused on his slightly less petrifying chin.

"They didn't send me," I repeated, hating the quaver in my voice. "I'm not supposed to be down here. I—I only came to read the books. Uncle Jack doesn't know I've been talking to you."

His glowing eyes narrowed to slits. "Then you are too stupid to realize they are using you."

"They aren't using me," I told the floor. When had I looked away? "I barely even talk to them, and when I do, it isn't about you."

Painful silence, pulsing with Zylas's rage, stretched through the room.

"When you speak to them again," he snarled softly, "tell them my bones will turn to dust in this cage, because I will *never* submit to a *hh'ainun*."

His vehemence drew my stare up, but black night had filled the dome, hiding him. My lips quivered and I pressed them together. With unsteady motions, I nudged the final piece of cake over the silver inlay, then collected the plate.

I looked back with every step across the floor, but Zylas didn't speak. The cake sat untouched. I slipped out the door and around the corner, then pressed my back to the wall and counted out a full two minutes.

Holding my breath, I peeked through a crack in the door. The slice of cake was gone, and as I watched, flames flashed inside the circle—Zylas burning the napkins to ash.

9

HOVERING AT THE WINDOW as though enjoying the view, I listened to Uncle Jack's and Claude's voices retreat down the hall. They were heading to the basement for their daily attempt at negotiating with the silent demon. I waited a minute to make sure they wouldn't return, then tiptoed down the hall to Uncle Jack's office and slipped inside.

Reconnaissance Mission, step one: complete. I had infiltrated enemy headquarters, just like the sorceress Celestina Peruggia from *A Study of Mythic Crime in the 20th Century*— some light reading I'd enjoyed a few weeks ago. Was I weird for admiring a notorious thief of mythic artifacts? She was just so tough and competent.

I scanned the large filing cabinets, imagining I was Celestina scoping her next heist. The cabinets would take too long to search; better leave them for now. I circled Uncle Jack's desk and dropped into his chair. Papers covered the desktop in sloppy piles, and I rapidly shuffled through them.

In the two days since Zylas had banished me, I hadn't returned to the library. I should have. I wanted to keep reading *The Summoner's Handbook* and I shouldn't let a demon that couldn't leave his circle stop me. But facing him again …

Besides, my priority was my mother's grimoire.

I sifted through envelopes, forms, printouts, bookkeeping records, receipts, and sticky notes with scribbled reminders. Where would a professional thief look for valuables? My hands fluttered indecisively around the desk, and I berated myself for hesitating. Celestina wouldn't have wasted time. Only the best of the best could've successfully stolen the Carapace of Valdurna from the terrifying dark-arts master known as the Xors Druid.

I opened the desk drawers. Basic office supplies in the top one. The second held envelopes, stamps, and a broken stapler. The final drawer was full of folders. I flipped one open, discovering a form headed with the MPD logo.

Hmm. MagiPol strictly enforced the laws that kept magic hidden and mythics safe, and they didn't like it when people, oh, you know, forged important paperwork. I skimmed a few forms, then folded them up and jammed them in my pocket.

Now what? I wiggled the computer mouse and the monitor flashed to life, requesting a password. I thought for a moment, then typed "admin" and hit enter. Nope. I typed "admin1" and hit enter again. The screen blinked to the desktop.

That had been easy. Technological dinosaurs like Uncle Jack didn't strain their brains worrying about password security. I opened his inbox and scanned subject lines and senders. Far down the list, a name jumped out at me—*my* name.

"RE: Robin Page arrival," sent by Claude Mercier—Uncle Jack's business partner. I clicked the email.

> Jack, I understand your concerns but if it's that much of an issue, you should have refused to let her stay with you. I doubt she'll be any help with the translation anyway. If you involve her, things could get messy.
>
> Claude

I scrolled down, but there was no chain of past emails under the message. Returning to the inbox, I searched for "Claude Mercier" and a short list popped up—too short. Uncle Jack was either archiving or deleting Claude's emails. Aside from the one about me, the others all contained attachments. I clicked the oldest one, a message from four months ago.

> heres the page...i think this is the 12th house??
> the sooner you get the name out of it the sooner we can get started. this is our big break.
> J.

I cringed over my uncle's horrible grammar. Claude's response was right above it.

> Jack, why are you sending this by email? Don't you understand what this page could be worth? Email isn't secure! No computer is! Delete these emails and the scans. I'll bring you the translation in person. Be more conscientious of security.

I scrolled down to the attachment—a JPG file—and double-clicked it. An image opened on the screen: a scan showing a single page of a very old book, the paper yellowed and the ink faded. Handwritten Ancient Greek scrawled across it, but that wasn't what had me leaning toward the monitor, my eyes wide.

Interspersed in the text were charcoal illustrations. A symbol took up one corner, and a sketch of a person, front and back view, filled the lower half. The illustrated man wore light armor, minimal fabric, and had a long tail ending in two barbs.

It was a drawing of Zylas. Or, if not him, a similar demon. Was *this* how Uncle Jack and Claude had summoned a demon that, according to them, had never been summoned before? Had they translated this page and learned a new name—Zylas's lineage name?

Footsteps thumped in the hall outside. Gasping, I ducked off the chair and into the dark gap under the desk.

The door opened. Shoes smacked across the hardwood, then a filing cabinet drawer slithered open. Had the person noticed the monitor, or was it turned far enough toward the wall to hide that the screen was awake? Scarcely breathing, I held my hands over my mouth as the unknown visitor rifled through files. I had to keep my cool, like Celestina had when she'd smuggled the Carapace out of the Soviet Union.

I grimaced at the absurdity of the comparison. This was hardly as terrifying as anything Celestina had done.

The cabinet drawer slammed shut, making me jump. Footsteps retreated, and the door banged. When all was silent again, I crept out and grabbed the mouse. A few quick clicks, and the printer hummed to life. A page slid through the machine.

I cleared my search and closed the inbox, then locked the computer. Printout in hand, I escaped the office and returned to the second floor. Only when I was back in my bedroom did I take a full breath.

Mission accomplished. Sort of. At least I'd made it safely out of enemy territory. Celestina had too, but a decade after she'd sold the Carapace to a British guild, the vengeful Xors Druid had tracked her down and murdered her. Maybe I should pick better role models.

I smoothed my stolen printout and stared at Zylas's likeness. This page had come from an antique book, which Uncle Jack had scanned and sent to Claude four months ago.

My parents had died six months ago.

I closed my eyes, fighting the heavy sickness rising in my stomach. *If* summoning ran in my family, and *if* my mother had kept important summoning details from Uncle Jack, chances were the grimoire was related to Demonica. And two months after my parents' deaths, Uncle Jack suddenly had two new, rare demon names.

It looked like Uncle Jack already had my mom's grimoire. He'd had it for months.

Fury, despair, and painful betrayal closed my throat. Uncle Jack had been stringing me along since the beginning. He knew what I wanted and he would never let me get it.

Fighting for composure, I glared around the bedroom. My gaze landed on the dresser, where my books were stacked. Shifting *Bronze Age History* aside, I picked up a worn textbook: *The Complete Compilation of Arcane Cantrips.* Pages were marked with bright stickers, corners were dog-eared, and a brown ring on the cover forever mocked me for setting a mug of hot chocolate on it.

My fourteenth birthday gift. *"This,"* my mother had said after I had opened it with a delighted gasp, *"is all the magic you'll ever need."*

The memory of her voice intensified my grief and doubt. I opened the book to a page with a large rune drawn in dotted lines. Cantrips were the most basic form of Arcana sorcery, and a paragraph of text described this one's purpose, power, pronunciation, and the proper method of drawing it.

Slipping a pad of paper from the back of the textbook, I rooted around for a pen, then drew a swift but small rendition of the rune. Holding the paper up, I whispered, "*Luce.*"

The rune blazed white. It glowed for twenty seconds, then faded.

With the stroke of a pen and a short incantation, I'd created magic. That simple. That easy. Not all Arcana was easy. In fact, most of it was painfully intricate. I knew, because from my fourteenth birthday onward, I'd read every book on magic I could get my hands on. Yet, despite the years I'd spent learning *about* magic, I'd never used it.

Stay away from magic and it'll stay away from you. My parents had etched that rule into my soul, had reinforced the fear of magic's power again and again.

But *why*? If our family included a long line of sorcerers dedicated to demon summoning, why had my parents been afraid of magic? If she'd wanted nothing to do with summoning, why had my mom cherished and protected the grimoire?

My only claim to fame was being the biggest, dorkiest nerd I'd ever encountered, yet for all my reading and studying and nerding out, I knew nothing. I had no idea why my parents had feared magic. Whether my family was a line of summoners. How summoning even worked—aside from a now pedantic understanding of the nuances of summoning rituals. I didn't even know what sort of contract Uncle Jack wanted to negotiate, or why Zylas was dead set against it.

Knowledge was power, and I needed more of it. I needed *The Summoner's Handbook* from the library.

I laid the grimoire printout on the light cantrip description, then pulled the stolen MPD forms out of my pocket and set them on top, covering the faded sketch of Zylas's doppelganger. I closed the cantrip textbook, the papers hidden inside, and stacked it with my other books.

One quick and silent trip through the house later, I entered the library, leaving the lights on their lowest setting. Ebony filled the summoning circle, nothing but silence inside it, and the soft thump of my socked feet was uncomfortably loud. Zylas didn't speak as I crossed to the sitting area, but the back of my neck prickled, warning that a predator was observing me—hunting me.

I pulled *The Summoner's Handbook* from under the coffee table, then said stiffly, "I can feel you watching me, Zylas. I'm not here to pester you. I'm just getting something."

As I headed back to the door, his low voice slid out of the circle. "Getting what?"

I should've kept walking. Should've gone straight to my room with my prize. Instead, I returned to the inky dome and held out the book in answer.

The darkness swirled, then faded. Zylas sat in the circle's center, looking bored. "A book?"

"A book about demons." Crouching so we were at eye level, I tapped on the cover. "I'm learning how summoning and contracts work."

He appraised me, suspicion creasing the corners of his mouth.

I lowered the book to peer more closely at him. His eyes were no longer what I'd call crimson—they were dark red, like cooling coals with only a hint of heat left. He watched me with dislike, but his snarling rage was gone. He seemed … tired.

"Um," I whispered uncertainly. "Are you … okay?"

A muscle in his cheek twitched, a suppressed reaction to my question. He opened his mouth to reply, then his gaze shot past me to the door and darkness whooshed through the circle. I launched to my feet and spun around.

Uncle Jack and Claude walked into the library.

"… won't wait much longer," Uncle Jack was saying. He swiped at the switch and lights brightened throughout the room. "But it shouldn't—"

He and Claude spotted me at the same time. I clutched the Demonica book, my brain frozen with panic.

"Robin?" Uncle Jack barked. "What are you doing in here? I told you to stay out!"

Claude's pale eyes moved from my guilty face to the black dome. "Were you talking to the demon?"

"No!" I gasped. "I—I—I just wanted to borrow a book."

Face reddening, Uncle Jack advanced on me. He wrenched the book out of my hands. When he flipped it open to read the title page, his eyes bulged.

"What are you doing with this? Have you read any of it?"

"N-no. I only just got it a minute ago—"

His fingers closed around my arm with bruising force. He dragged me across the room, shoving *The Summoner's Handbook* at Claude on his way past, and propelled me toward the stairs. I stumbled and almost fell.

"You're living under my roof," he growled, a vein throbbing in his forehead. "I will not tolerate any lies. Have you come down here before?"

"No," I whispered, staring at my feet as I twisted my hands together. "Not since you showed me the—the summoning circle. I wanted to learn more about Demonica so I came down just to … just to …"

He grabbed my upper arm again. "You don't need to know anything about Demonica. Didn't your parents forbid it? Stay out of the basement, Robin." His hand tightened, fingers grinding into my flesh, and tears spilled down my cheeks. "If I catch you down here again, I'll kick you out of my house in a heartbeat. Understood?"

"Yes," I choked out.

The moment he released me, I bolted for the stairs. My socks slipped and I pitched forward, bashing my knee against a step. Lungs paralyzed by pain, I heard Claude's say from the library, "I warned you about her."

I shoved myself up and ran. I didn't stop until I'd reached my room and slammed the door behind me.

I WAS GETTING GOOD at sneaking around.

For three days I hid in my room to demonstrate my obedience. That was as long as I could stand my boredom and restlessness. When I ventured out again, it was with a plan: sneak into the library and steal *The Summoner's Handbook*, or a similar book, without getting caught.

If Uncle Jack was determined to keep me away from Demonica and summoning, the information must be important. It could be he was afraid I'd realize he was breaking laws—as if I needed a book to tell me—or it could be more than that. I would find out.

Once I knew what I was dealing with, I'd devise a way to get my mother's grimoire back from him.

Stealing the Demonica book should've been easy, except Uncle Jack and Claude had developed a new obsession with the library. In the three days I'd been cloistered in my room, he and his partner had upped their visits to the summoning circle from once a day to every hour or two, day and night. Claude wasn't even going home—he was sleeping in a guest room between library sessions.

I'd been stalking them around the house for two days. They weren't following a schedule, so I couldn't guarantee a free window in which to sneak down there myself. Getting *The Summoner's Handbook* was important, but not getting caught was more important.

Crouched at the top of the basement stairs, I listened to the muffled echo of Uncle Jack's and Claude's voices coming from the library. When light flooded the hallway from the door opening, I darted into the kitchen. Sliding onto a stool, I took a huge bite of the apple I'd gotten out earlier and pretended to read the mystery novel I'd left open on the breakfast bar.

Uncle Jack's voice preceded him out of the basement, his tone frustrated and impatient. "Its breaking point should be any day now. We just have to keep checking."

"It should have come days ago," Claude replied.

"Which must mean the demon is exceptionally powerful." Uncle Jack strode into view. "We can't miss it or our last chance will be—"

Breaking off, he glared at me suspiciously.

"Good afternoon," I said politely, glancing up from my book.

He kept walking. Claude followed in silence, his mouth pressed in a thin line that pulled at the scar on his chin, and to my surprise, Travis trailed after them. I hadn't realized he was down there too, but I supposed it made sense. Travis was Uncle Jack's stepson, so why not train him alongside Amalia?

I listened to their passage through the house as I finished my apple, pondering my chances of making it downstairs and back again without getting caught. I was just thinking I should try when heels clacked down the hall.

Kathy swept into the kitchen. The way she glared in my direction before opening the oven to check on her casserole made me wonder if Uncle Jack had asked her to keep an eye on me.

I tossed out my apple core, washed my hands in the sink, grabbed my novel, and hastened out of the kitchen. As I stumped upstairs to my room, I mulled over what Uncle Jack had said. A "breaking point." Did he think Zylas would crack soon? Based on my interactions with the demon, I doubted he'd ever give in, but maybe the summoners knew something I didn't. Why hadn't I read *The Summoner's Handbook* from cover to cover while I'd had the chance?

My feet stopped of their own accord, and it took my distracted brain a moment to catch up. I was standing in front of Amalia's bedroom door. I pursed my lips. She was out most mornings but returned for the afternoon. I hesitated, then knocked.

A rustle, followed by footsteps. The door cracked open. "Yes?"

I peered at the sliver of her face. "Can I ask you something?"

"About what?"

"Summoning."

Her mouth twisted, then she stepped back. "Fine."

She opened her door wide enough to invite me in. Every inch of wall space in her room was covered in large photographic prints of … cloth. Dizzying close-ups of woven fabric, colorful silk rippling in the wind, patterns and textures, stitching designs, color combinations, even zippers.

She'd shoved her queen-sized bed with a patchwork quilt into one corner, and two very different work areas dominated the rest of the room. Back by the closet door, a flimsy desk buckled under the weight of leather-bound textbooks with Greek, Latin, and Sanskrit on the spines. In the other corner, a long utilitarian table was positioned under the window. On it, two sewing machines sat beside tumbled heaps of fabric and a rack of colorful thread spools. A dress form stood nearby, pins sticking out of the headless female figure.

"You sew?" I asked, surprised.

Her mouth thinned. "Problem with that?"

"No." I blinked, unsure how I'd offended her. "I think it's awesome. Do you make clothes?"

"Yeah." She dropped into the chair in front of the sewing machine and picked up a swatch of fabric. "I'm designing hex clothing."

I stepped closer to see the fabric. Sewn into the floral pattern was a discreet cantrip. I recognized it—*impello*, the push spell.

"Wow!" I exclaimed. "So this would be, like, a self-defense shirt?"

She grinned, pleased I'd caught on so fast. "Exactly. It's tricky, though. Not nearly as simple as drawing or etching a cantrip." She tossed the fabric onto the table and twisted her blond hair into a bun. "My dad thinks it's a waste of time."

I glanced at the books threatening to collapse her desk. "Because it takes away from your summoning apprenticeship?"

"I don't know how he expects me to study ten hours a day when I already spend every morning with my language tutor," she complained. Grabbing a fabric pencil off the table, she stuck it through her bun to hold the hair in place. "So, what do you want to know?"

I hesitated, then sat on the edge of her unmade bed. "On his way up from the library, I heard Uncle Jack talking about a breaking point. Do you know what that means?"

"Oh yeah, that's basic stuff." She held a hanky-sized sample of patterned cotton up to the sunlight streaming through the window. "Usually, demons agree to a contract within a few weeks, but sometimes, you'll get one that refuses to take a contract for whatever reason. So we wait."

She returned the cotton square to the pile. "Once a demon is summoned into a circle, it gets weaker as time passes. At around nine or ten weeks, almost every demon caves and agrees to a contract. That's the breaking point."

"What happens if Uncle Jack misses it?"

"The demon dies." Amalia reorganized a few thread spools on the rack. "They can't survive in those circles indefinitely. You have to catch them right before that, when they're most desperate. They usually give in. Demons have a strong survival drive."

My stomach twisted strangely. "So … you're saying … summoners call demons into this world, imprison them in a circle for weeks on end, force them to accept a contract, and if they don't, you let them die?"

Amalia shot me a scathing look. "Good god, how much of a bleeding heart are you? They're *demons*, Robin. You saw the one under the greenhouse. It'd kill us all in a heartbeat. Yeah, we let them die. We can't set them free—they'd massacre the entire neighborhood in the time it took the MPD to put out an alert."

"Why not send the demons back?"

"Summoning is a one-way ticket, and even if it wasn't, why would we send them back? If we did, no demon would *ever* agree to a contract."

"What does a contract involve, exactly?"

She studied me for a long moment, then answered with chilling simplicity. "Complete surrender."

She pushed to her feet and walked to her desk. After rooting around among the books, she tossed something to me. I caught it, fumbling the long silver chain. It was a round, flat pendant the size of my palm, with runes engraved over its surface.

"That," Amalia said, dropping into her chair, "is an infernus. It's the key to a demon contract. Assuming we're talking legal, MPD-sanctioned ones, a contract is pretty simple. The demon gives up its autonomy. Its spirit is bound to the infernus and the contractor's will. The contractor controls the demon like a puppet."

I stared at the silver pendant.

"Allow the demon any free will, and it'll find a way to kill its contractor."

"Why would a demon ever agree to that?" I whispered.

"Because of the slim chance they'll outlive their contractor and make it back home."

"How do they—"

"Amalia!" Kathy's buzzard call echoed up the stairs. "Travis! Dinner is ready."

Amalia plucked the infernus out of my hands and chucked it onto her desk. "Let's go eat."

I followed her out of the room, feeling numb. Zylas's vicious snarl replayed in my head. *Tell them my bones will turn to dust in this cage, because I will never submit.*

No wonder he refused to so much as speak to his summoners. I was surprised he'd spoken to *me*; I was a human, just like the ones who'd torn him from his home and were forcing him to choose between enslavement and death.

STANDING ON MY TIPTOES, I watched the car's taillights retreat up the long drive to the front gate. Uncle Jack, Claude, and Travis had loaded into the car before it set out. They probably wouldn't be gone long—Uncle Jack wouldn't want to miss Zylas's "breaking point"—but it would be long enough. I hoped.

I backed away from the window, scooted across the luxurious bathroom, and peeked out the door. On the main level, a TV talk show echoed from the family room. Kathy commented on something, and Amalia's softer voice replied. Good.

I snuck the long way around—sometimes the sheer size of this house was a blessing—and trotted down the basement stairs. Turning the lights up enough to see, I entered the library.

The usual pitch darkness filled Zylas's circle, and the room hadn't changed in the five days since my last visit. I zipped around the silent dome and was already crouching in front of the bookshelf when I realized what I was seeing.

The lowest shelves, where all the Demonica books had been stacked, were empty. Frantically, I pawed through the other titles. Arcana, Spiritalis, Psychica, Elementaria. That was it. Not a single book related to Demonica remained.

My hands tightened into fists. Damn it! Uncle Jack must have moved them! What was I supposed to do *now*?

I growled under my breath. All this time wasted planning and waiting for a chance to sneak down here, and my uncle was way ahead of me. I should've realized he wouldn't leave the books lying around. He'd beat me to this just as he'd beaten me to the grimoire.

Dropping onto my butt, I reluctantly scooted one-hundred-and-eighty degrees to face the black circle. "Zylas?"

As usual, he ignored me. In his mind, I was an enemy now.

"I have a question," I said, tugging the sleeves of my sweater over my hands. It was always so cold in here. "If you answer, I'll bring you something tomorrow night."

Silence.

"Did you see who moved the books from this shelf and where they took them?"

I was hoping Uncle Jack had hidden the books somewhere else in the library. He was lazy enough to half-ass it like that, and if he had, Zylas would've witnessed it.

The demon continued to give me the silent treatment. He must really hate me now that he suspected I was in cahoots with Uncle Jack.

"I know you don't trust me," I tried, feeling like I was talking to a wall. "I just need this one answer. I won't ask for anything else."

Again, nothing. I heaved a frustrated sigh, but beneath my irritation, concern sparked. Demons got weaker the longer they were in the circle, and Zylas had just hit ten weeks. Five days ago, when I'd last seen him, he'd seemed tired and his eyes had been dull. Had he reached his breaking point?

"Are you still there?" I inched closer to the silver inlay, my heart picking up speed. "I'm not leaving until you acknowledge me," I threatened. *He* didn't know I had to get back upstairs before Uncle Jack returned. "I'll sit here all night and annoy you."

Folding my arms, I counted to thirty, then opened my mouth to berate him again.

"Go away."

My breath caught. His voice was a dry whisper. I couldn't even hear his usual irritation.

"Zylas? Are you okay?"

He ignored me again.

"Let me see you." I scooted closer, my knees inches from the circle's edge. "Come on. If you do, I'll bring you something extra good next time I can sneak down here." I counted to thirty again. "If you don't reveal yourself, I'll throw a bucket of cold water on you."

To my surprise, the darkness in the circle swirled away, and my heart lurched again. Zylas lay on his side, arms wrapped around his middle, legs pulled up. He made no attempt to straighten as the last of the shadows faded. He didn't even open his eyes.

"What's wrong?" I gasped. "Are you …"

I couldn't finish the question, since the answer seemed obvious. The demon in the circle grew weaker and weaker, then …

His eyes cracked open. No longer crimson and glowing, they were dark, empty pits. "Come to watch me die, *payilas*?"

"No. No, I …" Demon or not, I didn't want to watch him die. I didn't want to see *anyone* die.

He hadn't asked for this. Human magic had dragged him out of his world and chained him to this room to perish slowly. He was dying … because Uncle Jack had gotten his filthy hands on my mother's grimoire. Without it, he could never have summoned Zylas.

"I will not submit," he whispered.

"I know." I swallowed. "Zylas, is there anything I can do?"

His eyelids flickered and those black, exhausted eyes slid to mine. "Do?"

"To help you. To—to—" I didn't know what I was saying.

"To keep me alive until I submit?"

"No. I know you won't become a contractor's puppet. I just …" I pressed my lips together. "It isn't fair that you're dying because they summoned you."

He closed his eyes again and curled into a tight ball on the floor as though he were freezing. His tail twitched half-heartedly. This didn't feel real. He'd seemed so invincible—a powerful, untouchable demon full of fierce arrogance despite his imprisonment. Now he was on the floor, unmoving, weak. Dying. He'd faded so much since I'd last seen him.

"Tell me how to help you."

A deep crease formed between his eyebrows, and his lips turned down as he fought an internal battle.

"Food," he finally muttered. "Heat. Light. Not fake light."

"Heat and light?" I looked around the cold, windowless basement. "And food? Those will help you?"

His head moved in the slightest nod.

"I'll be right back," I told him, shoving to my feet. "Hold on."

I rushed for the stairs. I couldn't get natural light to him— even if the sun had been up, the library had no windows. I hadn't seen a space heater anywhere in the house, and I couldn't light a fire indoors.

But I could bring him food. If food would help, then I would feed him.

As I raced into the kitchen, sudden understanding brought me up short. Uncle Jack and Claude didn't understand why Zylas hadn't hit his breaking point yet … but I had been feeding him. If food kept the demon alive, then I'd been prolonging his life with those insubstantial treats. Now I understood why he had played along with my questions … and why his strength had faded so quickly once I'd stopped visiting him.

I flung open the pantry doors and searched for something to feed a starving demon. My gaze whipped across boxed snacks and crackers, cereal and hard pasta, then landed on a pair of soup cans.

Hot soup. Food *and* heat.

I dumped both cans of vegetable soup into a large bowl and shoved it in the microwave. As the appliance whirred, I listened nervously to the sound of the TV from the family room and hit stop before the microwave could chime. The soup was still bubbling when I lifted it out, my sleeves pulled over my hands to protect them from the hot glass. Steam dampened my face as I carried the bowl downstairs.

My worry kicked up a notch when I saw Zylas hadn't darkened the circle. As I hurried across the library and knelt, broth splashed onto my arm, burning my skin.

Zylas's eyes slitted open, then widened at the sight of the steaming bowl.

"This is soup," I said. "It's hot and you can eat it, but you have to promise to give the bowl back and not break it or try to hurt me with it."

Motions slow and stiff, he uncoiled from his ball and pushed himself up. "I agree."

I pushed the bowl halfway across the line, and he reached for it.

"It's scalding hot," I warned as he wrapped his hands around the glass and drew it into the circle. "Be careful not to burn your—"

He lifted the bowl to his mouth and poured the soup down his throat. Steam swirled around his head as he drained the contents in seconds. If it burned him, he didn't show it.

His tongue swiped across his lips, catching a few escaped droplets, and I watched in amazement as his eyes lightened from midnight black to deep scarlet. He stared at the bowl, then set it down and sank back onto the floor. Curling up on his side, he watched me, his gaze intense and probing.

Feeling oddly nervous, like his attention was a blinding spotlight, I reached for the bowl. When my fingertips brushed the glass, I froze in sudden realization.

Zylas's eyes flicked down to my hands. To my pale skin a foot from his reddish-toffee skin. My hands were on the bowl—and the bowl was *inside* the circle.

My lungs were paralyzed but my heart careened in wild terror. I'd put my hands across the invisible barrier. I hadn't felt a thing, hadn't noticed a ripple of transparent magic. Could I pull my arms out before he grabbed me?

I stared at him, unable to exhale. He studied my hands, so close, within his reach. The end of his tail flicked, like a cat that had spotted a mouse in the grass.

Slowly, I wrapped my fingers around the cold glass. His expression didn't change, but a muscle jumped in his cheek. Despite his blank face, his jaw was tight.

Keeping my movements smooth and painstakingly sluggish, I drew the bowl across the silver line. My flesh cleared the invisible barrier and I let out an explosive breath, shakily pressing a hand to my chest to calm my petrified heart.

Zylas watched me pant, motionless and impassive.

I gathered my shredded composure and scooted back a foot to avoid making the same mistake twice. As I moved to set the bowl safely aside, I frowned. "It's cold."

The glass should've been hot from the soup. He'd only just drunk it.

Zylas settled more comfortably on the floor. "I took the heat."

I placed the bowl beside me and looked around. "Have you been taking the heat from this room, too? Is that why it's cold?"

"Only the heat in the circle."

The inner circle had been frigid. That's what had made me realize something was wrong—that I'd crossed the barrier.

"Demons need food, heat, and light to survive?" I asked.

"Food *or* heat *or* light," he corrected. "Heat and light are better."

I rubbed my forehead—and my soup-stained sleeve slapped me in the face. Cringing, I pulled my arm out of the sleeve.

"In books," I said as I peeled my sweater off, "demons are always described as creatures of cold and darkness, but you live off warmth and light?"

I tossed my sweater behind me and straightened my tank top. Zylas's gaze tracked the motion.

"What is that?"

"Huh?" I followed his stare. A purple bruise in the shape of grasping fingers, tinged with green and yellow where it had begun to heal, marked my upper arm. "It's a bruise."

"I do not know that word."

"A bruise is an injury." I shrugged self-consciously. "From being hit or squeezed or crushed by something."

His curiosity waned. "*Hh'ainun* are fragile."

"Compared to demons, I guess we are." I resettled on the floor. "I can't stay much longer or Uncle Jack will catch me again. Will you be okay now?"

"*Eshathē zh'últis.*" He closed his eyes. "*Īt eshanā zh'últis.*"

I waited to see if he would say anything comprehensible. "What does that mean?"

"You are stupid … and I am stupid."

My gaze dropped to my hands in my lap, and I didn't ask him to explain. His meaning was obvious. The hot soup would merely prolong the inevitable … and prolong his suffering. He would die anyway. Keeping him alive in his half-dome prison was a cruelty in itself. I was stupid for giving it to him, and he was stupid for accepting it.

"Don't enter into a contract," I blurted.

His eyes flashed open.

"Don't do it," I repeated, the hoarse intensity of my voice surprising me. "My uncle—the summoners are waiting for you to get weak and desperate. They'll try to convince you to do it to save your life, but you can't let them win."

He stared at me, then a wolfish grin revealed his pointed canines. "Do not fear, *payilas*. I will laugh at them as I die."

"Good," I said fiercely. "They deserve to fail. I'll laugh at them too."

He smirked, but the expression swiftly faded. Exhaustion lay over him like a heavy cloud. The soup had helped, but not much.

"I'll come back tomorrow night," I whispered, "and remind you that you'll never submit to one of us *high-nuns*."

"*Huh-ah-i-nun*," he corrected with a spark of irritation.

A choked giggle escaped me, and I blinked rapidly. "I'll see you tomorrow night."

"Go away, *payilas*."

I clambered up, collected the bowl and my sweater, and crossed the room. At the door, I looked back.

"Zylas," I called softly. "Darken the circle."

His tail flicked, then the circle faded to black, hiding his prone form. I switched the lights off and crept up the stairs.

Only when I had closed my bedroom door behind me did I allow the burning tears to fall. I stumbled to my bed and fell onto it, an ache burrowing deep into my heart.

I'll see you tomorrow. If he made it that long. He might not. He was so weak. Fading fast. Soon, he would be gone, and his torture would be over.

I pushed my face into my pillow, muffling my quiet sobs. I cried because this world was so cruel—cruelty inflicted by and upon demons and humans both. I cried because I was a fool to pity a demon, to inflict pain and grief on myself over a heartless monster. I cried because I was alone with no one to turn to, no one to ask what I should do, no one to comfort the aching grief. I would've happily died myself if, just for tonight, my mother could hold me one more time.

My tears eventually ran dry, but sleep didn't come for many hours.

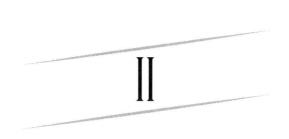

II

ZYLAS SURVIVED THE NEXT DAY.

I hadn't snuck down to the library yet, but I didn't need to see him to know he was still kicking. Standing at the kitchen counter, I suppressed a bitterly satisfied smirk as Uncle Jack's shouts rang down the hall.

"*How?*" he bellowed. "How is that thing still defying us? It should be halfway comatose! How is it maintaining the darkness in the circle? We haven't even *seen* it!"

Claude's calm voice answered him too quietly for me to make out any words.

"I know that!" my uncle roared. "It has to break soon! If it dies before we get it into a contract, I'll—I'll—" he spluttered, in search of a suitable threat.

"Oh, shut up, Dad," Travis snapped. "We're all frustrated."

"Talk back to me again and I'll break your jaw," Uncle Jack snarled. "You're an apprentice and if you ever want a demon name from me, you'll start acting like it."

Terse silence spread.

"We need a break," Claude decided. "Let's go out for something to eat."

Uncle Jack grunted and their voices receded. I strained my ears, and a minute later, the front door opened and closed with a thump.

I looked down at my white mug. Steaming cocoa filled it to the brim, and I'd topped the dark liquid with a dollop of whipped cream. Cradling the warm mug in my hands, I slunk out of the kitchen and down the basement stairs.

I turned the library lights up, crossed to the black dome, and knelt. "Zylas?"

The darkness faded out of the circle. Lying on his side, with his head pillowed on one arm, he looked more comfortable than last time—but his eyes were black again.

"*Payilas.*"

"How did it go today?"

He gazed at me tiredly. "They are more *mailēshta* than before."

"What does that mean?"

His brow scrunched and he closed his eyes as though struggling to translate the word. "Annoying. They are annoying."

I hesitated, staring at the steaming mug, then held it up. "I … brought this. You don't have to drink it if you don't want to, but it's hot."

He let out a long breath, then pushed himself into a sitting position, the metal armor on his lower legs scraping the floor. I set the mug on the silver inlay, with the handle sticking into the circle, and he picked it up. His eyes squinched as he prodded the whipped cream with one finger, making it bob in the hot liquid.

Maybe the whipped cream had been overkill.

He tipped the mug back, downed the contents like a shot, then replaced the mug on the inlay. I slid it out of the circle and set it aside.

"What do you want?" he asked, still looking exhausted.

"What do you mean?"

He flicked his hand at the mug. "For that."

"I don't need anything."

A snarl slid into his voice. "Ask."

"But …"

It was clearly important to him that he not accept charity from me. If it made him feel better … I tried to come up with an easy question. He watched me think, the sconce lights illuminating one cheekbone and the side of his jaw but casting deep shadows over his dark eyes.

"I want to touch you." I spoke without thinking—and instantly regretted it.

His face twisted. "*Touch* me?"

My cheeks flushed hot. "Just—just your hand, or—" I cut myself off and took a moment to regain my composure. "In that circle, you're like a … a vision or a dream. I want to touch you so I can feel that you're really there."

He stared at me like I'd sprouted a second head. "*Ch.* Fine."

My pulse quickened. Dangerous, dangerous. It was far too risky, yet … I wanted to do this. Touching him would make him real in a way that seeing him and hearing his voice couldn't.

I skooched closer until my knees were six inches from the inlay. "Put your hand against the barrier."

He pressed his right palm flat against the invisible dome and shimmers spread outward like ripples on a pond. My heart climbed into my throat, where it continued its frantic beating. I swallowed it down and lifted my hand. My arm quivered. I hesitated, my body so tense it hurt.

I touched two fingertips to the heel of his hand.

His skin was disconcertingly cool. Cautiously, I slid my fingertips up to the center of his palm and pressed, feeling the give of living flesh. As I traced his index finger to the top, wonder ballooned inside me, pushing my fear aside.

I followed the line of his thumb, then warily curled my finger around to feel the bony knuckle below his first finger. The back of his hand was firm and taut, his skin different from anything I'd felt before—tougher, with less give and stretch than a human's, yet soft and smooth.

Tipping each finger was a dark nail, its curved point resting flush against his fingertip. It wasn't razor sharp and seemed too short to be dangerous, but that didn't lessen the thrill in my center.

With the barrier rippling like liquid light, I spread my fingers and pressed my palm to his, my small hand dwarfed, my slender fingers so fragile in comparison, my fair skin white against his reddish-brown tone.

I raised my eyes, wide with awe, to his dark ones. He watched me, his expression unreadable.

It happened in an instant.

He pulled his hand back—and because I was pressing my palm to his, my hand moved too, dipping forward. It crossed that invisible line and the strong fingers I had traced snapped tight around mine.

Adrenaline flooded my body. Panic screeched in my head, but I couldn't move. Frozen like a rabbit in the wolf's teeth, I stared at him in horror.

He held my fingers in a tight grip, then pulled.

I had lamented his obvious weakness—but he wasn't weak. Not compared to my pathetic strength. I locked my limbs but my knees slid across the floor. My wrist crossed the invisible line, then my forearm, then my elbow.

Tears flooded my cheeks. Why was I so stupid? Why had I gotten so close? Why had I put myself within his reach? He would drag me in and tear me apart—the perfect finale to his long imprisonment. A demon's most exhilarating send-off—murdering a helpless human girl.

His other hand closed around my wrist. I expected him to wrench me the rest of the way into the circle. Expected him to tear into my flesh, to sink his predator's fangs into my throat and rip it out.

Instead, he flipped my hand over and pressed two fingers to my palm.

Between one hammering beat and the next, my tremoring heart threatened to stop.

He examined my palm, then each finger. He brushed the pad of his finger across my thumbnail, feeling the texture, then flicked his claw against it to test its strength. He felt the bumps of my knuckles, then stroked the back of my hand.

I trembled violently, scarcely breathing, not understanding.

He pinched my skin, his head tilting as he pulled. It hurt but I kept quiet. Pushing my sleeve up, he studied my inner wrist, then lightly traced the shadows of veins under my pale skin. His head dipped and his nostrils flared as he inhaled my scent.

Inhaling again, he licked my racing pulse. His tongue was warmer than his cool skin.

His black, starving, dying eyes lifted to mine.

Then he tightened his hold and dragged me into the circle.

My paralysis broke. I gasped wildly and scrambled for purchase on the smooth hardwood floor, but he hauled me easily across it. I crumpled inward, instinct driving me into a protective ball before he could strike.

He yanked on my arm, pulling me straight, and his other hand caught my jaw. Forcing my head up, he leaned down, his face filling my blurring vision. My breath wheezed from my lungs too fast and my head spun.

A low, husky laugh rumbled from his throat, his breath brushing across my tear-streaked cheeks, and he whispered, "What does your blood look like, *payilas*?"

My limbs turned to liquid. A sob shook my torso.

His head snapped up, his gaze flashing to the library door. In the brief second his attention shot away from me, his hand on my wrist loosened.

With strength I didn't know I had, I wrenched backward and threw myself out of the circle. My butt hit the floor as darkness flashed through the dome and the demon vanished from sight. I shoved away from the silver line.

"*Robin?*"

I jerked toward the door. Travis stood in the threshold, gaping.

Another sob burst from me, and trembling too badly to stand, I twisted onto my hands and knees to crawl away. Travis rushed across the room and knelt beside me, touching my shoulder.

"Robin, are you okay? Are you hurt?"

I shook my head. My voice had deserted me when Zylas caught my hand, and I still couldn't find it.

"Did the demon grab you? Why would you get that close?"

I drew in a shuddering breath. "I—" The word was a feathery croak. "I didn't ..."

He put his arm around my waist and pulled me to my feet. I couldn't support myself, the adrenaline having reduced my muscles to quivering jelly. He propped me against his side.

"Dad mentioned you'd come down here to get a book," Travis muttered as he scanned the black dome. "Robin ... the demon lured you over, didn't it? It tricked you into getting so close."

My lower lip quivered. Ducking my head, I pushed my glasses above my eyes and wiped my face with my sleeve to hide my humiliation.

"Did it talk to you? What did it say?" His voice sharpened with urgency and I cowered away from him. He tightened his arm around me. "It's not your fault. You didn't know any better. Demons can be very manipulative."

I nodded numbly, staring at my feet as the trembling subsided.

He drew me toward the door. "Come on. Let's get you out of here before Dad gets back."

I forced my head up. "You won't tell him?"

"No, I won't tell Dad or Claude, but ... Robin, if the demon spoke, I need to know what it said."

Cold prickles washed over me. How could I tell him anything about my conversations with Zylas? Not that I cared to protect the demon—not anymore—but I didn't want to incriminate myself. Travis waited expectantly for my reply.

"I heard … whispering," I invented. "I went over to try to hear, but the words … weren't English."

Pursing his lips, Travis led me up the stairs. "The demon should be able to speak English. The language rite was the first thing we did." At my blank look, he added, "A series of spells that imparts the basics of our language to the demon. Without it, negotiations would be impossible."

So *that* was how Zylas knew English.

"Maybe it was?" I revised hastily. "I couldn't really hear."

"Huh." He walked me to my room. At the door, he smiled wanly. "You're lucky you got out of there in one piece."

So, so lucky. Lucky that Travis had come down when he had. Lucky that Zylas had hesitated and he'd loosened his grip. Lucky that I'd reacted fast enough to escape.

"But," he added, "how many times have you been in the library? Has the demon tried to get your attention before? Have you ever—"

"No," I cut in, too shaken for politeness. "That was the only time. Thanks for your help."

Shoving away a flash of embarrassment over my rudeness, I closed the door on him. Weak and cold, I walked woodenly to my bed and sat on the edge, staring at the wall.

Zylas was a demon. He was famished, dying, isolated, and ten weeks into torturous confinement. He had a day or two left to live—and I'd offered myself on a silver platter. I'd given him the chance to get me, and he'd taken it. I shouldn't have expected anything different.

He was a demon. He'd obeyed his nature. *Profoundly immoral and wicked … an apt description of the demonic psyche.*

I knew that. I understood it.

I still felt betrayed.

Most of all, I felt like the biggest fool on the planet. A bleeding heart, like Amalia had said. I'd thought, in his own demony way, Zylas saw me as an ally, or at least an odd, annoying cohort in his lonely imprisonment.

So unbelievably naïve.

I flopped onto my bed, exhausted and wrung dry. As my eyelids grew heavy, I lifted my hand and stared at it, remembering Zylas's clawed fingers sliding so carefully across my delicate skin.

What does your blood look like, payilas?

Shuddering, I rolled onto my face and hoped, cruelly, selfishly, that Zylas wouldn't survive the night. If he died before morning, I would never have to think about him again.

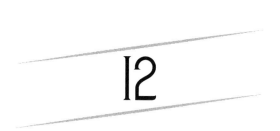

12

AT A KNOCK ON MY DOOR, I closed the self-help book I was reading in the hopes of learning not to be an impulsive, naïve idiot. So far, it wasn't helping.

The knock sounded again and I sat up in my bed. "Yes?"

My door cracked open. Travis stuck his head in. "Hey."

Warmth rushed into my cheeks and I surreptitiously slid the blankets higher. I wasn't wearing a bra under my tank top. "What's wrong?"

"I just want to check on you." He crossed to my bed. I couldn't tell if he did it on purpose, but he swung the door hard enough that it clacked shut behind him. Dropping onto the foot of my bed, he grinned at me. "How are you feeling after that scare? Did you sleep okay?"

"Pretty well," I mumbled. Post-adrenaline exhaustion could do that. I didn't mention that I'd woken up at 6:30 a.m. from a nightmare involving Zylas, the circle, and my gory death. I'd been reading in bed ever since, afraid to go back to sleep.

"That's good." He cleared his throat. "While I'm here … I've been meaning to apologize. Amalia told me you aren't a summoner or an apprentice or anything. I'm sorry I bought into Dad's bullshit and gave you the cold shoulder for so long."

"It's okay," I told my blanket, unable to meet his eyes.

"I want to make it up to you." His smile returned. "The rest of the family is going to a meeting at noon, but I'm on demon-watching duty. I have to stick around the house, so why don't we hang out?"

I blinked up at him, confused. "Um … sure."

"Cool. I bet there'll be a horror movie on—can you believe Halloween is tomorrow? Month, gone." He hopped up. "I've got a few errands to run, but I'll be back home around one o'clock."

"Okay."

He breezed out and closed the door, leaving me blinking in anxious bafflement. Why did Travis suddenly want to hang out? Was it a ruse to interrogate me about my "demon encounter" last night?

Dragging myself out of bed, I slouched into the attached bathroom and turned on the shower. I'd hoped the hot water would relax me, but I spent my whole shower planning various cover stories and evasions in case Travis questioned me about Zylas. Maybe I should pretend to have the flu?

I blow-dried my hair so it hung straight and neat around my heart-shaped face, the ends brushing my shoulders, then wandered down to the kitchen and made myself a small breakfast of fruit and yogurt. I ate at the breakfast bar, my self-help book propped in front of me but my focus completely shot.

Kathy marched in and out, busy with preparations for her excursion. Amalia passed by once, her usual jeans and oversized sweatshirt replaced by a sexy halter-top dress, its mid-thigh hem showing off her long legs. Her hair was twisted up into an elegant bun.

"Where are you headed?" I asked as she strode in the opposite direction.

She swerved off track, coming over to investigate my food. "The annual general meeting for our guild. It's a good time for networking, otherwise Dad wouldn't go while the demon is so close to breaking."

The MPD required all mythics, even those who didn't actively practice magic, to be guilded. It was a crucial part of the system of checks, balances, and accountability that hid mythics and magic from the public, but it could also be a pain in the butt.

Stealing a slice of apple off my plate, Amalia added, "Dad hates leaving Travis to watch things."

"Why?"

"Because it's Travis," she drawled with an unhelpful eye roll. "See you later, Robin."

"Have fun."

She laughed sarcastically but gave me an almost friendly smile as she sauntered out of the kitchen on four-inch heels.

A few minutes later, the clamor of the family leaving quieted. I rinsed my dishes and left them in the sink, then resumed reading my self-help book in my bedroom. Unsurprisingly, "10 Foolproof Reasons Not to Trust Hellish

Incarnations of Evil" wasn't a chapter. I needed a book specific to people with chronic, life-threatening inquisitiveness.

Thoughts of last night wormed into my focus, but I stomped them down. I wasn't giving Zylas another minute of my time or consideration. Dragging out a pair of earbuds, I put on music and continued reading.

One o'clock arrived without my noticing. Clueing in twenty minutes later, I tossed my book on the bed and headed down to the main level. The family room was empty, so I curled up on the leather sofa and selected a remote. After figuring out how to turn on the eighty-inch flat-screen TV, I channel-surfed for a quarter of an hour, my anxiety growing by the minute. Maybe Travis had forgotten. Should I go back upstairs? Better yet, should I use this time to search the house for my mom's grimoire?

A door clattered. Footsteps thumped, then Travis wheeled into the room, looking frazzled.

"Sorry, Robin!" he said breathlessly. "Got held up."

"It's fine."

"I need to check on the demon." He waved at me. "Come on."

I blinked. "Huh?"

"Come with me. Won't take long."

"Uh." I shrank into the sofa. "I'd rather not."

He grinned encouragingly. "You'll be perfectly safe. It's good to face your fears."

I hesitated, debating whether a flat-out refusal would look suspicious. He extended his hand in offer, his feet set like he intended to wait there all afternoon. Not knowing what else to do, I reluctantly climbed off the sofa and straightened my white t-shirt.

"Atta girl! Knew you were tough." He caught my hand even though I hadn't offered it. "Let's get this done."

He pulled me across the room. I looked at my hand in his, my stomach churning with apprehension. Why were my instincts screaming at me to run away?

As Travis reached the stairs and started down them, firmly tugging me along, I told myself it would be fine. If he tried to interrogate me about last night, I would leave. He wouldn't stop me from leaving … would he?

We reached the hallway at the bottom and my eyes darted to the open library door. Light spilled across the hardwood. Travis just needed to check on the demon. The circle would be filled with impenetrable darkness, like always, and we'd …

Why were the lights already on?

The disquieting question had scarcely pierced my thoughts before Travis pulled me into the library. My gaze flashed across the black dome and the podium in front of it, then caught on the three people waiting for us.

I recognized two of them: short, brusque Karlson and his huge, silent companion, whom I'd dubbed Hulk. Uncle Jack's clients, the ones waiting to buy a contract with Zylas. The third man was tall but not looming, with a military buzz cut and muscular arms displayed by his tight t-shirt.

My feet rooted to the floor. Travis turned and smiled. It wasn't a warm smile. I suddenly doubted whether it had ever been warm.

He slung his arm around my shoulders and dragged me forward. "Come on, Robin, don't be shy."

The three men assessed me with cold calculation.

"This is her?" Karlson snapped impatiently.

"Yep." Travis forced me to stand in front of the men like a model on display. "*This* is the only person the demon has spoken to. It lured her close enough to grab her."

"And she survived?" the third man inquired flatly.

"My arrival must've startled the demon. She fell out of the circle in complete hysterics."

I stood mute. Whatever was happening, it was bad. I needed to get out of here, but Travis was holding my shoulders and the three men were blocking my escape.

"Is she an apprentice?" Karlson barked.

"Nope. Doesn't know shit about demons. She's a sleeper."

A sleeper—a mythic who didn't practice magic. It wasn't a flattering term.

Karlson grunted, then stepped toward me. "All right, girl. I don't like wasting time, so I'll make this quick. We want that demon to talk, and you're the one it wants to talk to, so you're going to help us, understood?"

"H-he didn't talk to me," I began. "I—"

Karlson's hand flashed out and pain exploded through my head. I fell back into Travis, a scream lodged in my throat. My cheek throbbed violently.

Karlson lowered his arm. "Didn't I just tell you I hate wasting time?"

"Hey," Travis growled as he helped me straighten. "There's no need to hit her."

"I'll decide that. Keep your mouth shut and let the adults handle this." He folded his arms. "Now get the demon talking."

I trembled, my mind spinning in a desperate search for a way out. Travis turned me around and steered me toward the circle, stopping a foot away. I stared into the pitch black.

"Talk to it, Robin," Travis said, then added in a mutter, "This isn't going how I expected."

"Why did you bring me here?" I hissed.

"Because I'm the *stepson*. Dad will never give me a demon name, so I need money to buy one." He raked a hand through his hair. "Look, we can help each other, okay? Amalia told me Dad is hoarding your inheritance. I can help you with that. Once I get the contract bonus from these guys, I can hire a lawyer. Whatever you need."

I craned my neck to stare at him. He returned my look, earnest but also afraid. Was it dread over betraying his father or fear of his new business partners?

"Get on with it!" Karlson commanded.

Travis let out a sharp breath. "Please, Robin."

Did I have a choice? I cleared my throat. "Uh, demon? Would you say something … please?"

Silence. Of course. Why would Zylas respond? He probably hadn't been this entertained since being summoned.

"Demon, if you'll talk to me, I'll give you … uh … something … at your request." I waited a moment, the three men's stares boring into my back. My cheek throbbed in warning. "You don't have much time left. This is your last chance to get something you want."

Ignored again.

"The demon isn't stupid," I said over my shoulder, desperate for someone to understand. "He knows what you're doing. He won't speak while you're here listening."

Travis looked questioningly at the three men.

"This is moronic," the new man said in a rumbling voice. "The demon doesn't want to *talk* to the girl. It was trying to get her in the circle. It wants blood, not conversation."

Karlson rubbed his jaw. "Fair point. Let's see if we can tempt the beast, then."

He gestured at Hulk and the man lumbered toward me and Travis. I tried to step back, but Travis stopped me—the circle was right behind us. Hulk bore down on me and his thick hands seized my upper arms. He spun me around to face the circle, his fingers bruising my skin.

"Whoa, hey!" Travis exclaimed. "What are you—"

"I told you to keep quiet," Karlson interrupted. "Vince, take over."

The third man strode forward and stopped beside me. I squirmed against Hulk's hold, breathless with terror. I wanted to scream at them to let me go, but I couldn't speak. Why was I so timid? So helpless?

"Demon," Vince said to the circle. "You want this girl. Show yourself and you can bargain for her."

"*What?*" Travis blurted. "You can't—"

"Were you planning to let her walk out of here and tell your father how you went behind his back to steal his demon?" Karlson asked dismissively.

"I—I'll pay her to keep quiet—"

Karlson snorted like Travis was hopelessly naïve. "Get out of the way or we'll remove you—and our deal is over."

Travis snapped his mouth shut. I stared at him pleadingly, but he moved aside, eyes downcast.

"Well, demon?" Vince prompted. "Do you want to bargain for the girl?"

Silence from the circle. The darkness didn't shift.

"Maybe it doesn't think you're serious," Karlson suggested.

Grunting, Vince stepped closer and took my wrist. While Hulk held me immobile, Vince stretched my arm out. Silver flashed in his hand, but I didn't comprehend what I was seeing. A … knife? Where had he gotten a knife? What did he plan to do with—

The eight-inch blade flicked upward. I watched it pass across my inner forearm, just below my elbow. Felt the razor-edged steel part my flesh. Saw bright blood bloom across my skin.

Then the pain hit and I screamed.

Hulk's hands tightened as I convulsed. Vince pressed the flat of his knife against my arm, coating it in dripping blood, then flicked it at the circle. Red droplets disappeared into the darkness and splattered across the surrounding hardwood.

"Have a taste, demon," Vince said, holding my arm out so the bloody slice was fully visible. "You can have the rest. Just show yourself."

Blood ran down my arm. I quivered violently, panting for air.

"Let me go," I gasped. "*Let me go!*"

Like Zylas, they ignored me. Travis was looking in every direction but mine, his shoulders hunched and face crumpled with indecision. Or maybe resignation.

"Please," I wept as my blood dripped steadily onto the floor. "Please let me go."

"Demon," Vince called. "Your time is running out. Or rather, hers is. If you want her fresh and kicking, answer me now."

How could they talk about me like that? How could they throw me to the demon like a piece of meat? They were as evil as the creature in the circle. As heartless. As monstrous.

"Travis, help me," I begged through my tears. "Don't let them do this!"

Vince squeezed my wrist. He raised the blood-smeared knife again.

"No!" I screamed, thrashing against the hands holding me. "The demon will never talk to you! He'll never do it! Let me go. Just let me go!"

Vince sliced the knife across my arm again.

My scream shattered my eardrums. Blood ran. I was going to die. They were going to kill me. I would bleed out while they all watched—the three men, Travis, and Zylas.

I should never have come to this place. Should never have talked to Zylas. My parents had warned me: *stay away from magic*.

Adrenaline surged through me and I wrenched my body in a violent spasm. Hulk's hands slipped. Tearing free, I flung myself away. My socks slid on the hardwood and I grabbed the podium for balance. As it tipped over, a heavy tome tumbled off and a flat silver pendant skittered over the hardwood.

I surged past the falling objects toward the door—and hands grabbed my sweater. They hauled me backward. Spun me around. Vince's cold face blurred in my vision, and the knife flicked upward a third time.

Hulk threw me down. I hit the floor, the breath knocked out of my lungs. The flat pendant from the podium caught under my hand, the cold chain tangling in my fingers. My vision wavered with tears and panic and light-headed shock. It didn't hurt anymore. That was probably a bad sign.

"Last chance, demon. You have about ten minutes until she bleeds out. We'll wait."

I lay on the floor, shaking, weak. Weak in so many ways. Useless. Pathetic. Too powerless for this world of magic. What use was knowledge? How would book-learning save me?

Blood pooled under my arm, my racing heart pumping it out of my sliced veins. Zylas had wanted to see my blood. He'd gotten his wish.

Behind me, Karlson and his cronies murmured as they waited, conversing like gentlemen at a party, cocktails in hand. Travis had retreated and hovered halfway to the door.

In front of me, a foot away, the circle's silver inlay gleamed faintly. I lifted my gaze to the darkness within.

And looked into Zylas's black eyes.

13

I STARED into the demon's obsidian eyes.

Scarcely two feet away, Zylas crouched at the circle's edge. The darkness inside swirled and eddied, revealing his shape in faint glimpses and flashes of reddish-toffee skin. The barrier rippled as he pressed against it, his dark gaze fixed on my face.

Behind me, Karlson said something and his two associates laughed. They *laughed*. Too busy chatting, they hadn't noticed that Zylas's shadowy form was so close, pushing against the barrier, straining to reach me.

Bloodlust rolled off the demon. I could taste it in the air, as potent as the coppery tang of my blood. Crouched in his prison, he silently, lustfully watched me die from inches away. If he'd spoken, if he'd said something to the men, could he have saved my life? Did he even want to?

A monster before me. Three different monsters behind me. I was dying, and one would be my executioner. But which?

Karlson and the others were trading my life for a demon contract. But was my blood enough to break Zylas's resolve? Would he stay silent and hidden while I died in front of him, or would he give in so he could take my life himself?

My arm trembled as I slid my hand across the hardwood, leaving a smear of blood in its wake. The barrier rippled more violently as Zylas pressed against it. The conversation behind me stuttered.

My fingertips brushed the silver inlay.

"What's she doing? Stop her!"

Footsteps erupted, vibrating the floor as the men scrambled toward me. Hands grabbed my ankles to tear me away from the circle. Zylas's black eyes bored into mine.

I wouldn't give those bastards the chance to win. I would laugh at them as I died.

I thrust my fingers through the barrier, my human flesh passing effortlessly into Zylas's prison. His hand clamped around my wrist, cold and steely. His gaze held mine without faltering.

He wrenched me into the circle.

His strength tore my legs from the men's grasping hands. I flew into the hellish night within the dome, my vision darkening, frigid air sweeping over me. Scents filled my nose—earthy leather, the tang of metal, and something smoky and aromatic, almost like hickory.

I tumbled to a stop, my limbs splayed. An object jangled and clanked, the sound of metal hitting the floor. Hazily, my brain identified the orientation of my body—half sitting, half slumped, something supporting my back, solidity against my side.

Zylas's arm supported my back. Zylas's chest pressed against my side.

His cool hand closed around my sliced arm and squeezed. Pain flared hot and deep. A sob shuddered out of me.

"Zylas," I choked out, praying that somewhere in his demonic psyche he could find a shred of mercy. "Please kill me quickly."

"Is that what you want, *payilas*?" His husky whisper brushed across my cheek. His face was close, but I couldn't see anything in the freezing darkness. Outside the circle, male voices buzzed angrily, the words jumbling in my ears.

"I did what I could to help you," I whimpered. "Please don't make me suffer."

"What do you want?"

My arm was on fire, blazing with agony, and I didn't understand his question. My crumbling composure gave way.

"I don't want to die," I sobbed, shaking and gasping.

His hand squeezed harder and fresh torment cascaded through my nerves. "What do you want from me?"

I couldn't think. I didn't know. One need, one primal urge dominated my mind—survival. I wanted to live. I wanted to keep breathing. I wanted to live and—and—

And ... what?

Did I want to escape this circle? Did I want to face those men again? Did I want to survive them, only to face Uncle Jack's fury? Did I want to fail to get the grimoire, to fail my parents?

Tears flooded my cheeks. What I truly wanted was an ally. I didn't want to struggle alone anymore, to fight alone with no one at my side, no one at my back. No one to step in front of me and shield me, as my parents once had.

"*Payilas.*" His whisper demanded my answer.

"Protect me."

I didn't arrive at those words. They simply fell from my mouth, called out by his demand.

His breath cooled the tears on my cheeks. "What will you give me?"

My head was spinning. I didn't know if I was staring into the featureless darkness or if my eyes were closed. My heart thundered with growing desperation.

He was waiting, and through the overwhelming pain and fear, only one thing came to mind. "Cookies. I made you cookies before."

"Cookies?" His arm pulled me closer and his mouth pressed against my ear, his whispered command shuddering down to my bones. "Promise me your soul, *payilas.*"

My *soul?* The floor rolled and tilted under me. "No … I can't give you …"

"Would you rather die?"

"I … but I can't …"

"I need your soul, *payilas.*"

"But *I* need my soul," I insisted thickly, barely coherent but certain of one thing: my soul, whatever it was or whether I even had one, wasn't something I was giving away to *anyone.*

A harsh exhalation rushed through his teeth. He seemed to hang on something, his body rigid, his powerful hands bruising me with the tension in his grip. As the seconds slid past, my lungs heaved in shallow pants and my limbs tingled with growing cold.

"*Fine,*" he snarled furiously. "I accept."

My pulse drummed in my ears. He accepted what?

He released my arm and hot blood flooded my skin. His slick fingers pressed something flat and round into my weak grasp, then his hand closed over mine, compressing the cold disc between our palms. Pulling me hard against his side, he raised our entwined hands.

"Now seal it." His husky voice filled my head like the shadows that surrounded us. "*Enpedēra vīsh nā.*"

I was beyond thought or decision, but my mouth moved, my tongue forming the alien words without my instruction. "*Enpedēra vīsh nā.*"

As the last sound left my lips, new pain erupted—burning agony in my palm. The hard disc erupted with deep crimson light, shoving the shadows back. Zylas's fingers, entwined through mine, gripped hard, preventing me from releasing the scorching metal. The fire tore down my arm and into my chest, ripping a scream from my throat.

"What was that?" a voice outside the circle demanded, sounding far away. "Did you see that light?"

"The demon is killing her and recharging its magic," another voice spat. "Now we'll have to wait for it to weaken again."

The light died and the burning heat in my arm vanished. Zylas's fingers uncurled and I snatched my hand away, tucking it to my chest as I shuddered.

"Now, *payilas*," he crooned in my ear. "I need strength. How much heat can you spare?"

"Heat?" I slurred.

"Not much," he mused as his cool fingers touched the base of my throat.

My skin tingled—then cold hit me like a wave of arctic ocean. The heat sucked out of my body and I convulsed in a desperate attempt to get away. He caught my flailing arms—and his hands were warmer than my chilled skin.

Crimson eyes glowed in the darkness.

Zylas stood up, hauling me with him. Everything spun and I didn't know where the floor was. His hand brushed my hair, then something thumped against my chest with the jingle of a chain. Hunching under the dome, he pulled my back against his torso, his arms around my middle to support my trembling legs. The metal plate that protected his heart dug into my spine.

"Stand, *payilas*," he breathed in my ear. "All you must do is leave the circle. I will do the rest."

I shook violently, hypothermic, anemic, disoriented. "Leave?"

"Yes." His hands gripped my waist. "Are you ready?"

No. No, I wasn't—

With an eddying swirl, the darkness in the dome melted away. Light blasted my eyes, half blinding me.

Held by Zylas, I faced the fallen podium, the floor splattered with my blood. Beyond it, Karlson, Hulk, and Vince had frozen at my sudden reappearance. Travis sat against a bookshelf beside the door, hunched over his drawn-up knees. His mouth hung open.

Zylas threw me out of the circle.

As I flew forward, streaks of red light leaped with me, shooting all around my body and coalescing at my chest. I hurtled across the silver line and slammed into the floor on the other side, sprawling face down.

I wanted to lie there and die, but not with the three monstrous men watching me. Trembling, I braced my hands against the floor. As I pushed myself up, the flat metal disc swung from the chain around my neck.

Behind me, the summoning circle was empty. My head buzzed with dull confusion. How could it be empty? Where was Zylas?

Crimson light burst from the pendant around my neck like spouting liquid. It hit the floor and pooled upward, as though filling an invisible mold—a human-shaped mold. Flaring brightly, the light dissipated to reveal a figure in its place.

Zylas stood in front of me, facing the three men.

Outside the circle. He was outside the circle.

He lifted his arms away from his body and curled his fingers. His short claws unsheathed, doubling in length until they'd extended well past his fingertips.

"*Ahh*," he half sighed, half growled, his husky voice sliding through the silent room. "It feels good to move again."

Terror pulsed through the library.

"It's unbound!" Karlson roared. "Call your demons!"

Vince and Hulk yanked silver pendants from beneath their shirts. Crimson radiance bloomed across the metal.

Zylas's tail lashed—then he leaped. Fast. A reddish blur. He soared over the podium, took a springing step, and landed beside Hulk. His hand flashed out, closed around the man's pendant, and tore it away. The disc bounced across the floor.

Zylas spun behind Hulk. The man pitched forward, blood spraying from his back. Zylas whirled across the man's other side, claws flashing again. As he fell, Hulk's throat disappeared, replaced by gushing gore. The man collapsed.

Three seconds. It had taken Zylas three seconds to kill him.

"Run!" Vince bellowed.

Run, I thought vaguely. I should run too. My vision blurred in bright ripples. Pain jarred through me and I realized my arms had given out; I'd collapsed to the floor. This time, I didn't try to rise. The temperature had plunged, the room so cold that frost sparkled across the floor, dancing in my fading sight. Men were shouting. Screams. Footsteps, thundering impacts with the floor.

The sounds blurred too, mashing together until I couldn't hear anything but the roaring blood in my ears. My body had gone numb. Was I shivering? Was I trembling? Was I still breathing?

"Do not die, *payilas*."

I was lying on my back.

A hand was pressed to my chest and heat was flowing into me.

Another hand was pushing my bleeding arm into the floor as power crackled against my skin. My eyelids fluttered.

Zylas was crouched over me. Crimson light veined his right hand and crawled across my chest, sinking into my body like water into sand. Under his other hand, the one crushing my arm, a two-foot-wide red circle glowed across the floor, its interior filled with shifting runes.

At the edge of my vision, beyond the fallen podium, Hulk lay face down in a puddle of blood. Vince was slumped spread-eagle against a broken bookshelf, surrounded by scattered leather tomes and his head resting unnaturally on his shoulder. His dead eyes stared at the empty summoning circle.

Red magic blazed around me. Concentration tightening his face, Zylas murmured rapidly, the words flowing in the rhythm of an incantation. Power coursed down his arm and flooded the spell. Luminous magic gathered in my bleeding wounds.

His eyes, bright with power, caught on mine. Then he snarled a final command, electric heat exploded through his spell, and heart-stopping agony cleaved through my arm.

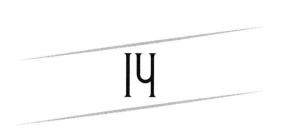

"ROBIN," *Mom sighed as she dabbed ointment on my hand, "what have I told you about getting Daddy or me to help when you want to try something new?"*

I stared glumly at my sliced finger, tears brimming in my eyes. On the table beside me, an old book with its cover removed was splattered in scarlet droplets. A box knife lay beside it, abandoned when I'd cut myself.

"I'll teach you all about restoring books when you're older," Mom promised as she wrapped a bandage around my finger. "Let's clean this up, all right?"

I helped her gather the tools, and we carried them from the kitchen into her home office. Her dark ponytail bobbed with her lively steps, dark-rimmed glasses sliding down her small nose. Her blue eyes were just like mine.

She opened the cabinet in the corner and set her tools in the bin— the same bin I'd "borrowed" them from. I guiltily added my armful.

She reached for the top shelf and lifted down a small object wrapped in crisp brown paper. "When you've mastered book restoration, you can help me with this."

She opened the wrapping. Inside was a thick journal-sized book. A tarnished buckle held the ancient leather cover closed, and sheets of white paper stuck out the top, revealing glimpses of my mom's loopy scrawl.

"This book is very special, and someday, it'll be yours. Before you inherit it, we'll finish restoring and translating it." She beamed at my awed expression. "It'll be a mother-daughter project, just for us, and when you have your own daughter, you'll pass this book on to her."

I frowned. "What if I don't have a daughter?"

She tweaked my nose playfully. "A worry for another day, Little Bird. Shall we find Daddy? He's lost in yardwork again."

As she ambled out of the office, I blinked up at the cabinet, the secret, special book hidden on the top shelf.

"Robin!"

My cut finger twinged painfully. I held it up—and terror flooded me as red liquid spurted through the Band-Aid.

"Robin!"

Cuts opened on my thin arm, the three gashes pouring blood over the hardwood floor. I screamed—

"Robin!"

Hands shook my shoulders roughly. My eyes flew open.

Amalia leaned over me, her face pale. The library lights blazed, illuminating the horrific scene. The empty summoning circle. Blood everywhere. Two bodies. I gagged on the stench of death.

"Is she awake?" Uncle Jack's shout made me jump. He appeared beside Amalia, his face splotched with pink and a vein throbbing on his bald head. "*What happened?*"

I cringed back from his furious holler.

He stooped, grabbed the front of my t-shirt, and yanked my torso off the floor. "Robin, where's the demon?"

"That's your first question?" Amalia yelled. She shoved his hands away and put her arm around my shoulders, helping me sit up. "If you won't ask if she's okay, at least ask about Travis before the goddamn demon!"

"Someone stole it," Uncle Jack spat. "I want answers! Robin, tell me what happened!"

"I—I heard noises in the basement, so I came to see and I saw … I saw the bodies." My gaze darted to Vince and Hulk. "I don't remember anything else. I think I fainted."

"What about the demon?"

"What about Travis?" Amalia burst out, glaring at her father.

I swallowed painfully. "I d-don't know. I … I never saw Travis. The circle was empty when I came in."

Swearing, Uncle Jack stormed across the room. "Those backstabbing bastards! They stole my demon! How did they get it to agree to a contract? Travis is in league with them, I know it."

"Or he's missing because he's *in danger!*" Amalia cut in loudly. She lifted her arm off me, her nose wrinkling. "You're drenched in blood, Robin. Are you sure you're not hurt?"

I peeked at my inner elbow. Dried blood coated my skin, and barely visible fingerprints smudged the gore where a hand had gripped my arm. I couldn't see the wounds from Vince's knife.

Amalia was watching me anxiously, so I stammered, "I—I guess I fell in the … the …"

Determinedly looking away from the bodies, she muttered, "Come on."

She helped me stand, keeping a firm grip on my elbow. The hem of her pretty purple dress was stained red.

"Where do you think you're taking her?" Uncle Jack stalked toward us, blowing air through his nose. "I want answers! I want—"

"No one cares what you want!" Amalia shouted. "I can't believe you! Kathy is upstairs in hysterics, trying to find *her missing son,* and all you care about is the demon!" She hauled me past him and spat over her shoulder, "I'm taking Robin upstairs. Do something useful while I'm gone."

Uncle Jack swore at her. As we left, I stared at my feet, unwilling to risk glimpsing the bodies.

Amalia steered me directly to my bedroom. "You should clean up. I'll check on you in a few minutes. You ... you sure you're okay?"

When I nodded weakly, she retreated into the hallway and closed the door. I stood there, numb and shivering, then looked down. My white t-shirt was drenched in crimson that had dried to brown at the edges. Blood everywhere.

My stomach jumped. I bolted into the bathroom just in time to throw up in the toilet. Panting, I washed out my mouth, then stripped off my shirt and wet a towel in the sink. I vigorously scrubbed my arm, then paused. Lowering the towel, I stared at my inner elbow.

Three pink scars marked my skin where Vince had cut me. I prodded one, surprised it didn't hurt. Healing sorcery could close wounds but it took intensive work ... and no healers had been present in that basement.

A visceral memory hit me in the gut: Zylas leaning over me, a hand on my chest, another on my injured arm, red magic crawling over the floor and sliding into my body. My stomach twitched threateningly and I grabbed the sink, breathing fast. Demon magic. He had healed me with his demonic magic.

My eyes fluttered closed. "*Protect me,*" I had said.

"*What will you give me?*" he had asked.

An exchange. A trade. That's how demons worked. I'd asked him to protect me, and in return … I'd set him free. I hadn't realized that's what I was agreeing to, and a violent shudder shook me from head to toe. I'd set a demon loose in the city. He was so fast, so deadly. Where was he now? How many people had he killed already?

Gulping down my nausea, I finished cleaning the blood off my torso, then unbuttoned my jeans and shoved them off my hips. As they slid down my legs, something fell out of the back pocket and hit the floor with a clang. A flat, circular pendant on a silver chain lay across the tiles, its surface smeared with blood like everything else. Warily, I picked it up.

Zylas crushed the pendant between our hands. "Now seal it."

I rubbed my thumb across its rune-etched surface. It was an infernus—the key to a demon contract, Amalia had said. The demon's will and spirit were bound to the infernus, and through it, the contractor could control the demon.

That was a real contract, though. Whatever weird bargain Zylas and I had made didn't come close … did it? He'd already fulfilled his end, even going a step further to heal my injuries—not merely repairing my arm, but a full healing. Though I should've been lightheaded and woozy from blood loss, I was simply tired—and parched with thirst. I turned on the faucet and drank from the flow, gulping down water until my stomach threatened to rebel again.

Finished with cleaning, I carried the infernus back into my room and tossed it on the bed. I needed to hide the pendant before anyone noticed I had it. That'd be hard to explain.

I pulled on clean clothes—a soft green sweater and stretchy yoga pants—then sat on my bed. Exhausted and sick with guilt and anxiety, I picked up the infernus again. My thumb traced the centermost rune—a spiky, circular sigil. I hadn't looked closely at the one Amalia had shown me, but I would've remembered such a strange marking.

Flopping back onto my pillow, I swung the infernus like a pendulum. Golden beams from the setting sun streaked through the window, illuminating floating dust motes and sparkling across the silver disc. How long had it been since Travis led me into the basement, since those men had nearly killed me? Where was Zylas now?

Red light sparked in the infernus's center.

The scarlet glow burst out of it in bounding streaks. They pooled and condensed, solidifying into a humanoid shape. Weight settled on my waist, and the light dispersed with a final shimmer.

Zylas grinned down at me, crimson eyes glowing and his pointed canines on full display.

For an eternity, I could neither move nor breathe. Gasping in blind panic, I shoved away from him—but he was straddling my hips, his weight pressing me into the bed. All I managed to do was writhe pathetically.

"*Payilas*," he crooned.

"What are you doing here?" I demanded breathlessly, fighting my panic. "I thought you'd left!"

"Left?" He canted his head, then flicked the infernus I still held in the air, sending it swinging. "I am bound to this, *payilas*. So are you."

"What?" I dropped the infernus like it was contaminated with a deadly disease. "No."

Bracing his hands on either side of my head, he leaned down. I pushed back into my pillow. "Are you not pleased? I have obeyed our terms."

I gulped, my mind spinning frantically. Bound to the infernus. Obeying the terms. A terrifying new understanding dawned, followed by the urge to howl in denial.

"You mean by protecting me?" I stammered.

"*Protect*." He seemed to taste the word, his eyes gleaming dangerously. "What does this word mean, *na?*"

He lowered his face until all I could see were his glowing eyes. Fresh adrenaline surged through my veins. A *demon* was pinning me down. He could kill me before I could draw breath to scream.

"What does it mean, *payilas?*" he whispered, his breath warm on my lips.

"It—it means you can't hurt me."

"Is that all?"

"And … and you won't let anyone else hurt me." I wanted to close my eyes but I was afraid to look away from him. "Would you move?"

"That is your meaning?" His wolfish grin returned. "You did not tell me this when we made our contract."

"*Contract?*" I mouthed silently, terrified by the word—by the confirmation of my new worst fear.

"So," he concluded with vicious delight, "*your* meaning does not matter."

No. No no no. This wasn't happening. "Zylas, *get off me!*"

With a husky laugh, he slid off the bed. I leaped off it after him, my shaking knees barely holding me up—but now we were standing in the whole five square feet of floor space between the bed and dresser. It wasn't nearly enough room.

I planted my feet and lifted my chin, fighting the urge to cower as he circled me. His movements were smooth and fluid, and the sunlight flashed on the armor that shielded his left shoulder, forearm, and a small square of his chest. Where metal or fabric didn't cover him—meaning most of his abdomen and half his right arm—powerful muscles rippled and flexed beneath his reddish-toffee skin.

He stopped behind me and my panic spiked again.

"You agreed to protect me," I said shrilly. "You have to—"

"You did not explain your meaning." His fingers caught a lock of my hair and tugged. "So *I* get to decide what *protect* means."

That answer was significantly worse than I'd been imagining.

He let the lock slip between his fingers—then suddenly slid both hands into my hair. "Why are you so soft?"

I jerked away, tearing my hair free, and spun to face him. "Keep your hands off me!"

"*Na?* But *payilas.*" He stepped closer and I retreated. My back hit the dresser. "*Protect* ... does not mean *obey.*"

I recoiled into the dresser as he leaned over me. He was of average height for a man—a human one, at least—which meant he towered over half a foot above my diminutive frame. With mocking deliberateness, he sank his hands into my hair again, cupping my head. He leaned into me, his body hard and heavy and warm. Terrifyingly solid. Strong. Dominating.

Suppressing the urge to shove him away, I let my arms hang at my sides. That's what this was. Domination. He was stronger, he could do whatever he wanted, and he was proving it.

What a bully.

"Must I keep you from *all* hurt?" he mused, as though there'd been no pause in our terse exchange. "Or only keep you alive?"

There was a distressingly large difference between those two interpretations.

His taunting smile returned. "You did not explain your promise either."

My promise? I hadn't promised him anything. "You don't get my soul. I didn't agree to that."

An edge sharpened his smile—angry displeasure. New fear skittered up my spine, but he didn't attack. Though he could show off his superior strength, I was guessing—or rather, desperately hoping—that whatever his interpretation of "protect" was, it didn't allow him to hurt me.

But what had *I* agreed to? I only remembered refusing to give him my soul. Since I hadn't promised to get him out of the circle, that couldn't be what he meant, and I didn't recall offering him anything else in exchange for …

My eyes popped wide as my fuzzy memory handed me the answer.

"*Cookies?*" I blurted shrilly. "*That's* what you agreed to?"

In my befuddled terror, that was the only offer I'd made. If I hadn't been half out of my mind, I never would've suggested something so ridiculously worthless.

"Why on earth would you *agree* to that?" I added, too flabbergasted to think before speaking.

His lips peeled back, flashing his canines, and his narrowed eyes sparked like angry flames. Yes, he'd agreed to my cheapskate offer, and he was *pissed*.

I might have gotten the better end of our deal, but he hadn't walked away with nothing. He'd escaped the circle without enslaving himself. Though he wasn't completely free—he was still bound to the infernus—he had survived a death sentence while keeping his mind and will intact.

Because, as he'd said, *protect* didn't mean *obey*.

Amalia's voice echoed from the main level as she called something to Kathy. Zylas's head turned toward the sound. His fingers flexed, then began to withdraw from my hair.

I grabbed his wrists.

"You promised to protect me," I hissed urgently, "so you need to know this: if anyone—I mean *anyone*—discovers we have a contract, I'll be put to death. Do you understand? The MPD—the organization that rules over mythics—will kill me. They'll kill you too. We'll both be executed. You can't protect me from them. No demon is that strong."

He listened, his expression inscrutable.

"The only way to protect us both is to stay hidden. You can't let anyone see you or hear you or—or *anything*. We can't let them find the infernus. We can't draw attention to ourselves or we're dead!"

His eyes squinched. "Attention?"

"That means we can't—"

"I know what it means."

He leaned close again, pressing me back into the dresser. I'd never felt so small and powerless—exactly what he wanted. I dug my fingernails into the back of his hands, but my nails couldn't pierce his skin. He didn't acknowledge my attempt to wound him.

"No attention," he pondered. "That is a problem."

"What? Why? Has anyone seen you?"

"Not a *hh'ainun*." Abruptly releasing me, he stepped back. "We should leave this place."

"You did something!" I realized with a gasp. "What did you do?"

He opened his mouth to answer—and magic exploded somewhere outside my window, the detonation shaking the mansion walls.

"WHAT THE HELL!" Amalia's frightened yelp rang out from the stairs.

"Zylas!" I grabbed his arm. "What did you do?"

He shook me off like I was a kitten clinging to his sleeve. "We should leave now."

"Not until you tell me—"

Feet thudded up the stairs. Someone was coming.

I dove for the bed and grabbed the infernus. "Get back in this thing!"

His face twisted with contempt.

"Hurry! Before she sees you!"

The disgust on his face intensified. The pendant heated on my palm, then red light ignited over his hands and feet. As his body dissolved into luminescence, the swirling glow sucked into the infernus and it vibrated before cooling. That fast, the demon was gone.

"Whoa," I whispered, holding up the pendant. Zylas was *inside* this thing? How did that even work?

A second explosion rocked the house. I staggered sideways and caught myself on the dresser. Dropping the infernus around my neck, I tucked it under my sweater with one hand as I threw my door open.

Amalia was picking herself off the floor. White showed all the way around her eyes as she spotted me. Her terror sent mine skyrocketing.

"Amalia, what—"

"The other demon is loose!" she shrieked. "It got out!"

"*What?*"

Slamming through her bedroom door, she shouted over her shoulder, "It blew the greenhouse sky high and now it's starting on the house. We have to get out of here!"

I gawked as she disappeared into her room, then I bolted back to mine. I tore my clothes off the hangers, rammed them into my suitcase, threw my books in on top, grabbed my phone, and zipped the bag up. Hauling it by the handle, I launched back into the hallway.

Amalia burst out of her room ahead of me, a backpack over her shoulder, and I chased her down the stairs. Another detonation shuddered the floor and my heart pummeled my ribcage. I remembered the huge winged beast, its magma-like eyes radiating bloodlust. It was out there. It was coming for us.

Amalia tore outside but I skidded to a stop to grab my runners from the closet. I stuffed my feet into them, then extended the handle of my suitcase to pull it. What about my mother's grimoire? It was probably in the house. I couldn't leave it behind when—

A fourth blast shook the walls, and I hurtled through the door. Recovering the grimoire would be pointless if I died. I would worry about it later.

Outside, the evening air was crisp and chill, the final beams of the setting sun peeking over the trees at the property's western edge. My suitcase bounced down the steps as Amalia ran across the drive toward the four-car garage.

Crimson light flashed.

A blazing orb hit the garage like an armor-piercing rocket. The building exploded, the doors rupturing and fire bursting from its interior. Amalia was flung backward and landed painfully on the concrete drive.

"Amalia!" I cried.

With a sweep of dark wings, the demon landed on the burning garage roof. Huge horns rose off its hairless head and its thick tail swung like a mace. Scarlet magic veined its forearms as it raised them. A glowing circle spiraled out of its palms, hovering vertically above the roof. Runes flickered through it, power building. Arctic cold spread out from the beast and the flames licking at its legs shrank and disappeared. Ice frosted the charred wood.

The air throbbed with power. The flowing runes swelled and the demon barked a command.

A red beam launched from the spell and struck the house. The power ripped through the walls, tearing a ten-foot-wide hole. A cacophony of crashes and shattering glass erupted from within, then the alarming creak of breaking wood. With a groan, a section of the roof caved onto the second floor. Flames snaked through the rubble and water sprayed from broken pipes.

The demon's glaring magma eyes swept over me and it raised its hands again. A semitransparent circle, filled with flickering runes, flashed around its wrist as it began a new spell.

Paralyzed with terror, I realized I was about to die.

The demon veered around, focusing on something behind the garage. It hurled its spell into the backyard. A crimson-striped blast boiled into the sky.

Panting and lightheaded, I rushed to Amalia and grabbed her arm. "Get up. Get up!"

She woozily pushed to her feet, her elbows bleeding from road rash. The demon on the roof summoned another explosive spell and chucked it at whatever target lay behind the garage.

"Quickly!" I dragged her down the drive. We broke into a jog, fleeing the destruction.

A pair of wrought-iron gates blocked the driveway's entrance. Amalia punched a code into the pad and they slowly opened. The instant the gap was large enough, we squeezed through and pelted down the sidewalk.

The neighborhood, filled with walled properties and sprawling mansions, wasn't intended for foot traffic. We had to jog the equivalent of three blocks before reaching an intersection. We stopped on the corner, wheezing. My legs shook from exertion.

In the distance, sirens wailed. Fire trucks? Police? If they approached Uncle Jack's home, the demon would kill them. It would kill everyone in and around the house, then extend the battlefield to Uncle Jack's hapless neighbors.

Zylas had done this. It must've been him. For some hideously stupid reason, he'd freed the other demon. That meant every atrocity the winged demon committed was ultimately my fault.

"Come on," I panted. "The bus stop is just up this street."

"Eh?" Amalia stumbled after me, her plastic flipflops snapping. "I didn't know buses ran in this neighborhood."

Probably because she had a car—or she used to. The demon had just blown it up.

The streetlights blinked on, pushing the shadows away and filling the street with a warm orange glow. Still catching my breath, I speed-walked to the bus stop, where a teenager was glancing between his phone and the wailing sirens. A boom vibrated the ground and his eyes went wider.

If he could have guessed the sound was not caused by construction or an accident but by a raging demon, he would've run in the opposite direction. I squeezed my eyes shut, debating internally, then summoned my courage.

"Excuse me," I said to the boy. "Can I borrow your phone to send a text?"

He scanned me, no doubt debating whether I could outrun him if I tried to steal it. Deciding there was no way—he, like everyone, was taller than me—he tapped on the screen, then held it out.

He'd already opened a messaging app. I entered the MPD's emergency number and typed a swift text alerting them to an unbound demon at Uncle Jack's address. I sent the message, deleted it out of the phone's history, and handed it back.

"Thanks," I told him.

Amalia grabbed my arm and dragged me a few paces away. "What did you send?"

"An anonymous tip to the MPD," I whispered.

"Are you insane?" Glancing at the kid, she lowered her voice. "The MPD will investigate our house! They'll confiscate everything! We'll lose all our—"

"*You'll* lose?" I retorted angrily, surprising myself. "You'll lose your big house? Your favorite possessions? Your ten cars?" I glared up at her. "What about the first responders who are about to lose their *lives*? What about your neighbors? What about the innocent people who'll die because your family was illegally summoning demons in a residential neighborhood?"

She recoiled from my vehemence.

"No one else was going to take responsibility," I muttered, my furious intensity fading into dread. "I guess I didn't need to make it anonymous. They'll probably figure out I was there, won't they?"

"No," Amalia sniffed, tossing her head. "My dad's not stupid. The house isn't in his real name. Nothing is. It can't be traced to us."

"Oh."

We waited, Amalia and I fidgeting and exchanging terse looks. The sirens had gone quiet, but I didn't know whether that was a good sign. A red glow smeared the horizon in the house's direction, illuminating columns of billowing smoke. The boy was staring at it.

A blue-and-gray bus trundled around the corner and rolled to a stop. Amalia and I climbed on after the boy. I dug my wallet out of my suitcase and dropped coins into the slot, but Amalia stood there blankly. I fished out another few coins for her fare.

We took seats at the back and the bus rolled into motion. Amalia and I kept silent as it rumbled down street after street, carrying us steadily away from the burning mansion. When we sped across the long arch of the Lions Gate Bridge, putting a mile of ocean between us and the escaped demon, I breathed easier.

The view outside the bus grew darker and business complexes replaced the residential streets. I had no idea where the bus was taking us. Other passengers got on, then disembarked ten or fifteen minutes later, while Amalia and I stayed in our seats.

Several times, I opened my mouth to speak, then chickened out. The infernus rested against my ribs just below my bra, warm against my skin. I prayed Zylas would stay put.

Eventually, the bus groaned to a stop and the driver opened both doors.

"This is the end of my route," he called back to us. "You'll need to catch the next one."

Amalia jumped up. I followed her out the door and we stepped onto a stained sidewalk. Skyscrapers towered all around us, and I eyed them warily as the bus doors closed. Amalia marched away from the bus stop, the skirt of her dress fluttering. I scrambled after her with my suitcase bumping along behind me.

"Where are we going?" I asked.

"I'm going to find a hotel." After a beat, she added, "You can come too, I guess."

I tried to match my pace to her longer stride. "Do you know where we are?"

"No idea. You?"

"I'm from Burnaby. I've only been downtown a few times." I half jogged beside her, then prompted cautiously, "What happens now?"

She plucked bobby pins out of her updo. "We hole up somewhere and wait for Dad to contact me. He and Kathy will set up in one of our safe houses and we can join them there."

"Oh, okay." That didn't sound so bad. Once we reunited with Uncle Jack, I could get my mom's grimoire. He would save it from the demon, I was sure. He was too greedy to let it be destroyed. And he, unlike us, wasn't entirely helpless either. As I'd learned from *The Summoner's Handbook*, to be a demon summoner, you had to become a demon contractor first. Uncle Jack had his own enslaved minion to protect him.

She dropped her arms and her blond hair unraveled from its bun, spilling down her back. "What the hell happened back there? Demons don't just *escape* summoning circles. They can only pass through the barrier if they're carried inside an infernus, which requires being contracted, or if the circle is physically damaged."

Well, I knew which method Zylas had employed then.

"*Who* stole the demon from the library?" she growled. "Dad's clients? But how did they get a completely unresponsive demon to take a contract?"

By feeding him cookies and cake for two weeks, I silently answered. Just thinking it caused hysterical laughter to bubble up in my throat. I gulped it down and cleared my throat.

"And *where*," Amalia added, "is Travis? That dickwad better turn up soon."

I made a noncommittal noise. Travis's disappearance worked in my favor. He and Karlson—assuming they'd survived Zylas's attack—were the only two people who could guess I was now contracted to the "stolen" demon.

A demon contractor. Me, Robin Page. *A demon contractor.*

There was so much wrong with that. Firstly, my contract with Zylas was *completely ridiculous*. He would protect me in return for *cookies*? I couldn't believe such a flimsy pact even counted as a binding magical covenant.

Secondly, our contract was illegal as well as ludicrous. If anyone realized the truth, the MPD would put a bounty on my and Zylas's heads. We wouldn't last long. Bounty hunters knew how to kill demons.

Lastly, I didn't practice magic. I *avoided* magic. Now I was bound to an extremely magical demon. Contractors were universally feared, with reputations as power-hungry bullies. After all, nice people didn't sell their souls for a demon's power.

I glanced around the dark street. "Uh, Amalia? Are we going the right way?"

"I told you I don't know this area. My phone has eleven percent battery and I'm not wasting it on GPS."

"But …" My gaze skipped from a graffitied wall to boarded-up windows. "I think we're going the wrong way."

"We just need to find a hotel. This is downtown. There are hotels everywhere."

She strode onward, flipflops smacking her heels. I dug my phone out of my bag and ran to catch up with her. The streetlights buzzed in the hush of nightfall. A few cars sped past, their headlights flashing over us. A truck slowed on its way by and the passenger wolf-whistled.

Hunching my shoulders, I pulled up a GPS app and waited for it to load.

"We aren't in the downtown core." I squinted at the screen. "This is … the Downtown Eastside?"

Her steps hesitated and our eyes met in shared realization. The Downtown Eastside was the worst neighborhood in the city. And we—two girls, alone and on foot—were lost in the middle of it.

16

"WE SHOULD GO WEST," I said urgently. "Toward the downtown core."

"I'm not walking all the way back," Amalia groused. She pointed at a glowing orange sign, the text partially obscured by a scraggy tree. "Look, there's a Travelodge right there. We'll get a room for the night and find a better place tomorrow."

I squinted at the "LODGE" visible through tree branches. We hastened up the sidewalk, ducked under the tree's lowest boughs, and stopped. My suitcase rolled into the back of my leg.

"Booty … Lodge," I read, repulsed by the neon outline of a yellow butt under the letters. A lightbulb glowed above the business's open door, and a dance beat trickled out. Smokers clustered around the entrance in hazy clouds.

Amalia swore under her breath. "A strip club, ugh."

"Hey there, pretty ladies," a heavyset man at the door called. "Coming inside?"

"Eat a dick," Amalia snapped.

Another man whistled. "Got a firecracker here, boys."

Male gazes burned my skin. The club's patrons had a sleezy, disreputable air to them, and I didn't like what they were seeing—not confident, in-control women, but two girls who were clearly lost and frazzled, one in a short dress, the other dragging a suitcase.

I grabbed Amalia's arm and hissed, "Let's get out of here. Quickly."

She nodded and we hurried back the way we'd come.

"Where ya goin'?" the whistler called. "You girls lost?"

We kept walking. I fumbled with my phone, looking for the nearest hotel. There was nothing nearby. Not even a gas station where we could take shelter and get our bearings.

"Hey girlies. What's the rush?"

My head whipped around. Four men from the Booty Lodge trailed after us, still smoking. Amalia muttered a vile curse and hitched her backpack up her shoulder. She kept her pace steady and I matched it, my heart racing.

For two blocks, the men followed us, laughing and bantering in drunken slurs. Breathing hard, I checked my phone again. There was a twenty-four-hour convenience store a block and a half away. We could hide in there.

"Come on, pretty ladies," one of our stalkers called. "Let us buy you some drinks."

Amalia's jaw tightened and she glanced back. Her head snapped straight again, her face paling, and she extended her stride.

"Yeah, baby. Work that ass. Whatchya wearing under the dress?"

I rushed after her, my suitcase clattering after me, and glanced back too.

The men were gaining on us.

Fear cut through me. I didn't want to find out what they'd do if they caught up. The street was dark, abandoned except for our urgent procession. The convenience store wasn't in sight yet and I stretched my legs, taking the biggest, fastest steps I could without running.

"I call dibs on the little pixie girl."

My nerve broke and I bolted.

Amalia was a step behind me, and raucous laughter rang out as the men gave chase. My suitcase bounced on its wheels, dragging at my arm, but I couldn't bear to release it. Amalia drew ahead, her longer legs pumping—then her flimsy sandal twisted.

She fell in a sprawl. I skidded around to help her, and then the men were on us.

Amalia shoved to her feet as the group formed a half circle around us. My heart hammered in my throat and my voice had vanished again. Even Amalia had run out of insults.

The men advanced. As Amalia and I backed away, shadows closed in—we were retreating into an alley. No, the men were *herding* us into an alley. My throat closed. Stupidly, I was still clutching the handle of my suitcase. I couldn't let it go. It was all I had left.

The two closest men lunged and I stumbled backward, smacking hard into a brick wall. Amalia screamed as the other two men went for her.

Leering drunkenly, a greasy, bearded man grabbed the front of my sweater and pushed me into the wall, his hot, cigarette-stale breath bathing my face.

"No!" I cried.

Heat scorched my stomach and crimson light burst through my shirt. The glow coalesced between me and the man, shoving him backward. The light flared then faded, and suddenly, a warm body was pressed against mine.

Zylas. He stood with his back against me, facing my assailant.

"What the—" the man spluttered.

Zylas seized him by the throat and threw him. The man soared ten feet, crashed into the opposite wall, and slumped to the ground, stunned. My second attacker backed away, his face a mask of horror.

The other two creeps looked around at us. "Who the hell is that guy? Where'd he come from?"

Zylas turned his glowing red eyes on them and his husky laugh rolled through the dark alley. Silence shivered between the men, then they bolted. The one Zylas had thrown scrambled after them, groaning with each pained breath.

Eyes gleaming, Zylas bounced lightly on the balls of his feet, as though warming up for a sprint, then stepped after them.

Panic gripped me and I flung myself at him. I smacked into his back, and when he didn't stop, I grabbed him around the middle, my hands clamped over his stomach.

That he noticed. He twisted to peer at me over his shoulder.

"Stop!" I gasped. "No one can see you, remember?"

"Then I will make sure I am not seen." His mouth curved up. "A challenge, *na*? Will be fun."

"No! Just stay here. You can't protect me if you're chasing them." I unwrapped my arms from his bare stomach. He needed clothes with better coverage.

His tail flicked. "*She* has seen me. I can kill her."

I jerked around.

Amalia was pressed against the wall, her face white and mouth gaping in a horrified O. When we looked at her, she sidled away from us.

"Uh," I squeaked. "I—I can explain—"

"You're a contractor?" she whispered in disbelief. "You said you didn't know anything about Demonica …"

Zylas canted his head. "I should kill her, yes?"

"No!"

"The demon is talking," Amalia added, her voice faint. Her legs gave out and she sat heavily on the dirty pavement. "Contracted demons can't speak. They give up their voices when they give up their autonomy."

Zylas's fingers curled, his claws extending past his fingertips. I grabbed his arm and clutched it to my chest. He probably wouldn't hurt *me* but Amalia was in danger.

"Zylas," I said shrilly, "you can't kill her!"

"It will be easy."

"I mean you *shouldn't* kill her! She's—she's my cousin. My family." I tightened my hold on his arm, knowing it wouldn't stop him. "I need her help to survive this."

Tail lashing in annoyance, he relaxed his hands. His claws retracted.

Amalia stared at us without blinking. "You said you weren't a summoner and I believed you. I believed you!" Anger burned through her shock and she pushed to her feet, speaking right over my weak protest. "You *did* come to steal Dad's demon names, didn't you? You wanted the glory of a new lineage for your—"

She broke off, her eyes widening in sudden realization.

"No way!" she burst out furiously, pointing at Zylas. "That's Dad's demon, isn't it? That's the hidden one from the library!"

"Wait, Amalia," I pleaded. "You don't understand—"

"How did you even—no, I don't want to know." She shoved away from the wall. "Your 'sweet, naïve girl' act is good, Robin, but you should've put more effort into your summoning apprenticeship instead. That demon is going to kill you."

"Amalia—"

"Forget it, Robin." Venom coated her voice. "I'm done. I never should've believed you."

Slinging her backpack over her shoulder, she took a step toward the street, realized she'd have to pass Zylas, then spun and marched deeper into the alley. I watched her go, my heart racing faster and faster.

Zylas pulled his arm from my weak hold. "*Now* should I kill her?"

"No," I gasped. "Don't—don't touch her. She—she's—she's my—"

I broke off, panting desperately, and wrapped my arms around myself. Panic built in my head. I couldn't take a proper breath.

I was alone in a reeking alley in the middle of the night. I didn't know where I was. I had nowhere to go. Amalia had left and I was all alone. What was I supposed to do? All I had was my suitcase, cellphone, and a demon who wanted to kill everyone nearby.

Tears streamed down my face and I sank into a crouch, holding myself and fighting to breathe. I couldn't do this alone. I needed help—but there was no one. Amalia had left. My parents had died. Any other mythic I turned to would report me to the MPD—assuming Zylas didn't kill them first. I couldn't go near *anyone*, not with Zylas. Anyone I exposed him to would be in danger.

A shadow blocked the streetlight. Zylas crouched beside me. "What are you doing?"

I shook my head, gasping and crying and losing my mind with panic.

He prodded my shoulder. I tried to pull myself together, but I was caught in a spiral that was dragging me deeper and deeper. Every time I fought its pull, the realization that I was alone and had nowhere to go or anyone to help hit me all over again.

"*Payilas*," Zylas growled. "Stop it."

I hunched inward and pressed my face against my knees, hiding from him.

He pulled on my shirt to make me sit up. I lost my balance and fell on my butt, then curled into an even tighter ball. I couldn't breathe right. The ground was rolling and tilting.

"What are you doing?" he snarled. "Stop it!"

"I—I can't! Leave me alone!"

He sprang to his feet and whirled, the barbed end of his tail just missing my face. He paced away from me, glanced back with his teeth bared and eyes blazing, then disappeared into the alley's dark depths.

Now I was *completely* alone. The maelstrom of panic spiraled deeper, my pulse racing and heart heaving in my chest. If only getting rid of the demon were as easy as sending him away, but he was bound to the infernus. Just like me. I was an illegal contractor bound to a demon I couldn't control.

Mom, what should I do?

My heart broke all over again, and I wept into my knees. Minutes crawled by, and my sobs weakened until I was sniffling pathetically, my cheek resting on my knee. I stared blearily into the darkness where Zylas had vanished.

A black shape appeared among the shadows, drawing closer. Two points of crimson glowed—demonic eyes.

Zylas stalked down the alley, irritation radiating off him with each gliding step. And under his arm …

Amalia hung from his arm like an oversized sack, her hands scrabbling vainly at his wrist. Her hair was a wild tangle, her face pasty white beneath her makeup.

Zylas swept over to me and tossed Amalia onto the ground. She hit the pavement in her third painful impact of the evening, a gasping whimper rushing from her throat. She shoved onto her hands and knees—and Zylas stepped on her back, flattening her. Her sharp cry echoed off the alley walls.

Leaning his weight on her, he grabbed her hair at the scalp and bent her head back to look into her terrified face.

"Listening, *hh'ainun?*" he snarled. "The *payilas* wants your help, so you will help her. If you don't, I will take you apart piece by piece by little piece. Sounds fun, *na?* Or would you rather help her?"

Amalia's mouth moved but no sound came out.

He pulled harder on her hair. "Answer or I will decide for you."

"Zylas!" I shrieked, breaking my horrified silence. "Let her go!"

His glowing eyes didn't shift from Amalia's face.

She whimpered weakly. "I'll help. I'll do whatever you want."

"Smart *hh'ainun*," he crooned, opening his hand. He stepped off her and folded his arms expectantly.

I stared at him, then at Amalia, my limbs quivering. Her teary glare burned with hatred as, wincing and cringing, she gingerly sat up.

"I—I didn't tell him to do that," I choked. "I didn't, I swear."

Her mouth trembled as she fought back tears. Sucking in a breath, she straightened her spine. "I dropped my backpack. I need to go get it, then we should find a hotel."

Just like that, she was tough-Amalia again, pretending nothing had happened and a vicious demon wasn't one word away from ripping her apart. I wished I had half her backbone.

"Okay," I mumbled, climbing to my feet.

Amalia got up far more slowly, each movement triggering a wince. Without the contract, without Zylas's promise, he could have done the same to me. His interpretation of "protect," whatever it might be, was all that kept me safe from his strength, his claws, and his merciless brutality.

He watched me, arms folded, tail lashing impatiently.

I was bound to him. He was *my* demon. And if I couldn't control him, he would kill a lot of people before he and I landed in an early grave.

17

AMALIA SCRUBBED BOTH HANDS over her face, then dropped them into her lap.

"Let me see if I've got this right," she said. "You were feeding the demon in the library because ... I still don't understand your reasoning, but whatever. You were feeding it. Travis saw you."

I nodded.

"This afternoon, while we were out, Travis took you downstairs and Dad's clients were there. Travis had made a deal with them."

I bobbed my head again.

"And then ..." She took a deep breath. "And then you made a contract with the demon to save yourself."

"Yes," I whispered, not minding that she'd skipped over the worst part.

We were sitting side by side on a stiff bed, heads bent together to hear each other's quiet murmurs over the blaring television. This was the first motel we'd found and we'd checked into the double-queen room thirty minutes ago. Amalia had cleaned and bandaged her scraped elbows and knees with the first-aid kit from the front desk while I told her the whole story.

"You couldn't have had much time to lay out a contract," she muttered, picking at a tear in the skirt of her dress. "You definitely missed a few key clauses."

"What are the key clauses?"

"There are a lot. What *did* you include in your contract?"

"Well, he …" I fidgeted with the infernus's chain around my neck. "He has to protect me."

"That's vague. What else?"

"In exchange, I'm supposed to … make him cookies."

She stared at me expectantly, waiting for the joke's punchline. "Are you serious?"

"I was bleeding to death," I mumbled in embarrassment. "It was all I could think of."

"You're supposed to promise the demon your soul when you die."

"Why would I give him my soul?"

"Don't you know what the Banishment Clause is?" When I shook my head, she sighed. "Okay, so once a demon is summoned to Earth, it can't return to its own world—except with a soul it's bound to. When you die, the demon is supposed to use your soul to escape our world. The Banishment Clause is crucial to a contract because without it, your demon is set loose when you die."

"Zylas wanted my soul, but I said no."

She huffed. "The demon must've been more desperate than you to agree to that. What else did you negotiate?"

"That's it."

"No, I mean, what other clauses did you two agree on?"

"None."

"What do you mean, *none*?"

I shrugged self-consciously. "He protects me in exchange for baked goods. That's … that's the whole contract."

Horrified disbelief twisted her face and she turned toward the room's opposite end. I followed her gaze.

Zylas was crouched on the dresser, his tail swishing back and forth in front of the drawers. His nose was an inch from the wall-mounted TV, his head tilted. As we watched, he leaned sideways to peer behind the screen, trying to figure out where the picture and sound were coming from.

"*Protect* you," Amalia whispered with a shudder. "You know a proper contract is about fifty pages long, right? You have to cover every possible scenario or the demon will find a loophole. Did you even define what 'protect you' involves?"

"No. He says he gets to decide what it means."

Shivering again, she lowered her voice to a whisper. "Do you realize that demon doesn't have to obey you? It can do *whatever it wants,* as long as you aren't hurt in the process. I don't understand why it isn't already on a killing spree."

Zylas's tail lashed, thudding against the dresser. He peered around the other side of the television.

"I explained to him how I'd be executed if the MPD found out I'm in an illegal contract," I told her. "I think that's why he's behaving so well. If he draws attention to himself, it would put me in danger."

"And putting you in danger would violate the protection clause," Amalia murmured. "That's a good sign."

"What happens if he violates a clause?"

"Demons never violate their contracts. The magic binds them somehow. *You* can violate it, though. If you do, the contract magic weakens, so make sure you bake that bastard all the cookies it wants." Her face hardened and she leaned close to whisper in my ear. "You'd better keep that demon one hundred percent convinced you can't survive without me."

I nodded earnestly. If Zylas decided Amalia wasn't necessary anymore, he'd kill her.

She sat back against the headboard. "All right, first things first. You're an illegal contractor, which means you're officially a rogue and—"

Crunch.

Zylas, still crouched on the dresser, now held the television, which he'd ripped off its wall mount. As a crappy made-for-TV movie blared from the speakers, he studied the television's back, then tore the cord out. The sound cut off and the picture went dark.

Amalia continued as though we hadn't witnessed anything out of the ordinary. "You're a rogue, so your best bet is to find a rogue guild and—"

"Wait," I interrupted. "Doesn't Uncle Jack have a system for forging his clients' paperwork? So they can be legal contractors?"

"Yeah, but he uses special forms that his MPD contact has prepared, and without those …"

She trailed off as I jumped up. Zylas paused midway through prying the plastic backing off the TV to watch me dig through my suitcase. I pulled out my cantrips textbook and flipped it open. Taking the folded papers, I closed the book on the copy of the grimoire page and handed Amalia the forms.

She unfolded them, her expression incredulous. "How did you…?"

"Uh …" Admitting that I'd considered blackmailing her father seemed unwise.

"Whatever," she sighed. "This is good. We can register you as a legal contractor, but you'll also need to join a guild with a Demonica license."

"A Demonica license?"

"Yeah." She unplugged her phone from the wall charger and pulled up an app. "Guilds need a special license to have Demonica members. Most guilds don't bother with it—they don't want contractors. Let's see … guilds with a license …"

I recognized the MPD app on her screen. Along with making and enforcing laws, the MPD required anyone with magic to join a guild by eighteen years old. Guilds provided support but also monitored their members, helping enforce the rules and laws.

Since I wasn't a practicing sorceress, being a guild member was kind of like having a gym membership I never used. I paid a monthly fee and scheduled an annual checkup every spring, but not all guilds were that passive. Some were tight-knit communities, some were weekend clubs, and some were businesses with members doubling as staff.

"Okay," Amalia said. "There aren't many around here. Your options are the Grand Grimoire, Odin's Eye, M&L, the Crow and Hammer, and the Seadevils. That's it."

"The only one I recognize is M&L." That guild was also an international bank—the same one my father had worked for.

They employed a lot of mythics, and most of us did our banking with them.

"You don't want to join M&L. They're sticklers for rules, and I think they only take Demonica mythics for security jobs. Let's see ... the Seadevils guild has one contractor and the Crow and Hammer has none. That's no good. You'll need to blend in."

Unease churned in my gut at the thought of transferring to any of those guilds, but this was my new reality. Until I could get rid of Zylas, I had to accept I was a contractor. An illegal one.

"So that leaves the Grand Grimoire and Odin's Eye—oh, but Odin's Eye is a bounty-hunting guild. You'd never get in, and you want to stay far away from bounty hunters anyway. It's gotta be the Grand Grimoire. They're a Demonica guild, so you'll blend right in with the rest."

"Okay," I mumbled.

"Let's get this form filled out and—" Her phone beeped loudly. She tapped the screen and read something, her full lips pressing into a grimace. "The MPD just sent out the alert."

"What alert?"

"For an unbound demon. Took them long enough. You sent in that tip hours ago. They must've lost the demon, but now they've located it and they need the combat guilds. See?"

She held out her phone, the message displayed in bold text.

MPD Emergency Alert: --CODE BLACK--
Suspected unbound demon active in your area. All CM assemble at GHQ ASAP. NCM take shelter. PROCEED WITH UTMOST CAUTION.

Unused to MagiPol acronyms, it took me a moment to parse the whole message. Combat mythics were to assemble at their guilds, while non-combat mythics should take cover. With that alert, every mythic in the city now knew about the escaped demon, and they'd be either terrified or preparing to face the creature's unchecked magic in the hope of killing it. I squirmed, painfully aware of my role in the demon's escape.

"Anyway," Amalia said, tossing her phone onto the mattress, "let's get these forms filled out. Dad made me do his paperwork all the time, so I have the MPD guy's email memorized."

We busied ourselves filling out the form while Zylas systemically gutted the television. Amalia scanned the paperwork with her phone, sent it off, then stood and stretched.

"As soon as we get confirmation that he's inserted your paperwork into the system, you can apply to the Grand Grimoire. You need to move fast or it'll look suspicious."

I nodded. "Thanks, Amalia. I would've been screwed without your help."

Her gaze darted to Zylas. "None of this will save you if your demon doesn't behave as if it's properly contracted. That part is for you to figure out. I'm going down to see if the front desk guy can recommend any late-night delivery options."

Giving Zylas a wide berth, she swung the door shut behind her. I sighed, figuring she wanted to get away from the demon more than she wanted to visit the front desk. Unconcerned by her absence, Zylas snapped a chip board out of the TV's innards and examined it from every angle.

"Having fun?" I asked him dryly, flopping onto the mattress.

He tossed the board into the gutted television and hopped off the dresser. Gliding over to the bed, he looked down at me, his dark pupils constricted to slits in the yellow glow of the bedside lamp. I wondered if he wanted to break me open and examine my insides the way he had with the television.

"You have a plan?" he asked in his strange accent.

"I think so."

"Join a guild? Blend in?"

"You were listening?"

His hand closed over the front of my sweater and he pulled me upright. My head spun from the sudden movement—and my breath caught when I found myself nose to nose with him.

"You expect me to *behave*?" He sneered the word. "I must be obedient? What is the difference between surrendering my will and pretending to?"

I cringed back but he didn't release my shirt. He towered over me, his upper lip curling to reveal his sharp canines. "I have to, Zylas. It's the only way to—"

"What if I refuse to behave, *payilas*?"

Alarm shot through me. "You—you have to protect me!"

"*I* decide how." His unsheathing claws pierced my shirt with a tearing sound. "I did not give you my will."

My pulse thundered in my ears. "Zylas ... what do you want?"

"*Ih?*"

"Back in the circle ... you asked me what I wanted and I said protection. But what do *you* want? I know it isn't cookies."

"I wanted your soul, *payilas*, but you would not give it to me."

I let out a slow breath. "You want to go home."

Without my soul, he couldn't escape this world. When my death released him from the contract, he'd be set adrift here. Though he'd escaped the circle alive, he now faced a human lifetime spent babysitting a helpless girl, then however much longer wandering my world until he died or someone killed him.

"I'll find a way for you to return home." Only after I'd said the words did I stop to consider them—and the magnitude of the offer I was making.

Zylas went very still. Watching me. Waiting.

"There has to be a way for demons to get in and out of this world," I plowed on. "If there wasn't, how would the first human have learned how to summon demons?"

"You think you can discover this?"

"I can't promise I'll succeed, but I promise to try." I stared up at him anxiously. "It'll take time—a long time, maybe years."

"Years," he scoffed. "What do you know about those, *payilas* of twenty years?"

"What do *you* know? You can't even tell me how old you are."

He leaned down, his warm breath brushing my cheek, and I recoiled. He moved with me until I tipped over and landed on my back. Bracing a hand on the mattress, he tapped the infernus under my sweater.

"Our contract is sealed." His red eyes drilled into me. "But you will promise to find this—a way I can return home?"

"I promise to try my best."

He searched my face for a sign of deception. "Then I will try to … *behave* … so the *hh'ainun zh'ūltis* will think I am obedient."

I hadn't picked up many of the demonic words he peppered through his speech, but that one was easy: stupid humans.

"Deal," I said. "Now would you get off me?"

"Why? I am not hurting you." As though to prove his point, he pushed a hand into my hair, his warm palm against my cheek.

I grabbed his wrist to yank his hand away—assuming I could—and the sensation under my palm belatedly registered in my brain. My eyes popped wide and I shoved myself up.

My sudden movement startled him and he released my hair. I caught his arm and ran my palm from his elbow to the strap that crossed his right shoulder, then pressed both hands to his bare stomach below his leather-and-plate chest armor.

"You're warm!" I exclaimed. "Even warmer than me! Your skin was so cold before. Are you sick? Do you have a fever?"

"I do not know those words."

"Are you ill? Unwell?" Warmth radiated from his skin into my palms. His temperature had to be at least two degrees higher than mine. "Are you supposed to be this warm?"

"Yes. I recovered *vīsh* in the light. Outside."

"You … you powered up your magic in the sunlight?" I realized. "That's what you were doing after healing me … before you set that other demon loose. Why did you do that, by the way?" I added, my tone hardening.

He shrugged dismissively. The motion caused his abdomen to tense under my palms—and I realized I still had my hands pressed firmly to his bare stomach.

His bare stomach of hard, taut muscles that could put any non-demonic man to shame.

I snatched my hands away, heat flushing through my cheeks. He didn't seem to have noticed—or didn't care—that I'd been touching him in a way human females did not touch human males they weren't intimately familiar with.

His face appeared in front of mine, a curious frown tweaking his lips. "What is wrong with your head? Your skin is changing color."

"It's nothing!" My cheeks, of course, grew even hotter. "I'm fine."

"*Na?* But why—"

"It's nothing!" I scrambled across the mattress to the bed's farthest edge, then rolled onto my side with my back to him. "I'm tired. I need to sleep."

Quiet spread through the room. I switched off the light, plunging us into darkness, then settled back down and forced my shoulders to relax.

"*Payilas dilēran*," he muttered.

That one I couldn't translate, but I would bet my measly savings it wasn't complimentary.

18

I CLEARED MY THROAT. "Are you sure this is the place?"

Standing beside me in the sheltered doorway, Amalia looked at her phone for the third time. "This is the address. And it says right there, 'Grand Grimoire.'"

Across the street, a plain three-story building with a faded white exterior sat next to a narrow alleyway. The road slanted downward and the main level of the building was embedded in the hillside, giving it a weirdly crooked appearance. Steady rainfall pattered the asphalt, and muddy rivulets followed the curb as they raced down the slope.

A faded green awning boasted the guild's name, and matching green bars covered the main-level windows. The building's exterior had been recently painted but graffiti tags covered the glass panes.

"They might not be open," I hedged. "It's a holiday."

"Halloween isn't a real holiday." She shot me a stern look. "Quit being a chicken. You need to act like a proper contractor."

She marched into the rain and I reluctantly skittered after her. Regardless of how I acted, no one would believe a five-foot-one waif with glasses was a demon contractor.

The entrance was set back from the sidewalk and green gates blocked the alcove. I stubbornly hoped they'd be locked, but Amalia pulled them open with ease.

The dim interior revealed a few shelves and racks half stocked with board and card games. Guilds were required to masquerade as legitimate public or semi-public businesses—so the comings and goings of their members didn't draw suspicion—but this was a poor effort. Dust liberally coated all surfaces.

Amalia swept to the counter and slapped the small bell beside the abandoned cash register—a model from the eighties, by the look of it. It took a solid two minutes of bell abuse before a lock clattered and a door at the back flew open. A burly man with a thick beard and shaved head scanned us, his dark eyes glaring.

"We're closed today, girls," he barked. "Shop somewhere else."

"We're not here for your shit games," Amalia shot back. "Is your GM in? We sent an email about doing an interview this morning."

"What hole did you two just climb out of? We ain't doing interviews today. There's a code-black alert in effect. The MPD shut down most of the Eastside and every combat guild has teams on a search rotation."

The Eastside? But the demon had been blowing up Uncle Jack's house in West Vancouver when Amalia and I had fled … to the Eastside. Had the winged demon tracked our departure? I shuddered at the thought of that thing stalking us.

"So …" Amalia drawled. "Your GM isn't in, then?"

"Shit," the man growled. "We're busy, princess. Half the guild was up all night. Come back when the alert is off."

She folded her arms. "We're here now. If your guild wants a shot at recruiting a newly discovered, one-of-a-kind demon, you'll make time for an interview."

My eyes bulged. That boast was the opposite of *blending in!*

The man reassessed Amalia, taking in her tight black jeans and leather jacket—purchased this morning to replace her ruined dress. Her dirty blonde hair fell down her back in loose, messy waves, and makeup—borrowed from me—darkened her eyes. She looked like a total badass.

Then he shifted his appraisal to me. As his gaze traveled from my shoulder-length brown hair to my powder-blue raincoat and snug jeggings, his eyebrows bunched together. He gave my white sneakers a final disapproving grimace.

"You should've left your little sister at home," he told Amalia. "Our guild isn't kid-friendly. This way."

Amalia followed him through the door and I trailed after them, fuming. Just because I was short didn't mean I was a child. I adjusted my glasses, wishing I could take them off.

Beyond the dusty shop was a maze of equally neglected offices. Our guide led us up a dimly lit staircase to the second floor, where we entered a large room scattered with comfy sofas and chairs. A projector screen occupied one wall and a few tables, jumbled with computers and laptops, lined the back.

Large windows let in abundant light, brightening the space despite the dark maroon walls.

A dozen people were slouched in chairs or lying across sofas. If I were stereotyping them, I'd go with "biker gang." Leather, tattoos, beards. Big guys with big muscles. There were no women.

"Tae-min," our burly guide called. "We've got visitors."

A head appeared over the back of a sofa. Black hair poked out from beneath the man's vivid orange beanie as he scrutinized us. He pushed off the sofa, a gray-and-white plaid shirt hanging open over his plain t-shirt. A pendant bounced against his chest but it wasn't an infernus.

Burly waved at him. "Tae-min, our first officer."

Guild hierarchy was straightforward. The guild master, or GM, was the ultimate authority and responsible for everyone in the guild. He was supported by one or more guild officers, who were like the shift supervisors—or camp counselors, or maybe army lieutenants. It depended on the guild.

I blinked bemusedly as Tae-min joined us. He wasn't what I'd expected—neither bearded nor tattooed nor muscly. At maybe thirty years old, he was young for an officer.

"What's up?" he asked.

On closer inspection, he appeared exhausted. So did Burly; he mustn't have been exaggerating about being up all night. Every guild in the city was hunting the winged demon.

"This chick wants to interview for membership. She claims to have a newly discovered demon line on contract."

Tae-min's brown eyes brightened with interest. "A new lineage? There hasn't been a new one in, what, a century? Who's the summoner?"

"Confidential," Amalia replied promptly. "Is your GM here?"

"No. It isn't a great time, you know, with the alert." He flapped his hand like it was no big deal, the unbound demon loose in the Downtown Eastside and probably slaughtering innocent people. "But I could call him—if you and your demon are legit."

Other guild members, listening in on the conversation, wandered closer. I edged behind Amalia, my heart pounding. Things I hated: confrontation, any form of spotlight, and not knowing what I was doing in a strange place in front of strange people. This was my social-insecurities nightmare.

Amalia folded her arms, boldly staring Tae-min down. "We aren't here to entertain you."

"Look, we'd love to add a new contractor to our ranks, but Rocco is busy managing our teams for the demon hunt. I'm not calling him based on your claim alone. All things considered, I shouldn't call him at all."

"Yeah," someone muttered, "but for a new demon line ... that'd put us on the radar for sure."

My nervous gaze roamed across the gathering crowd. It wasn't a big group, but the men were so tall and beefy that it felt much larger. Was every person here a contractor? Had they all sold their souls to control a demon's brute power?

"Show us your demon," Tae-min prompted, "and I'll call Rocco. If you're for real, he'll induct you over the phone."

Show them? I squashed my alarm. Oh no. Definitely not. Zylas was safely confined to the infernus and I planned to keep it that way.

Amalia nodded. "Yeah, sure."

What? No!

Tae-min grinned and the other mythics drew closer, eagerness and greed livening their faces—until Amalia pulled me out from behind her.

"Call your demon, Robin," she ordered.

A ripple passed through our observers.

"Wait," Burly growled at her. "You're the contractor, aren't you?"

"Hell no."

A dozen pairs of disbelieving eyes fixed on me. I shrank in on myself.

"Her?" someone said in an undertone.

"She's tiny."

"Is she even legal?"

"No way she's a contractor."

"Robin," Amalia cut in firmly. "Do it. We don't have all day here."

Her gray eyes lashed me with warning. I needed to play my part. I wasn't a non-practicing sorceress who read lots of books and only knew basic cantrips. I was a contractor now.

Swallowing hard, I tugged my infernus from beneath my jacket. The silver runes gleamed as I settled it on my chest. All eyes followed the motion.

Breathe. I could do this. Amalia had spent over an hour coaching me and Zylas on how a demon and its contractor were supposed to behave. It would be simple. Easy-peasy. I grasped the pendant, as Amalia had instructed, and waited for Zylas to appear in a swirl of red magic.

Nothing happened.

Tae-min glanced at Amalia, then back to me. "Are you calling it or what?"

I squeezed the infernus tightly, adrenaline flooding my veins. Why wasn't Zylas appearing? He could detect some of what went on outside the infernus, couldn't he? He'd popped out at exactly the right time to save me and Amalia last night.

Should I call his name out loud? No, Amalia had explained that a normal contractor controlled his demon through a telepathic connection, puppeteering the demon's body in silence.

Angry rumbles grew among the watching mythics. The infernus cut into my palm as I gripped it harder.

Zylas, get out here! I silently shouted. As the words rang through my head, red light bloomed over the infernus. It streaked to the floor, then flowed upward into Zylas's shape. The glow died away, revealing his solid body.

He stood utterly still, arms hanging at his sides, expression blank and eyes staring straight ahead. Not even his tail twitched, exactly as Amalia had told him. His imitation of an enslaved puppet was perfect, and a mixture of pride and relief swept through me. We could do this!

I looked up eagerly, but the Grand Grimoire mythics were gawking at Zylas in disbelief. Had he done something wrong?

Burly burst into laughter.

Roaring guffaws erupted from the others, and they exchanged gleefully derisive looks as they slapped their thighs with mirth. Only Tae-min kept his composure.

"*That's* your demon?" a man called between chuckles. "That little thing?"

"Is it even full grown?" someone else asked mockingly. "Did the summoner catch an adolescent by mistake?"

"I've never seen such a pathetic demon!"

"Mine would tear it apart in half a second."

"If the demon isn't bigger than a human, what's the point?"

Burly snorted. "A new line, eh? Now we know why. Who would bother contracting such a weak demon?"

My hands curled into fists. "He's not weak!"

My loud protest silenced all the laughter and I stiffened under the weight of the group's judgement.

"You think your baby demon can compete in our guild, little girl?" Burly scoffed. "*This* is a real demon."

He dragged an infernus from under his leather jacket and crimson power leaped off it. The light pooled on the floor, then crawled up—and up and *up*. When it reached seven and a half feet, the light dispersed to reveal the demon.

Thick gorilla arms were bound by heavy muscle. Spikes protruded from its elbows and shoulders, and its tail was thick and powerful and tipped with more spines. Two pairs of six-inch horns curled off its head, its scalp covered in bristling black hair, and its eyes glowed like lava in a swarthy, reddish-brown face with a heavy jaw and protruding fangs.

In comparison, Zylas looked like a toy version of a demon. Burly's beast was so huge that Zylas could've walked under its outstretched arm without ducking.

"Aw, look, you scared her," a guy said with feigned sympathy. "Take your pet demon and go home, girl."

"A demon like that wouldn't put us on the radar," Burly told Tae-min. "It'd make us a laughingstock. I'm sorry for bringing them up here."

My fists tightened. "My demon isn't weak!"

Burly laughed again. "Should I demonstrate for you?"

His attention turned to his spiky demon. The creature, who'd been standing as statue-still as Zylas, lifted its huge arm. Its monstrous hand zoomed toward its smaller cousin's face.

Zylas! I silently screamed.

That gigantic, talon-tipped hand reached for Zylas's head—and he ducked. The demon's hand closed over nothing but air. Legs already coiled, Zylas sprang up and grabbed the demon by its horns. He vaulted over the demon's head and landed lightly in front of Burly.

Before the man could do more than widen his eyes in shock, Zylas grabbed him by the throat. He lifted the taller, heavier man off the floor with an easy flex of his arm.

"No!" Tae-min shouted, whipping out a small, rune-marked wand. "*Ori imped—*"

Still holding Burly in the air, Zylas pivoted and slammed his foot into Tae-min's chest. The officer flew backward and crashed into two other guys.

The Grand Grimoire mythics shouted furiously. They surged into motion, infernus pendants appearing everywhere. Someone began an incantation and electric magic crackled up another's arms.

Zylas hurled Burly into the crowd—then leaped in right after the man's tumbling form.

Chaos reigned. Shouts, bellows, flares of crimson light as contractors tried to summon their demons. Zylas was a spinning flash of reddish-toffee skin, shining armor, and dark fabric. I couldn't follow his movements.

All I knew was the men were falling.

It lasted maybe thirty seconds, and by the end, Zylas was the only one still standing. Well, him and Burly's demon, which couldn't move unless Burly commanded it.

Zylas leaped out of the tangle of groaning men and landed neatly beside me. He resumed his statue imitation, gazing blankly at nothing. I stared at him, then at the heap of mythics.

No one was dead. I didn't see any blood either. Zylas had merely beaten them into the ground.

Amalia elbowed me and hissed, "Stop looking so shocked. You were controlling his attacks, *remember?*"

I cleared my expression as Tae-min heaved himself off the floor, straightened his shirt, and glowered at me. Grumbling and swearing, the other mythics got to their feet and formed an angry, muscly ring around us. Would it look bad if I hid behind Zylas? He was my demon. I was allowed to use him as a shield, right?

"One of a kind," Amalia remarked into the silence, buffing her nails on her jeans and looking bored. I was so jealous of her acting skills.

Tae-min stepped in front of Zylas. He and the demon were the same height, and the guild officer stared into Zylas's crimson eyes. "You have a legal contract? I've never seen a contracted demon move that fast."

"Yes," I lied, wishing I could sound as cool and bored as Amalia. "It's legal."

He nodded as he reached under the back of his shirt. When his hand reappeared, he held a short knife with an engraved hilt. Did *all* mythics carry hidden knives around?

"What are you—" I began shrilly.

His dark eyes skimmed my face, then his hand snapped out—the sharp, deadly blade slashing at Zylas's throat. I lunged forward.

Blood splattered the floor.

The knife pressed against Zylas's cheek, dark blood running down the blade. My hand was clamped over Tae-min's, stopping the weapon from cutting any deeper.

I scarcely remembered moving—I only recalled the piercing urgency that had driven me forward to grab the knife. Sharp pain dug into my inner thumb and a tremor ran through me, but I didn't loosen my hold.

"What are you doing?" My hard, chilly demand surprised me.

Tae-min pulled his weapon back, easily breaking my hold, and I curled my fingers into a tight fist. Tucking the blade under his shirt, the guild officer assessed my demon. Through it all—the sudden attack, my lunge, the cut—Zylas hadn't so much as twitched. He must have nerves of steel.

"I had to be sure it's fully under your control," Tae-min explained casually. "Your handling of the demon is superb. How do you do it?"

My mouth opened but I had no idea what to say.

Amalia jumped to my rescue. "We aren't about to reveal our family secrets to you plebeians."

An annoyed grumble ran through the mythics.

"Well …" Tae-min rubbed his smooth jaw. "I'll talk to the GM."

As the officer walked off to a private corner to make the call, I looked up at Zylas. Blood darker and thicker than a human's dripped off his chin.

My fist tightened, pain flaring through my palm, and I hoped no one noticed the slow dribble of blood squeezing between my fingers, its tempo matching Zylas's almost perfectly. Something told me a contractor slicing her hand open to stop a blade from touching her demon might raise suspicion. Even *I* could hardly believe I'd done it.

19

"I'M SORRY," I muttered for the fourth time.

Arms folded, Amalia glared across the road. We were standing in the alcove outside the Grand Grimoire's front door, waiting for Tae-min to join us. Pattering rain coated the pavement and heightened the colors of the spray paint that marked the opposite building.

No matter where I looked, the street was ugly, but I should get used to the view. This was my guild now.

Whatever Tae-min had told the GM had done the trick. I was officially a member of the Grand Grimoire, and Tae-min was putting through the preliminary paperwork right now. More forms and waivers awaited us but until the MPD lifted their "escaped demon" alert, no one would process anything.

I assessed the heat level of Amalia's glower. "I really am sorry. When he asked if you were my champion, he seemed to expect a 'yes.'"

Her scowl deepened.

"You never said you weren't planning to join the guild with me," I added.

"Of course I wasn't!" she blurted furiously. "I was already in a guild! But you had to go and tell him I'm your champion and it would've looked suspicious if I'd corrected you."

My hands tightened and pain flared. I'd balled a few tissues against my cut thumb to stanch the bleeding, but it hurt a lot. "Why didn't you explain champions to me before?"

"I forgot you didn't know," she replied grouchily. "But don't you think it's kind of obvious? Controlling a demon in a fight takes concentration. Contractors can't defend themselves at the same time, so they need a protector."

And that protector was their "champion," a mythic partner who guarded the contractor's back.

"It's a good thing your crazy demon can fight on its own," she added, "because I'll be a useless champion. But remember"—she leaned close and lowered her voice—"if he fights, he can't use *any* magic. It'll be a dead giveaway that he's not—"

The door behind us opened, causing Amalia and me to jump. We exchanged alarmed looks and I vowed to be more careful about what we discussed in public.

Tae-min stepped outside, accompanied by another man—almost as thick and muscled as Burly, but several inches shorter. "This is George. We're partnering for the search. Let's go."

Since Tae-min was a sorcerer—he'd been waving around sorcery artifacts earlier—that would make George a contractor. The guild was half contractors, half champions.

The officer led us out of the alcove, and I pulled my jacket tighter around me as I followed him into the cold rain. His car was parked in the alley adjacent to the guild and we piled into it. As the vehicle pulled out onto the quiet road, I hunched in my seat, wishing I could wake from this nightmare.

Thanks to Zylas, there was a demon loose in the city, and every combat mythic from every guild was hunting it. The Grand Grimoire, as the city's primary Demonica guild, was crucial to the hunt—and Amalia and I were now part of the search effort.

The wipers swept across the windshield, chasing the rain. Six months ago, I'd been living with my parents, going to college, and studying mythic history in my spare time. Two weeks ago, I'd been losing sleep over Uncle Jack stealing my mom's grimoire.

Now I was bound to a demon, newly inducted into a Demonica guild, and about to hunt the most dangerous adversary a mythic could face. And until I dealt with that, I couldn't do a thing about the missing grimoire.

GLUMLY, I WIPED RAIN off the lenses of my glasses.

Oblivious to the downpour drenching the abandoned intersection, Tae-min squinted at the MPD app on his phone for the "grid" we were supposed to search. The neighborhood had been cleared for the combat teams hunting the demon, and the MPD was coordinating every team's search zone.

"Our grid is three blocks," Tae-min declared, pocketing his phone. "We'll search it from west to east, then they'll assign us a new grid."

"I can't believe we don't have central communication yet," George complained in a chain-smoker's gravelly voice. "We should have headsets."

"That's not in our budget," Tae-min muttered. "Anyway, let's split up. Check everything, then come back here. Remember, unbound demons are fast and in full command of their magic. Shout if you see any sign of it."

With that, he and George strode away.

I stood blankly in the middle of the street. Um … were we supposed to just … walk around, then? Uncertainly, I started in the opposite direction. Amalia followed me onto a narrow street lined with businesses, then ducked under the awning of a health food store.

I stopped, cold water pattering on my head. "What are you doing?"

"Waiting here." She pulled out her phone. "I'm not wandering around in the rain, searching for an unbound demon. It's suicide."

"But," I spluttered, "your dad is the one who summoned it. If *anyone* should be—"

"Yeah, but *I* didn't summon it. Look, Robin." She put a hand on her hip. "We're no match for an unbound demon and you know it. It isn't killing people, so let's just chill and let the pros handle things."

"It isn't killing people? Then what's it doing?"

"No idea. Demons on the loose usually go on killing sprees, but this one is just lurking around the Eastside." She waved her phone. "Either way, I checked the latest MPD update. The demon has injured a few mythics but no one's died. We don't need to get involved."

"We're already involved, and we have a responsibility to—"

"Ugh." She rolled her eyes. "Knock yourself out, then. I'm staying here."

Huffing, I marched down the sidewalk. I *would* search for the demon, especially since I was partly responsible for its escape.

The constant drumming of the rain deadened all other sound and shadows encroached on the streetlights' glow. My stubborn determination to do the right thing withered beneath a wave of apprehension, but I continued to the next intersection. Where did our grid end? This seemed awfully slapdash for a highly organized, multi-guild search.

As I stood there, unsure of what to do, movement caught my eye.

Four people were jogging down the adjacent street, two on each side. As they reached an intersecting alley, the pairs swept into the shadowy passageways with the determined proficiency of a SWAT team. A minute later, they reappeared, giving each other hand signals that I assumed meant, "All clear."

I hurried behind a bus stop shelter and peered out as they reconvened in the street, pausing while one checked his phone. They all wore black clothes, lots of leather, and what appeared to be bullet-proof vests. The three men stood beside a short blond woman with something sticking up over her shoulder.

The man on his phone pressed a finger to his ear. "Copy that, Felix. We're almost finished this grid."

"I'm beat." Stretching her arms over her head, the woman turned to her teammate, revealing the sword strapped to her back. "How much longer on this shift?"

"Two more hours."

"Damn." She stifled a yawn. "I haven't gone on this little sleep since the Lynn Creek shifter stakeout."

A guy chuckled. "That was a fun one!"

"Let's get back to it, guys," the leader said.

Reforming their pairs, they set out in a swift but cautious jog. I watched the woman's retreating back with hungry awe. She was petite—almost as short as me—but she oozed toughness with each step. Could I ever be like that?

I watched the team methodically sweep the street until they disappeared in the rain. Wow. So *that's* what we were supposed to be doing. Did Tae-min know how this search should be performed? I retreated half a block and peered down a dark alley. Going in there alone struck me as a dumb plan.

Heat flared against my chest, radiating from the infernus, and Zylas materialized beside me in a burst of red light. Ignoring my shocked gasp, he peered upward. Rain peppered his face and he frowned as though the weather's daring offended him.

"What are you doing?" I hissed in alarm. "You can't just pop out whenever you feel like it!"

Crimson eyes glowing in the dim light, he cast me a dismissive glance. The cut on his cheek was a dark line, no longer bleeding. "Why not?"

"Someone might see you!"

"I knew you were alone."

"How?"

He stretched lazily, arching his back. "You thought about it."

"You—you can *hear my thoughts?*"

"In the infernus, there is nothing." He wrinkled his nose. "Quiet and dark. Boring. But I can hear you."

I didn't know how to react. Crawling into a sewer and dying of humiliation was appealing. "Don't eavesdrop on my thoughts! That's—that's private!"

He studied a streetlamp as though wondering if he could climb it, then wandered into the alley.

Ignoring me. Completely.

I stalked after him. "Zylas—"

He spun around. Seizing my wrist, he forced my hand up, a bloody tissue pinched against my cut thumb.

"Do you mind?" I asked as I tugged on my arm.

He ripped the tissue out of my grasp and tossed it aside. "You are *still* bleeding? How much are you hurt?"

I reluctantly opened my hand. Fresh blood welled in the deep cut and a drop spilled over, running down my palm.

Watching the bright red line snake over my wrist, Zylas pulled my arm closer to his face—then licked the blood, his hot tongue running up my wrist to the cut.

"*Aaagh!*" I squealed, wrenching my arm free. "What are you *doing*?"

Gaze unfocused, he worked his mouth as though experiencing a new flavor.

"That's disgusting," I whined, vigorously wiping my wrist on my jeans. "I can't believe you—"

He spat on the ground. My jaw dropped, my complaint forgotten as his face contorted with complete and utter revulsion.

"*Guh!* Does all human blood taste like that?" he demanded.

"Of course it does."

He stuck his tongue out like he wanted to wipe it clean. "Tastes like *metal*."

I glared at him, unreasonably offended that he thought my blood was gross. "Serves you right for licking me."

"*Hh'ainun* blood is supposed to be the finest flavor." He shot me a look like I'd severely disappointed him. "A stupid rumor."

He grasped my wrist again. Turning my palm up, he pressed two fingers into the cut. I flinched, but before I could draw away, red magic glowed across his hand. A miniature swirl of lines and runes flashed out, and he whispered a few words.

I gasped as searing pain burrowed into my palm. The magic brightened, then drained into the cut. As the light faded, he wiped away the blood, and we peered at the new pink scar at the base of my thumb.

"That happened last time," he muttered, prodding the slight ridge with one finger. "Your skin does not grow right."

"You healed it," I whispered, lifting my gaze to his. "Why?"

"Your blood smells as bad as it tastes."

The soft, confusing feeling of gratitude in my chest snuffed out. "Ugh." I yanked my hand away. "You're awful."

"But I do not taste bad."

"I *never* want to know what you taste like." I pulled myself together. "We're out here because we need to stop the escaped demon. Do you know how to find it?"

He glanced skyward, his pupils constricting to near-invisible slits against the muted light.

"Zylas?" I prompted impatiently. "How do we find the demon?"

"*Mailēshta.*"

"What?"

"Annoying," he translated.

"What's annoying?"

"You."

I gritted my teeth. "Very mature, Zylas."

He focused on the lower portion of a rusty fire escape two feet above his head.

"Don't even think about climbing that." I folded my arms. "The demon is on the loose because of you, so the least you can do is help stop it."

"No."

"Why not? Are you afraid you'd lose in a fight?"

His attention snapped to me. He bared his teeth, but I couldn't tell if it was a snarl or a smile. "*Vh'renith vē thāit.*"

I waited a moment. "What does that mean?"

"It means I never lose."

My eyebrows rose at his arrogance, but who was I to question him on it? From everything I'd seen, he was utterly lethal. Uncle Jack and Claude had said this mysterious demon could be the strongest ever summoned.

His gaze shifted away again as he scanned the alley.

"In that case," I continued firmly, attempting to draw his attention back, "you shouldn't have any problem helping—"

"Quiet, *payilas.*"

"Would you stop—"

He clamped his hand over my mouth and swept me against his chest with his other arm. "*Quiet.* I am listening."

Mashed against him, I halted in the midst of digging my fingernails into his abdomen. Sucking in air through my nose, I stilled, ignoring the discomfort of being pressed against him. Warmth radiated from his body, his hand hot on my mouth, his other arm across my back, holding me in place.

He smelled like leather and sweet hickory smoke. The thought crowded into my head, heightening my discomfort.

Nostrils flaring as he scented the damp breeze, he looked one way then the other. After a long moment, he stepped backward into the shadows beneath the fire escape, pulling me with him. A faint buzz of power passed over his body, then the surrounding air cooled—and the shadows thickened like black fog.

We stood in chilly darkness, Zylas holding me tight against him as though I might bolt straight into danger. "Danger" was the only conclusion I could draw from his sudden desire to hide.

A soft footstep crunched on broken glass, the sound traveling down the alley.

"Where are they?" a male voice asked, the rain muffling his quiet words.

"I'm not sure," another voice answered. "I lost them."

"Let's keep moving."

The glass crunched again. I strained my ears but only heard the increasing downpour. What the heck had *that* been about? Were those men part of another search team?

Zylas held his position, only his head moving as he tracked sounds I couldn't hear. I waited. One minute stretched into two, then three, and my discomfort grew. When no other sounds came from the alley, I tugged on his wrist. He didn't release my mouth. I tugged harder. He ignored me.

Growling against his palm, I dug my fingernails into the back of his hand as hard as I could.

He looked down, surprise widening his crimson eyes. "What are you doing, *payilas*?"

Let me go! I thought at him, since I couldn't speak out loud.

He tilted his head curiously—then a husky laugh rumbled from his throat. "*Na*, you are trying to hurt me? So I let you go? Too soft, *payilas*."

Outwardly, I glowered with extra force. Inwardly, I shriveled. My attempt to hurt him was so ineffective he hadn't understood my intent? Why was his skin so impenetrable?

"Robin? Where are you?"

Amalia's voice rang out over the drumming rain. Zylas graced me with his taunting smirk, then red light glowed over him. His hand disappeared from my face as his body dissolved into sweeping red light that swirled into the infernus. It vibrated, hot and electric, then returned to an inanimate metal disc.

I clenched my jaw. Stupid jerk of a demon. A bully. That's what he was.

Grimly pleased that he could probably hear me insulting him, I hastened to join Amalia and resume our hunt for the escaped demon.

20

THIS WAS STUPID.

The thought repeated more and more as the afternoon dragged on. Tae-min had no idea how to manage our search. We wandered around at a quick walk, gazing pointlessly into alleys. Anytime we split from the two men, Amalia chose the driest spot and waited, letting me search on my own. Like we'd ever find the demon this way.

I marched alone up another street, fuming at them. Tae-min for his incompetence. George the Contractor for failing to recognize how futile this was. Amalia for refusing to help. And Zylas for … for *everything*.

The rain had softened to intermittent spitting—the only bright spot in this crappy day. As I glared across an intersection, the traffic light blinked from red to green, but there were no vehicles. The neighborhood was eerily deserted and the quiet was so intense I could hear myself breathe.

As I turned to go back the way I'd come, a glimpse of movement brought me up short. Had I just seen a human-sized shadow duck out of sight, or were my eyes playing tricks on me? Maybe it was another search team.

"Hello?" I called. "Anyone there?"

I waited a minute, but no one answered. I must've imagined it …

The phantom memory of Zylas's hand on my face shivered through me. Those men in the alley had said, *"I lost them." Them.* Not "it" or "the demon." Who had those men been looking for?

"Hello?" I shouted again.

Half a block away, a shadow moved. A man in dark clothes, his shape blurred by the misty rain, stepped out of a shop doorway and raised his arm.

Green light flashed over his hand—and shot toward me.

I lurched backward and my heel caught on the pavement. As I tumbled to the ground, the green light whizzed over my head. A sorcery spell? Was he *attacking* me?

Shoving to my feet, I yanked out my infernus. Pivoting, the man whipped around a corner and vanished from sight.

"Heyo!"

The call came from behind me. I spun around.

Three men, also in dark clothes but with reflective patches on their upper arms, were jogging up the street. Weapons were strapped over their torsos and they wore protective vests like the other search team, but these men were older—in their fifties, I was guessing.

"Are you the one who was calling?" the lead man asked as they neared me. "What are you doing out—"

His gaze caught on my infernus and surprise blanked his face. His rain-dampened hair was dark, but dry, I suspected it would be salt-and-pepper gray like his close-cropped beard. Four silver daggers were belted around his waist.

His teammate, a man with wavy, shoulder-length hair, let out an impressed whistle and grinned through his luxuriously thick beard and mustache. "Well I'll be damned. A contractor?"

I pretended the contractor label didn't bother me.

"Are you part of the search?" the leader asked, his gray eyes flicking over my decidedly non-combat-ready outfit. "What's your guild?"

"Grand Grimoire," I muttered. "Did you see the sorcerer? He shot a spell at me then ran off down that alley."

"Someone attacked you?" the third man rumbled. His bare arms were tattooed and coated in rain, but he didn't seem to mind the cold as he rested a long, rune-carved staff on his shoulder.

The leader appraised the empty street. "Where's your team?"

"Back that way." I waved over my shoulder.

The leader made a swift gesture at his teammates. Nodding, they broke into a jog, heading in the direction the sorcerer had fled.

"I'll escort you back to your team," the remaining mythic told me. "It isn't safe out here alone."

I hunched my shoulders, embarrassed. I knew it wasn't safe, but what was I supposed to do? Tell Tae-min he had no idea how to lead a team? I started down the street, the man matching my pace. I could feel his gaze but kept mine on the ground.

"I admit I'm curious," he ventured. "You don't seem like the usual contractor type."

Watching my mud-splattered shoes, I said nothing. What could I say? "Stop stereotyping contractors"? Or maybe, "Petite, bespectacled bookworms can be power-hungry, soul-selling contractors too"?

He tried again. "How long have you been a contractor?"

I almost said, "Twenty-four hours," then remembered my fake paperwork. "Six months."

"Robin, are you done—" Popping out of her alcove, Amalia spotted my new comrade and froze. "Oh! There you are, Robin! Why didn't you wait for me? We're supposed to stick together."

I glared at her.

"Would you be this young lady's champion?" the man asked.

"Uh, yeah."

The leader directed his full attention at Amalia. Her careless defiance, which I'd only seen falter when Zylas had threatened to kill her, crumbled under this man's stern disapproval. Her guilty stare flicked away.

With slapping steps, Tae-min trotted out of an alley, George trailing after him.

"What's going on? Who—oh." Tae-min slid to a halt.

"Tae-min," the man said. "Unpleasant circumstances under which to meet again. How are you?"

"I—I'm fine, thank you, Darius."

Darius smiled. I blinked, amazed by how he could look so warmly amicable *and* like a panther about to pounce.

"I'm delighted to hear you're well. Before that changes, may I ask why you're failing to follow basic protocol?"

Tae-min cringed. "Uh—"

"No mythic should be alone in the combat area, and team members should remain within each other's sight lines at all times. I assume you're leading this team?"

"I—yes, I am, but—"

"You're responsible for the lives you expose, and as an officer of a Demonica guild, you should understand the intense danger present on these streets—but what I'm seeing suggests you don't."

Tae-min stiffened.

"How much of your shift do you have left?" the mysterious mythic demanded.

"We—this is our last grid."

"Then you are dismissed, Tae-min. My team will cover this grid."

The officer's eyes blazed. "You can't just—"

"Escort these two young women back to your guild," Darius continued without pause, his commanding tone silencing the officer. "All else aside, I expected you and your GM to have better sense than to—"

"We know what we're doing!" Tae-min cut in furiously. "That girl"—he pointed at me—"and her demon will be the ones to take out the unbound demon. I'd bet my guild's treasury account on it."

"That isn't much of a wager. Take them back, Tae-min. I will be speaking with your GM about this as well."

Tae-min glowered, his jaw so tight a muscle was twitching in his cheek.

Darius offered me a warm smile. "I commend your bravery, Robin, but there will be other opportunities to test yourself against dangerous opponents."

To my surprise, I found myself returning his smile. As he strode back the way he'd come, Tae-min growled in the departing man's direction.

"Who was that?" I asked.

"Darius King," the officer answered grudgingly. "The guild master of the Crow and Hammer."

The Crow and Hammer? Damn it. Why hadn't Amalia and I joined Darius's guild instead of the Grand Grimoire? *He* knew what he was doing.

"The Crow and Hammer is a joke." Tae-min pulled his beanie off and wrung it out. "A lecture on following protocol from *him*? His guild is notorious for breaking rules and skirting regulations."

"Yeah, but all the same," George remarked, "they take a big share of the bounties around here."

Tae-min sneered. "Let's get back to the car."

As I followed the others, my thoughts spun, replaying Darius's lecture. *The lives you expose. The intense danger present on these streets.* How many mythics were out here, risking their lives to hunt the escaped demon? How many people, like Darius and his comrades, like that other team I'd observed, were putting themselves in terrible danger?

Zylas could mow through a room of contractors in less than a minute. What damage could the winged demon do to the mythics on the streets? Or humans who crossed its path? Though Tae-min hadn't known what he was saying, I *was* the one who needed to stop the escaped beast. Or rather, Zylas was the one.

I was no pro, but Zylas was lethal—and unlike properly contracted demons, he could wield his unstoppable magic. He had the power to defeat the winged demon. If *he* stopped it, no one else would get hurt. No one would have to die.

This was my responsibility. I needed to fix it.

We returned to Tae-min's car. As everyone else got in, I hovered beside Amalia's open door. "Uh, I'm going to go ... a different way."

Tae-min twisted in his seat. "What?"

"I need to go home," I lied quickly. "It's in the other direction. I'll catch a bus."

"You can't just—"

"I'll be back in time for my next shift." I glanced at Amalia. "I'll catch up with you later."

She stared at me. "Uh ... sure."

I shut her door. My hands were trembling but I ignored them. While a panicked voice in my head screamed at me to go back, I started down the nearest sidewalk, pretending I knew where I was going. The car's engine revved, then quieted as it drew away. I kept walking.

I was alone.

The coiling fear in my gut intensified, but I raised my chin. If Zylas and I found and defeated the escaped demon, everyone would be safe. I *needed* to do this, even if it terrified me.

I cut into an alley and withdrew my phone from my pocket. As I opened the MPD app, the infernus heated. Light flashed and Zylas appeared beside me.

"*Payilas*? What are you doing?"

I pulled up a map marked with all the demon sightings so far. "We're going to find the escaped demon."

His eyebrows drew down. "Why?"

"Because we're the reason it's on the loose. Why can't you and Amalia understand this? I freed you from the circle, and you freed the other demon. People are being hurt, and it's our fault."

He examined my face, pondering me like I was some sort of puzzle. "So?"

"Right. Of course you don't get it. You're a demon." I refocused on the app. "The most recent sighting was eight blocks away. We're too far west."

Gastown, a busy tourist area, was only a few blocks farther west. And, I saw, the Crow and Hammer guild was almost as close—four blocks to the northeast. I had a long walk to reach the correct area and it would get dark soon. Maybe I shouldn't do this …

No. It was my responsibility. Shoving my phone into my pocket, I started down the alley.

Zylas looked up from the newspaper dispenser he'd been examining, then started after me. "Where are you going?"

"To find the demon."

"Just like this?" Mocking amusement joined his swirling accent. "Walk, walk. *Na*, a demon! So easy."

I realized I was clenching my jaw again. The more time I spent around him, the higher my dental bills would be. "Help me, then. I'm sure you have a better idea of how to find it."

"Why would I want to find him?"

"Why did you free him in the first place?"

"Because he is old. He knows more … and he wants to return home too."

Stopping, I turned to study the demon. "You freed him to see if he knows a way back to your world."

Zylas made an irritated sound. "But he does not know or he would not be playing games with *hh'ainun*. I should have left him in his circle."

"Games? What kind of games?"

"Stalking games. He likes to hunt weak things on the ground."

"Do you *know* this demon?" I asked incredulously.

"His name is Tahēsh. He is the *Dīnen* ..." His nose scrunched. "I do not know your word. He is ... king?"

"King?" I gasped. "He's a demon *king*?"

Zylas hopped onto a dumpster, crouched on its edge, and peered up into the erratic rain. "He is *Dīnen* of the First House. All of my kind know his name."

A memory stirred—Uncle Jack's email to his partner Claude. *I think this is the 12th house??*

"How many demon kings are there?" I asked.

He watched the sky, his nostrils flaring as he scented the breeze. "Twelve."

A king for each House. I rubbed my hands over my face, smearing raindrops across my skin. "Uncle Jack summoned a demon king. That's insane. And you set him free!"

"What is so impressive, *payilas*? He lived longest, so he became *Dīnen*."

"But ... a king! Does that mean he commands other demons?"

"He rules his House." Zylas's gaze traced the rooftops. "It is not a great thing."

I snorted. "Now you just sound jealous. You wish you were a demon king too."

"*Ih?*" He looked at me properly, his mouth thinning. "I am."

"You're what?"

"*Dīnen.*"

My expression froze. "Wh ... what? *You're* a demon king?"

His scowl deepened at my disbelieving tone and his tail lashed, hitting the dumpster's side with a clang. "Of course, *payilas*. Do you know anything?"

I stared at him, my heart thudding in a strange rhythm. "You're King of the Twelfth House …"

He glanced skyward, then hopped off the dumpster. "Finding Tahēsh is stupid, *payilas*. Leave now. Back to the other *hh'ainun*."

"What? No, we have to stop him. I just explained—"

Zylas stepped closer, his dark hair tangled across his eyes and dripping rainwater. "Go back to the *hh'ainun*."

"No, I—"

He pushed on my stomach, forcing me back a step. "Go now."

"Quit it! I'm not leaving until Tahēsh is stopped."

Zylas shoved me again—gently, but he was so strong I staggered.

"Stop it!" I seethed, skittering away from him. How did I make him understand our responsibility to stop this demon? *Could* he understand it or was it beyond his moral conception?

His eyes glowed menacingly as he herded me toward the alley's entrance, his teeth glinting, half bared. His contractual promise to protect me suddenly felt all too flimsy.

"Faster, *payilas*," he growled, shoving me with more force. As I grabbed a wall for balance, I almost missed the darting glance he shot toward the rooftops.

And I realized it wasn't aggression fueling his tension. It was muted urgency. Zylas was desperate to get me away from here without revealing the reason—but I could guess why.

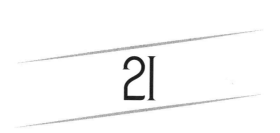

21

WHICHEVER DIRECTION Zylas didn't want me heading was the way I planned to go. Diving under his reaching arm, I bolted deeper into the alley—but he grabbed my jacket, hauling me back. I smacked into his chest, my feet dangling off the ground.

"What are you doing?" he snarled in my ear, his arms banded around me, squeezing my lungs.

"Tahēsh is nearby, isn't he?" I fought to inhale as his hold tightened. "That's why you keep looking at the sky and want to leave."

"If you know, why do you run toward him? Do you want to die?"

Determination eclipsed my fear. "You have to protect me."

If Tahēsh came after us, the contract's magic would force Zylas to fight him to keep me safe. He couldn't refuse to fix his mistake if I was in danger. And he'd told me himself—he never lost.

I sucked in a deep breath and loosed the loudest shout my lungs could produce. "*Tahēsh!*"

Zylas clamped his hand over my mouth and ducked backward into a dark nook where two buildings met. Satisfaction filtered through me, and I tilted my head back to see Zylas's face, silently gloating that I had outsmarted him.

He pressed against the wall, head turning, nostrils flaring wide. His crimson eyes were wide and ... alarmed. Almost ... *afraid*.

My smug feeling of victory faltered.

Zylas's head snapped back. Clutching me tight, he leaped out of the alcove.

Red light flashed and the doorway exploded. The force hit Zylas from behind, hurling us toward the opposite building. He twisted at the last second so that his back slammed into the wall instead of me, his body absorbing my momentum. Bricks shattered, the falling debris narrowly missing my head.

He shoved off the wall, threw me over his shoulder, and sprinted away. The buildings on either side blurred with his speed. He veered around a corner, feet sliding on the wet pavement and tail sweeping out.

A red glow bathed the alley.

Zylas dropped, the armor covering his knees and shins screeching across the asphalt. He slapped his hand against the ground and red magic shot down his arm, spiraling into a rune-filled circle.

The sky turned scarlet as power blasted downward. Zylas's magic arched over us and the two forces collided in a blazing detonation that threw him into me. His forearms hit the asphalt and he shuddered under the impact, braced above me like a shield—with hatred blazing in his eyes.

The ground was still vibrating when he lunged up. He seized my coat, heaved me off the asphalt, and clamped me against his side. Leaping onto a fire escape, he dragged us up with one arm, got his feet onto the steel grating, and raced for the top.

On a building across the alley, a dark shape appeared. Wings spreading from heavy shoulders, the demon stepped to the rooftop's edge. His eyes glowed as magic rippled up his arms—an attack taking form.

"Watch out!" I cried.

Zylas flung us off the fire escape just before the crimson blast hit it. Metal shrieked as the structure tore away and plunged down to the street. We soared through the air, then Zylas caught the wall with one hand. His claws ripped down the bricks and caught on a windowsill. He clung precariously to his narrow handhold, a three-story drop onto pavement and twisted metal below.

From his rooftop, Tahēsh loosed a deep, throbbing laugh. "*Eshathē gūkkinanin venarish antin hh'ainun taridis, Dīnen et Vh'alyir.*"

Zylas bared his teeth. He dropped off the wall, plunged downward, and landed on a parked car. The roof caved under his feet. He hit the ground running, his arm a steel band crushing my lungs.

I could hear Tahēsh laughing.

We burst out of the alley into a small parking lot surrounded by three- and four-story buildings. Zylas dashed toward a dumpster, probably to use it as a launching block to get onto a roof—high ground against the winged demon. I desperately clutched his arm.

A few yards from the dumpster, he sprang upward like a startled rabbit.

A blast struck the pavement right under us. Red power hurled us in a violent spin and Zylas hit the ground on his back. Torn out of his grasp, I tumbled to a painful, dizzying stop beside the dumpster.

Zylas flipped onto his feet, red magic spiraling over his arms. He thrust his hands up.

Wings flared wide, Tahēsh plunged out of the sky and slammed into the smaller demon. Red magic rippled out from them like a sonic wave and Zylas buckled under the attack. He rolled clear. As he sidestepped away from his adversary, crimson magic glowed over his hands and extended past his fingertips, forming six-inch-long talons.

Rumbling with amusement, Tahēsh raised his hands and even longer talons of magic sprouted off his thick fingers. "*Kirritavh'an Zylas nailēris? Eshanā agrēris.*"

Zylas didn't respond, his eyes glowing and body coiled in readiness. As he faced the winged demon king, I clutched the infernus. Seven feet tall, Tahēsh rippled with bulging muscles, his size magnified by his curved wings and thick tail. And Zylas, facing him, looked like a scrawny adolescent about to take on a wrestling heavyweight.

The two demons stared at each other—then Tahēsh attacked.

Zylas ducked away from the streaking crimson claws. The two demons blurred with speed, Tahēsh striking and slashing while Zylas dodged and retreated. I couldn't follow their movements—couldn't tell who was winning and who was losing.

Red power burst off Tahēsh. Zylas slammed into the ground—and the pavement caved under his body. The earth shook from the impact.

For two heart-stopping seconds, Zylas didn't move. Then he rolled, barely escaping Tahēsh's downward strike. As he sprang up, Tahēsh's tail swung around and the bony plate on the end caught Zylas in the stomach.

They blurred again, their slashing, dodging motions interspersed with glimmers of crimson light. Blood sprayed across the ground but I didn't know whose. Slamming blows, vicious snarls. They broke apart—blood running from deep gashes in Zylas's upper arm—then clashed again, magic flaring.

Zylas whirled away as the pointed tips of Tahēsh's talons ripped across his chest. He stumbled, tail lashing, balance lost—and as he faltered, Tahēsh pounced.

My mouth gaped in a silent scream as he slammed Zylas into the pavement.

All sound and movement and magic died. Tahēsh was a dark, motionless shadow, crouched low with his wings arching off his back. Laughing gruffly, he straightened and raised his muscular arm.

Zylas hung from the long crimson claws impaling his stomach. The points protruded from his back, coated in blood. Panting wetly, he clutched Tahēsh's wrist and crimson power shot across his hands.

Tahēsh roared. Magic exploded in a blinding flare.

A deafening crash boomed beside me. I flinched away as Zylas pitched forward, crumpling to the pavement a foot away. He'd struck the dumpster so violently the metal had split. Garbage fell through the fissure—beer bottles and fast food wrappers and stained cans of spray paint.

Dark, thick blood pooled under Zylas and flowed across his back from the five punctures. He didn't move except for his rapid, rasping breaths. Tahēsh started toward us, his teeth exposed in a hungry grin.

My mind seized with panic. I had to do something. I had to help.

I grabbed a can of spray paint and shook it as I jumped in front of Zylas. Squeezing the nozzle, I prayed for some small blessing of luck—and blue paint spat from the can. I swept it across the pavement, drawing rushed lines.

Tahēsh stalked closer, taking his time, laughing quietly.

I threw the can aside, grabbed Zylas's shoulder, and heaved. "Get up! He's coming! We have to get away!"

Zylas groaned faintly and lifted his head. His eyes, tight with pain, gleamed dimly, and he pushed up on his elbows, blood running everywhere. His arms shook under his weight.

Tahēsh was almost on us.

"Zylas!" I yelled. "You have to protect me! Get up!"

His head turned in my direction, his teeth bared.

Ready? I mentally called to him. His eyes burned in answer and red light lit his hands and feet, veining across his limbs.

Tahēsh's giant foot crunched on the pavement inches from the drying paint.

"*Luce!*" I screamed.

The two-foot-wide cantrip I'd painted on the ground blazed as bright as the sun. Tahēsh bellowed, recoiling from the blinding radiance.

Zylas's arms caught me, crushing me against his chest. Red power flashed and a spell erupted beneath his feet.

We were blasted into the air. The incandescent cantrip and crumpled dumpster shrank as we rocketed five stories above the earth. At the apex of our ascent, we seemed to float on the icy wind—then we began to fall.

I clutched Zylas's neck as we plummeted toward a rooftop. We slammed down, his feet smashing through concrete, legs bending to absorb the impact. A sound rasped from his throat—part agonized groan, part fierce snarl. Crimson power rippled over his lower legs, and he launched forward—unbelievably fast, his movements powered by magic.

As Tahēsh's infuriated roar sounded behind us, Zylas leaped again. We soared across a wide road and hit another rooftop. Below were dark streets and brown train tracks. A rattling transit train snaked along the tracks like a silver serpent.

Zylas dashed across the roof and sprang one more time. We plunged downward as the Skytrain sped beneath us, streaking away. We hit the last car. Zylas slid wildly across the slick metal roof—we pitched off the back—

Metal screeched and we jarred to a halt. Zylas hung from the back car, his claws embedded in a steel edge, his other arm locked around my waist.

The train sped along the tracks, carrying us away from the Eastside and the demon king.

22

WE HUNG OFF THE BACK of the train for a few minutes. When a grassy bank replaced the buildings and streets, Zylas swung sideways and let go.

We dropped off the elevated track and fell fifteen feet. He landed on the grass and crumpled, his arms constricting around me as we rolled down the slope. We came to a halt beside a paved bike path, and the moment we'd stopped moving, he went limp.

I shoved onto my knees and touched his arm. His skin was cold. "Zylas?"

Sprawled on his back, he squinted at me. Blood ran from the corner of his mouth and his eyes had gone dark as night. The rest of him was a gory mess that my brain denied was real. A horror movie prop, not a hideously wounded living being.

"Are you safe here?" he rasped.

I dragged my horrified stare off him and looked around. Cars zipped along the street at the top of the knoll and distant pedestrians ambled along the wet sidewalks with umbrellas.

"Yes, I think so."

He let out a pained breath. Red light sparked over his limbs—and his arm disappeared from beneath my hand. His body dissolved into crimson radiance that swept into the infernus. Suddenly alone, I crouched beside a patch of dark blood on the grass, my hands hovering over a demon that was no longer there. All my limbs went weak and I slumped forward, trembling violently.

So stupid. I'd been so stupid.

I wanted to close my eyes, but I couldn't stop staring at the blood-drenched grass. Zylas was badly wounded. Fatally wounded, if he'd been human. I wasn't sure what a demon could survive. He had amazing healing magic … if he could use it. Could he heal himself? Or was it too late? The last time I'd seen his eyes dark like that, he'd been near death.

Fresh panic swept through me. I sprang to my feet and sprinted up the slope.

Zylas was dying. He needed help and I was the only one who could keep him alive—if I was fast enough.

I BOUNCED IMPATIENTLY on the balls of my feet as the cab driver held out my credit card and receipt. I snatched them from his hand and ran into the motel parking lot, not caring what he thought. With dirt and splattered stains—Zylas's dark blood—all over me, I already looked like a freak.

It had taken me fifteen minutes to hail a cab, get a ride back to the motel, and pay. Had too much time passed? Was it already too late? I hadn't seen any other options.

I fumbled in my coat pocket for the key card to my and Amalia's room, jammed it through the lock, and shoved the door open. The drab room was dark and empty, the two beds unmade, our bags open against the wall, and the TV Zylas had dismantled shoved in a corner.

Kicking the door shut behind me, I ran into the bathroom and turned the shower on full blast. Icy water sprayed into the tub. The infernus chain tangled under my jacket when I tried to pull it out, so I unzipped my coat and threw it aside. Clutching the metal disc, I stuck my arm under the water. Warm. Getting hotter.

"Zylas." I spoke and thought the words as intensely as possible. "Come out. I have something to help you."

Nothing happened. No. I couldn't be too late.

I kicked my shoes off, set my phone on the counter, and stepped into the tub. Scalding water soaked my socks. Flinching, I held the infernus under the spray. "Zylas, come out, please!"

Hot water flowed across the metal—and a red glow suffused it. Instead of leaping energetically toward the floor, the magic spilled straight down. Zylas took form almost on my toes, his back to me as he faced the showerhead. The water ran red with blood.

His legs buckled.

I grabbed his shoulders but his weight dragged me down too. I thumped onto my butt, the demon half in my lap, his head against my shoulder and his back between my legs. Water cascaded over his torso, blood running everywhere. Steam rose from the spray and wherever the blood-stained liquid touched me, it burned.

With effort, I propped him up to get his face out of the water. "Zylas?"

A muscle in his cheek twitched but he didn't open his eyes. "It is hot."

"Yes," I whispered.

He lay limply as the water washed over him. My gaze darted across his torso, trying to assess the severity of his injuries, but I couldn't begin to guess. Five punctures straight through his abdomen, four deep tears in his upper arm, and shallow slices across his chest, nearly cutting through the leather straps of his armor. And who knew how much internal damage from impacts? A terrifying amount of blood was swirling down the drain.

"Zylas …" I swallowed against the catch in my throat. "Will you survive?"

"You will not be rid of me this easily," he growled.

"I'm not trying to get rid of you." A sob built in my chest, fueled by guilt and furious regret. "I'm so sorry."

He watched me through half-lidded eyes the color of cooling coals. "Sorry?"

"I thought you could beat him. I thought it would be easy for you. If I'd realized … I never would've tried to get you to fight him."

"Easy?" His mouth contorted with disgust. "You are *zh'ūltis*. Can you not see?"

"See what?"

He twitched his hand to indicate his body. "Why would you think I am stronger?"

"But … but you said …"

He pulled himself upright and leaned against the shower wall, one leg hooked over the tub's edge. Resting his head against the tiles, he fixed a cold, indecipherable stare on me. "Tahēsh is *Dīnen* of the First House. I am *Dīnen* of the Twelfth House. I am the weakest of them all."

My throat closed. "I'm sorry. I should've realized you had no chance against Tahēsh."

"No chance? Insulting me more, *payilas*." A hint of crimson glowed in his dark eyes. "I can kill anything. Any of them. I did not become *Dīnen* by losing. I survive because I never lose."

"But you just lost really badly."

"*Kanish!*" His hand snapped out and he sank his fingers into my hair. Teeth bared, he yanked my face toward his. "*You* are the reason I lost! You forced me to fight him when I could not win!"

I trembled, afraid to blink. He wasn't hurting me—but he wanted to. I could see it in his face, in the twist of his lips, in the curved canines that could rip through my soft skin with ease. Terror gripped my body like icy talons.

He released me and slumped backward. Tilting his face into the water, he closed his eyes.

I sucked in air to calm my palpitating heart and mumbled, "I don't understand."

He shifted more under the hot spray. The water wasn't running as red now.

I tried again. "You said you never lose, but you also said you couldn't win against Tahēsh."

"Winning," he growled softly, "and *not losing* are different things. If you lose, you die."

I exhaled slowly. "So you never lose? How?"

"If I am not certain I can win, I do not fight—and I wait. That is how I have survived the other *Dīnen*."

"What do you wait for?"

"*Dh'ērrenith*. It means … assured victory." His eyes opened, luminous scarlet. "I wait until they are weak, distracted, injured, alone. I wait until they have forgotten to watch for me. I wait until I can strike from behind, from above, from wherever they do not see me. And I kill them. I never lose."

I stared at him, chilled despite the hot water.

"Until you," he added with a sneer. "Now I have lost."

"I'm sorry," I whispered. "I made a mistake."

He ignored me.

Swallowing, I climbed out of the tub, water dripping from my drenched clothes. I pulled a towel off the rack, grabbed my phone, and left Zylas to soak up the shower's heat.

Shivering in the cool air outside the bathroom, I sent a quick text to Amalia, telling her I was back at the motel and wouldn't be returning to help with the demon hunt. Then, casting wary looks toward the bathroom, I hastily shed my wet clothes, dried off, and pulled on yoga pants and a sweater.

I was just putting on a pair of socks when Zylas walked out of the bathroom. Droplets glistened over his skin and his hair was plastered to his head, his small horns more prominent than usual. He was tugging on the buckle of the strap that ran over his right shoulder. The leather gave way and he pulled off the armor plate that protected his heart, as well as the fabric piece under it, and dropped both on the floor.

Nervously, I watched him unbuckle the bracer on his left arm and peel off his fabric sleeves. They joined the pile on the floor.

Naked from the waist up, he sat cross-legged in the middle of the carpet. Slashes and punctures scored his torso in dark lines. Unbelievably, the bleeding had stopped. Eyes half closed, he seemed lost in thought. Then he pressed a hand to the floor.

Crimson veins snaked up his arm. Magic ignited beneath his palm and spiraled out into a rune-filled circle, and the air went cold. The faint light leaking through the windows dimmed until all I could see was the glowing spell. He studied it as though checking its accuracy, then laid back.

His lips moved in a soft rumble—an incantation in his mother tongue. Power rose from the markings in a red haze, coiled over him, and gathered in his wounds. With a final whispered word, the spell flared. The magic sucked into his body and he arched off the floor, jaw clenched and muscles straining. When all the power had sunk inside him and the spell had faded, he slumped, panting.

Staring unabashedly, I crept toward him. His wounds were gone like he'd never been injured. Not even a scar remained. Breathing hoarsely, he sat up and kneaded his right bicep where it'd been sliced open just moments before.

I minced closer. "Does it still hurt?"

He ignored me. Climbing to his feet, he rolled his shoulders, then leaned down and pressed his palms to the floor. My eyebrows rose at his flexibility. He held the stretch for a moment before straightening—then he leaned over backward. My eyebrows climbed even higher, and when he pressed his hands to the floor again, body folded in a tight backward arch, I swallowed hard.

He pushed off the floor and casually resumed a standing position, as though bending his spine in half were completely normal. Frowning, he rolled his right shoulder again, water dripping off his skin.

I skirted around him and into the bathroom, shut off the shower, then gathered a pair of towels. Back in the main room, I shook one out and draped it over his shoulders.

His eyes narrowed suspiciously.

"You should dry off," I mumbled. "So you don't get cold."

Shoving the towel off, Zylas stepped away as though my nearness offended him. My shoulders sagged. Clearly, I was not yet forgiven for almost getting him killed. Not that I deserved forgiveness that easily.

"You can lie down if you want." I waved at the bed. "If … if that would be more comfortable than the infernus?"

Leaning down, he unbuckled the greaves that protected his shins. He pulled one off and examined the damage from scraping across asphalt.

I mopped up the carpet as best I could, then carried the damp towels back into the bathroom. When I came out, Zylas was reclined on my bed. His toffee-toned skin contrasted boldly with the pale blue duvet, the lines of his upper body unbroken by clothing or armor.

In all objectivity, I had to admit his body was … beautiful. The difference in his skin's tone and texture was subtle, but it gave him an airbrushed look. Combined with his sculpted muscles, he was as perfect as a magazine photo—except for his dimly glowing eyes, small horns, and tail hanging off the mattress's edge, its barbed end twitching like a cat's.

He made an angry sound, startling me out of my slack-jawed reverie, and rolled onto his stomach. Head turned sideways, he glared at me with one eye.

Face heating, I hastily busied myself by tidying up. I hung my wet clothes in the bathroom, straightened up my suitcase, and collected Zylas's discarded gear, stacking it in the bathtub to dry. Lying on his stomach, he watched my every move, radiating hostility.

I picked up his armguard. A round, spiky sigil was engraved on it, and recognition sparked through me. I lifted my infernus to peer at the symbol in its center. They were identical.

"What's this?" I asked, pointing at the sigil on his armguard.

"The emblem of my House."

His House. The sigil must have appeared on the infernus after we'd formed our contract. I gazed down at him, his arms folded and cheek resting on them. Fighting the urge to creep away and hide in a corner, I set his armguard on the bedside table and sat beside him.

"Zylas ..." I took a deep breath. "Once Tahēsh has been stopped—by other mythics—I'll start researching a way to get you home."

"Why not now?"

"It's part of blending in. All the guilds are hunting Tahēsh. Until he's stopped, anything I do will draw too much attention to us."

He assessed me coldly, then turned his head the other way. I wilted. Zylas had probably hated me all along, so I didn't know why his resentment bothered me so much.

Pointedly ignoring me, he kneaded his right shoulder to work out the stiffness. Without thinking, I pressed my thumb into the muscle that ran alongside his shoulder blade.

He shot up onto his hands and knees, teeth bared. "What are you doing?"

"Sorry!" I yelped, flinching backward. "I—I was trying to help …"

He glowered at me, then sank back down onto his stomach. His tail snapped sideways, betraying his agitation. "Go away."

I started to get up—then hesitated. He might have healed his injuries, but he was stiff and probably sore. Drawing in a steadying breath, I put a knee on the bed, then pressed both hands to his back and ran my thumbs over his shoulders with firm pressure.

He hissed like an angry snake. "Go *away*."

"My mom would spend hours hunched over faded grimoires," I said determinedly. "I used to give her a massage a few times a week. I'm pretty good at it."

He snarled and started to rise, but I found the muscle that was bothering him—a tight band that ran from his neck to his shoulder blade—and dug both thumbs into the knot. He tensed in place. As I pushed into the muscle, he sank down under the pressure until he was lying flat again.

Angling his head, he watched me work on the taut muscle group. His muscles were so toned it was easy to trace their lines and follow the tension. I kneaded his stiff shoulder, then worked down his back. He didn't move, warily observing as though I might pull a knife and jam it through his ribs. Maybe, in his mind, that wasn't a far-fetched possibility—nothing in our contract prevented *me* from hurting *him*.

Shifting onto the bed, I started on his left shoulder. As I searched out the tightest muscles, my mind skittered wildly over this bizarre situation. Massaging a demon was quite possibly even stranger than feeding a demon homemade cookies … especially since his back was all stunningly defined muscle and smooth, unblemished skin. Unease trickled through me and I peeked at his face.

He was no longer watching me. Instead, he gazed vaguely at the wall, eyes half-lidded, jaw relaxed, breathing slow.

Pleasantly surprised, I hid my smile and kept going. My hands were getting tired, but the ache in my fingers was nothing compared to the pain he'd suffered because of me. Resolutely, I massaged his left shoulder then shifted down that side of his torso. When I couldn't find any knots, I lightly traced his muscles, searching for tension.

His shoulders lifted and fell in a deep breath. I glanced up. His eyes were closed. My hands stilled, but he didn't move.

Was he asleep?

An odd flip of pleasure in my middle caught me off guard. He'd fallen asleep while I was touching him. If that wasn't a tiny step toward trust, I didn't know what was.

I settled more comfortably on the bed. His breathing was slow and even, his body limp and free of tension. I slid my hand up his spine to the back of his neck, quiet wonder displacing my discomfort. So close to being human, yet so different.

His skin was cooler than mine, meaning he'd yet to fully recover. Watching his face, I inched my fingers into his damp, messy black hair. My soft sense of amazement deepened.

We were bound together. I had saved his life and he had saved mine. Though it was the magic that forced him to protect me, he had fought and bled to keep me safe. I would never abuse the power I had over him again. He and I were in this together, and demon or not, he deserved as much respect and consideration as I would give anyone else who'd saved my life.

In the dark room, I settled beside him, keeping quiet watch over the sleeping demon.

23

HUNCHED OVER THE MOTEL DESK, I jotted notes on a pad of white stationary. My phone was propped beside me, the MPD app open on the screen. I'd spent the better part of the last two days researching every guild and mythic in the country that specialized in mythic history, knowledge, or magical study, plus everything I could find about Demonica.

The MPD archives weren't my best source of information, but it was all I had to go on. Once Tahēsh was dealt with, I'd visit these guilds and begin building out the puzzle of demonic gateways—or however demons entered and exited our world.

Beside my phone was a thick textbook—*The Complete Compilation of Arcane Cantrips*—pulled from my suitcase. In between research, I'd been reviewing its contents. Cantrips were the weakest form of sorcery but they were all I knew and recent events had convinced me to refresh my memory.

With nothing exciting going on, I'd expected Zylas to drive me insane, but he'd turned out to be an extremely accomplished lounger. During the day, he hid on the motel roof and absorbed as much sun as he could through the persistent cloud cover. In the evenings, he entered a sort of "low-power mode," where he lazed around the room, cat-napping and recuperating strength.

At night, Amalia insisted he return to the infernus. I was glad she'd taken that stance because I hadn't wanted to tell Zylas that neither of us could sleep with his crimson eyes glowing in the corner. He'd be delighted to learn he was extra terrifying in the dark.

He was currently sprawled across my bed on his stomach, face in my pillow. His armor was back on, and he'd repaired the damage to the leather and metal with a series of fine-tuned spells that I was dying to learn more about. Demon magic was unlike anything I'd ever seen. It was as powerful and complex as Arcana spellwork, but as fast as elemental magery.

Adding a final guild name to my list, I sighed at the daunting scope of this task. Cracking the mystery of demonic gateways, which had gone unsolved for centuries or maybe even millennia, should've had me freaking out, but I was as quietly excited as I was intimidated. Uncovering ancient history was one of my favorite things ever, and it was the best sort of excuse to read all kinds of fascinating new books. Yeah, I was that much of a nerd.

But it wouldn't be a quick process, and I hoped Zylas would be patient.

As though my thought had woken him, he rolled over and sat up, his attention turning to the door. A moment later, the handle clacked. Amalia slipped inside, a takeout bag hanging off her arm, and bolted the lock.

"Ugh," she grunted, dropping the bag on the desk beside me. "Would you believe some creeps in a car followed me to the bus stop?"

I opened the takeout bag to find two containers of Chinese food. "What did they do?"

"Nothing … just followed me. The bus came right away, so I didn't have to wait around." Flipping her hair over her shoulder, she lifted out a box and a pair of chopsticks. "I got you sweet and sour chicken."

"Thanks." I cracked the box open and dug into the rice with a fork. "How did it go at the guild?"

"Tae-min is pissed you won't come in." She shrugged. "But what're you gonna do? We can't tell him your demon got his ass kicked."

I regretted informing Amalia how badly Tahēsh had beaten Zylas. It'd only confirmed her suspicion that he was a weak and useless demon.

The demon in question appeared beside me, but he didn't acknowledge her taunt. His attention was fixed on my takeout box.

"Any updates on the demon hunt?" I pulled out a napkin. "I can't believe Tahēsh has evaded capture for three days now."

"They aren't going to *capture* the demon," Amalia corrected with a roll of her eyes. She used her chopsticks to lift a tangle of noodles out of her container. "They're going to kill it. Also, do you *have* to do that?"

I glanced up, then resumed scooping a few bites of saucy rice onto the napkin. I handed the sample to Zylas. He examined the offering, smelled it, then dumped it in his mouth and swallowed. I'd told him several times he'd get more out of food if he chewed it but he wouldn't take my advice.

As soon as he was done, I plucked the napkin from his hand. He had a terrible habit of dropping literally everything on the floor when he was done with it. At least he wasn't burning things like he had in the summoning circle.

As I stuffed the garbage in the bag, Amalia made a disgusted noise. "He doesn't need food. Why are you wasting it on him?"

"Because he likes to try it," I said simply. He wanted to taste anything I ate—except meat. Apparently, meat from this world tasted as bad as my blood and he was going full vegetarian for the duration of his earthly visit. "So? The hunt?"

"Quit indulging him. He's already useless. You don't need to—hey!"

In one swift move, Zylas had plucked her takeout container from her grasp. He dug his hand into it, lifted a glob of noodles, and tipped his head back to drop them in his mouth.

"That's *mine*, you horned freak of—*ahk!*"

Her chair tipped over backward and she slammed into the floor. Zylas unhooked his barbed tail from the leg and swished it innocently as he licked sauce off his fingers.

Amalia clambered off the fallen chair. "You promised not to hurt me if I helped Robin!"

"But are you helping?" he crooned malevolently. "Are you useful? How?"

Her jaw clenched, fear dilating her pupils.

I grabbed her noodle box from Zylas in case he was planning to drop it. When I held it out to Amalia, she stepped back.

"Not after he stuck his hand in it. Yuck."

I offered my sweet and sour chicken instead, and her eyes widened in surprise. She hesitated, then took it. I dug my fork into her noodles. Zylas had touched them, but … whatever.

"Demon hunt?" I prompted yet again.

She picked up a chicken bite with her chopsticks. "The body count is rising. Several combat teams have engaged it, but no one has had much luck."

My stomach twisted with guilt. As I'd feared, Tahēsh had escalated to killing his mythic hunters. I unenthusiastically hefted a forkful of slimy noodles, no longer sure I could stomach any food. "I don't understand what Tahēsh is doing. Why is he *only* roaming around the Eastside? He could go anywhere. He must have a goal or purpose in mind."

I glanced at Zylas, hoping he had a theory, but he was observing Amalia like a kid about to step on an ant hill.

"Does it matter?" she asked with a shrug. "Maybe he can't get away anymore. One team reported that the demon is injured and can't fly well."

"Injured?" Zylas repeated unexpectedly. "What injuries?"

"A broken wing and a damaged hand, according to the report. Its injuries aren't really slowing it down."

Zylas's eyes gleamed. He wandered to the window, his tail snapping back and forth.

"What about Uncle Jack?" I asked. "Any contact from him?"

"No." Frustration tightened her mouth. "I have no idea why. He must've reached a safehouse by now."

I nodded, squashing the question I wanted to ask. Amalia didn't need me to point out the most likely reason behind her father's silence.

"He isn't dead," she stated firmly, guessing the direction of my thoughts. "I snuck into Tae-min's office and used his MPD login to see the investigation on your anonymous text. The only bodies they found in our house were the two guys your demon killed. They don't know who the summoners are or who owns the house. They don't even know there were two demons."

That was good. I needed my uncle alive. Despite everything else, I hadn't forgotten about my mother's grimoire. It was right at the top of my priority list, along with getting Zylas safely back home.

"*Payilas.*" Zylas turned away from the window. "As long as Tahēsh wanders freely, you must stay here and *blend in*, yes?"

"Yes," I agreed warily.

"Then it is time to hunt."

My breath caught. "You mean … you want to go after him?"

"He is injured. I want to see how much."

"But …" I shook my head. "Even injured, he's too strong. He could kill you."

He glided closer, staring down at me. "Small and weak ones like us, *payilas*, we can still kill the strong."

My eyes widened. *Like us.* He was smaller and weaker than most demons, and I was smaller and weaker than most humans.

"I can sense it." His lip pulled up to reveal his sharp canines. "The time of *dh'ērrenith.*"

Assured victory. I swallowed hard. "Are you certain you want to do this? We don't have to."

His smile widened and he leaned down, bringing our faces close. "This time, we will hunt *him*—and this time, he will feel *my* claws."

"NOW WHAT?" I whispered.

Hunkered as low as possible, I peered across the sea of rooftops. We were perched on the roof of a six-story building that could've been an office complex or apartments, but I had no idea because we hadn't entered it. Zylas had climbed the outside of the building, carrying me under one arm.

Crouched beside me, he scanned the downtown view, his eyes glowing in the darkness. As it turned out, he *could* find the other demon if he wanted, though he had to get fairly close before he could detect his adversary's presence. That had taken us three hours, and it was now past nine o'clock.

"He is on that roof." Zylas pointed. Four structures filled the city block between us and the similar-sized building where Tahēsh waited. "He is not moving."

"Is he hurt?" My brow scrunched. "If he was injured, why wouldn't he heal himself?"

"It is the most difficult *vīsh* to master. He did not learn it."

"But you did?"

He cast me his taunting, wolfish grin, then refocused on his prey. I scanned the block, trying to get my bearings. I needed a map.

As I slid my phone out of my jeans pocket, I grimaced. Between rips, stains, and water, I was running critically low on clothing. For our demon hunting excursion, I was wearing a purple zip-up sweater and jeans with a flower embroidered on one hip. On my way out, Amalia had remarked that I looked ready for a hardcore book fair.

I opened the MPD map. Red X's dotted it—the reports of demonic activity—and I squinted as I worked out where we were and where Tahēsh was. Eyes widening, I lifted my stare to the pale building the demon was parked on.

"The Crow and Hammer guild," I whispered in disbelief, "is right across the street from Tahēsh. Why is he waiting beside a guild?"

Zylas shrugged. "Something to hunt?"

I remembered the guild master Darius and his comrades. Did they know the demon was stalking their guild? I hoped they were safe.

"Now what?" I asked again.

Zylas hunkered lower, his tail swishing across the gritty concrete. "Ambush him. I will attack from behind, but I must get close. Any closer than this and he might sense me. If I use *vīsh*, he will know."

I watched him, unnerved by the wicked cunning in his face as he plotted his attack.

"He might not come down, so I must go to him …" His stare turned to me and his eyebrows pinched together.

I leaned away from his intense assessment. "What?"

His mouth twisted. "You cannot do it."

"Do what?"

"Get close enough. If I am inside the infernus, he will not sense me, but you would not get close enough—not while he is up high."

I couldn't scale the exterior of buildings, but that wasn't the only way to reach a rooftop. "I could sneak through the interior."

He considered that, then whipped back to face the distant building. "He is moving!"

A dark silhouette appeared on the rooftop, then broad wings spread. Tahēsh sprang off the building and glided away—in the opposite direction of our hiding spot.

"Where is he going all the sudden?" I demanded.

"If he goes to the ground, it is my chance," Zylas growled, grabbing me around the waist.

He leaped. I choked back a scream as we plunged over the edge. He dropped down the side of the building and grabbed a windowsill. For an instant, my white face reflected in the glass, then Zylas let go. I clapped a hand to my eyes, holding my glasses in place as we plummeted another story. He jumped the rest of the way down, hit the pavement, and launched into a sprint.

Struggling for air, I yelped, "Stop! *Stop!*"

He skidded to a halt and I squirmed out of his arm.

"You're crushing me," I panted, massaging my ribs.

His tail snapped impatiently. "If *you* could go in the infernus, this would be easier."

I decided to ignore that as I stepped behind him, grasped his shoulders, and jumped. He caught my legs and pulled them around his waist—then he was running again. He whipped around the corner and sprinted up the middle of the street. If there'd been cars on the road, he would've matched their speed.

One block flashed by, then a second, then a third. Ahead, the buildings separated to reveal a park, where erratic white light was flickering through the surrounding trees. Zylas dashed toward it. A streetlight glowed across a decorative wooden sign that read, *Oppenheimer Park.*

He sprang over the sidewalk, landed silently on the grass, and ducked into the shadowy trees. Tahēsh's savage laugh floated out of the park, followed by the thud of a heavy body hitting the ground. I peered through the barren branches of a shrub.

Two vehicles were parked on the grass: a black van and an old red sports car, their headlights illuminating the scene. I blinked, then blinked again as though the sight might change if I focused my eyes differently.

The park was full of people and demons—three men in a cluster, one holding a heavy broadsword; two demons battling Tahēsh; and three other guys, one on the ground. The first three men were in mythic combat gear, but the others wore street clothes. They didn't even have coats. Civilians who'd gotten caught in the fight?

Tahēsh had already hammered one demon into the ground and he spun, slamming his tail into the other.

Zylas let out a vicious chuckle. "Tahēsh is slow. I will tear him into pieces."

"You can't use any magic," I warned him. "There are too many people. You have to pretend you're enslaved."

He grunted irritably—annoyed by the reminder and the restriction. Contractors couldn't wield their demon's magic, so even a single demonic rune would betray our secret.

The two non-combat guys had grabbed their friend—who seemed to be unconscious—and were heaving him toward the red car. The driver's door flew open and a redhaired woman leaped out.

"What's the plan?" I whispered.

"Wait," Zylas crooned. "Wait for the right moment."

Tahēsh and the upright demon were locked hand to hand, and the winged beast pushed into the other demon with superior strength.

"Get up!" one of the geared men yelled. "Get up, get up!"

The downed demon twitched pathetically, its tall, lean body gouged with wounds. It was contracted, I realized. Two of those men were contractors and the third was their champion.

The other group had loaded their friend in the car. Were they leaving? Good. The fewer witnesses, the better for—

"Demon magic! Get back!"

At the champion's bellowed warning, the contractor team scrambled backward. Crimson magic spiraled around Tahēsh, a circle of runes spreading across the grass as he summoned a spell—something that would shred his opponent and the surrounding humans, who were far too slow to get clear.

"Zylas!" I gasped.

He shot out of the trees. As Tahēsh's spell blazed, the magic seconds from detonating, Zylas streaked between the two vehicles and charged straight for Tahēsh. Reaching the glowing circle, he sprang, twisted, and landed in a backward skid.

His hand dragged across Tahēsh's spell, red light flaring over his fingers.

With another twist, he leaped away—and Tahēsh's spell exploded. Red power ballooned outward, throwing all the humans off their feet and hurling the contracted demon to the ground.

With a furious bellow, Tahēsh pivoted, searching for his new opponent.

Zylas paused for the briefest instant, his stare meeting Tahēsh's, then he streaked past his adversary. The winged demon whirled to follow, his movements markedly slower than they had been in the demons' last fight.

With a slash of Zylas's claws, blood spurted from the back of Tahēsh's thigh. As Tahēsh roared in pain, Zylas leaped onto his back. The much smaller demon rammed his claws between his enemy's ribs in swift strikes, then sprang away again.

Scarcely breathing, I clutched a tree as Zylas spun around the brutish demon, moving ceaselessly, darting in with tearing claws and jumping clear. Tahēsh turned clumsily, unable to keep up, unable to land a hit.

Dh'ērrenith. Zylas had been right.

Tahēsh's movements grew more frantic. Roaring again, he swung at Zylas—and missed. Zylas ducked in low and tore out the back of Tahēsh's knee, and I knew the fight was over.

It took three more gouging strikes for Tahēsh to realize it too. Screeching like a bobcat, he spread his wings and leaped into the air. Zylas looked up, tracking his enemy's ascent.

No magic, I reminded him with a loud thought.

He coiled his legs, then sprang upward. He slammed into Tahēsh in midair—lithe, agile, deadly. In the darkness, the faintest spark of red magic flickered off Zylas's hands. Then he and Tahēsh plunged back to the ground—and when they hit the grass, Tahēsh's head rolled away from his body.

It was over. That fast, that easy.

I understood now what Zylas had meant when he'd said he never lost; he waited for the odds to shift in his favor. But what had shifted the odds so far? In our last encounter, Tahēsh had seemed invincible, but over the last two days, someone had dealt the demon debilitating wounds. Who had injured him? What mythic could have done what Zylas couldn't?

Silence had fallen over the park. The combat team was staring at Zylas. So was the redheaded woman, who'd fallen to the ground a yard from Tahēsh's body.

Zylas rose out of his crouch and ambled woodenly toward my hiding spot. Right. His contractor needed to make an appearance or those mythics might assume he was an unbound demon too. Which he sort of was … but we didn't want anyone to know that.

Steeling myself, I walked out of the sheltering trees and into the glare of headlights.

Six pairs of eyes turned to me—the three mythics, the two maybe-human men, and the redhaired woman. Zylas walked to me and stopped. With his back to our witnesses, he flashed me a pointy-toothed grin full of victory and bloodlust, then turned to face the park, his expression blank.

Shivering, I turned my attention to the three mythics—a short older man, a super tall middle-aged guy, and an average-built young guy. I waited, but they did nothing but stare at me. Okay then.

I looked at the others. The redheaded woman was still sitting on the ground beside the car, her mouth hanging open. Behind her was another redhead—one of the two guys—and his pal stood beside an overturned motorcycle. Their unconscious friend must be in the car. I hoped he wasn't hurt.

They, like the mythics, didn't move or speak or … anything. Was no one going to react at all?

I glanced at Tahēsh's corpse, summoned another dollop of courage, and pulled out my phone. My audience silently watched as I dialed the MPD's emergency number.

It rang twice, then a cool female voice said, "MPD hotline, what is your emergency?"

"Um, hello," I mumbled. "Yes, um … this is Robin Page from the Grand Grimoire. I'd like to report the unbound demon, please."

"The unbound demon?" the woman repeated, startled. "Do you know its location?"

"Yes …" I tried to gather my thoughts, but the staring was getting under my skin. No wonder Zylas got angry whenever I gawked at him too long. "Um, it's in Oppenheimer Park."

"The demon is in the park?"

"Mm-hmm."

"What's it doing?" she barked urgently. "Are you in danger?"

"Uh, no, the demon is dead."

A long pause. I nudged my glasses up and glanced at Zylas. He stood motionless, looking bored.

"Are you sure the demon is dead?" the operator asked.

"Yes, I'm sure. It's definitely dead."

The clatter of a keyboard sounded through the phone. "Robin, stay right where you are. I'm sending agents to your location immediately. Please wait for them—right where you are."

Did she think I would wander off? "Okay, I'll wait here. How long will MagiPol take to arrive?"

I almost missed her reply as the mythics in the park snapped to attention. The contractors' demons lit with red magic, and as they dissolved back into their pendants, the mythics rushed toward the black van.

"Ten minutes or less," the operator replied. "I'm also alerting all GMs and officers. Some of them may arrive first."

The van's engine rumbled to life, and the wheels spun as the driver gunned it. The vehicle tore away.

"Robin? Are you still there?"

"Yeah," I mumbled, my confusion growing as the two civilian men and the redhaired woman also launched into motion. Two of them jumped into the car, and the dark-haired guy picked up the bike and started it. "I'll wait here."

I ended the call as the red sports car reversed off the grass and onto the road. The motorcycle followed, their engines roared, and a moment later, Zylas and I were alone in the park.

While I pondered the bizarre behavior of the witnesses to Tahēsh's defeat, Zylas relaxed out of his wooden stance—then let out a whoop that made me jump a foot in the air.

"*Vh'renith!*" he shouted, pumping his fist. "I killed the *Dīnen et Lūsh'vēr*! I killed Tahēsh of the First House!"

Eyes glowing and a broad grin stretching his lips, he spun on the spot like he couldn't contain his exuberant energy.

"That was *lalūdris, kirritavh' dahgan rūs hh'istaran*," he spouted, slipping into his native language. "I will be …"

He trailed off, his victorious outburst fading into a scowl, then he groaned and flopped backward, landing on the grass.

"Zylas?" I yelped. "What's wrong?"

Flat on his back, he glared at me. "No one will ever know."

"Huh?"

"I am the first of my House to kill a Lūsh'vēr and no one will ever know!" Heaving a sigh, he sat up and glowered at Tahēsh's body like it was all the winged demon's fault. "No glory for me."

"Glory? For killing another demon king?"

"It is the greatest victory for my kind—to kill a *Dīnen.*"

I crouched beside him. "Doesn't that mean that other demons try to kill you all the time?"

"*Ch.* Of course."

Hesitantly, I patted his shoulder. "Well, *you* know you defeated him, and that's what's important."

He squinted at me like I'd said something utterly moronic, then gazed across the park. "Maybe the other witnessed my triumph."

"The other what?"

"The other demon."

Confusion fizzled through me. "You mean the two contracted ones?"

"No. There was another." His nostrils flared. "I can smell his *vīsh*. Different from Tahēsh."

Vīsh. Magic. Zylas could detect the magic of another demon? But contracted demons couldn't use magic.

"I could smell him on Tahēsh," Zylas added. "This other demon ... he is the one who injured Tahēsh. The one Tahēsh was hunting. He is powerful. Second or Third House."

A chill washed over me. Another powerful demon, one capable of using magic, had injured Tahēsh. Did that mean there had been a *third* unbound demon in the park?

"I did not see him." Zylas pointed to the dark street where the red car had disappeared. "But his scent ... it disappeared with them."

I stared at the empty street. Two dark-haired men, one unconscious. A pair of redheads, one male and one female. They'd looked human to me, but Zylas didn't lie.

Who *were* they?

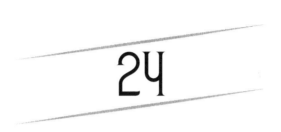

24

I SAT ON THE GRASS, bored and exhausted. More than a dozen MPD agents and high-ranking mythics—GMs and first officers from multiple guilds—swarmed the park.

Over the past couple of hours, I'd been questioned, questioned some more, then questioned again. The demon corpse had been bagged up and a nondescript van was parked beside it, back doors open to receive the body. Someone was pouring liquid from a large jug over the bloody grass, and silver vapor rose from it in unnatural corkscrews.

My phone buzzed in my pocket, but I ignored it. I had a dozen messages from Amalia and Tae-min—the former asking if I'd killed the demon, because rumors were flying, and the latter demanding, with growing urgency, that I return to the guild immediately to see the GM.

I pushed my glasses up my nose, nervousness skittering through my belly. This was way too much attention. Would the MPD investigate my paperwork and realize it was all a forgery? The Grand Grimoire guild master summoning me didn't seem like a good thing either. Hopefully he just wanted to congratulate me on a job well done.

Chewing my lower lip, I watched a tall woman in a crisp business suit bark orders at various agents. From what I'd overheard, she was the captain of this MPD precinct. That made her the biggest boss in the city, and I was extra glad I hadn't had to talk to her. Despite her waves of soft blond hair, she was inexplicably terrifying.

A man broke away from the crowd and strode toward me. I got wearily to my feet, trying to place his thick beard and longish gray hair. He seemed familiar.

"Robin?" He held out his hand. "Girard Canonach, first officer of the Crow and Hammer."

His guild jogged my memory; he was a teammate of Darius, the Crow and Hammer's GM. "We met a couple of days ago, didn't we?"

"Briefly," he confirmed as he shook my hand. "You did an excellent job on the unbound demon. Are you hurt?"

"Not a scratch. My demon did all the work."

"Glad to hear it. The entire city owes you a favor—though I believe the bounty for an unbound demon kill should go a long way toward that IOU."

Right. In return for completing bounty work, the MPD awarded bonuses that increased depending on the difficulty and danger of the job.

"I'm just glad no one else will be hurt," I said quickly.

"As are we all." He studied me, his gaze bleakly assessing, and I got the feeling he was skirting around something. "You're a new member of the Grand Grimoire, correct?"

I nodded. He waited to see if I would offer any more information about my recent guild transfer, but I changed the subject. "Did you ever find out what that sorcerer was doing? The one who attacked me?"

"I was going to mention that. Is there any reason someone might be stalking you?"

"N-no," I replied, startled. "I can't think of anything."

He considered me carefully, then shrugged. "We're still investigating the sorcerer. He wasn't part of a search team … and he wasn't alone."

Gooseflesh prickled my arms.

"Be careful, Robin. The demon is dead, but I'm not sure this is over yet."

I nodded numbly as he returned to the MPD group. No one was looking my way, so I cautiously backed toward the sidewalk. I was supposed to wait for permission to leave, but I'd been sitting around for an hour. If they needed me, they could call my cell.

Turning on my heel, I hurried away from the park. It was after eleven and darkness lay thick and heavy over the abandoned roads. Streetlamps glowed overhead, holding back the shadows. I should've been fearful of walking alone in a poor neighborhood at night, but I wasn't alone—not with the infernus bouncing lightly against my chest.

My thoughts spun, tangling across too many threads and puzzle pieces.

Tahēsh was dead, but the Crow and Hammer's first officer was concerned about something else … something more.

A sorcerer had attacked me in the streets, and he hadn't been alone.

Zylas and I had heard voices in an alley earlier that afternoon. *"Where are they? I lost them."*

A mysterious third demon had attacked and injured Tahēsh.

Tahēsh had been stalking the Crow and Hammer guild.

The seven people who'd been battling Tahēsh in the park had fled the scene once the demon was dead.

The mysterious third demon's scent had vanished with the red sports car.

I rubbed both hands over my face, almost knocking my glasses off. None of this made sense. Where had the third demon come from? Who were those people in the park? Who were the strange men we'd heard in the alley? Who was the sorcerer who'd attacked me?

And how did the Crow and Hammer fit into all this? They kept cropping up. Tahēsh had been watching their guild. Their GM had bumped into me during the search. Their first officer had sought me out a few minutes ago but hadn't said much of anything.

I didn't understand any of it, but at least I was alone with my thoughts instead of—

Heat washed through the infernus, followed by a flare of light. Zylas materialized beside me.

"Were you listening inside my head again?" I demanded accusingly.

"What else is there in the infernus?"

"I told you not to do that! I also told you not to pop out whenever you feel like it." I glanced around, but the street was abandoned. "You're lucky there's no one nearby."

He was unrepentant. "Where are you going?"

"To the Grand Grimoire." I resumed walking. "The guild is a few blocks down this street. I'm supposed to see the GM."

I drew several steps ahead before Zylas caught up and matched my pace. Noticing the undemonlike bounce in his step, I had to suppress a laugh. "Still feeling good about defeating Tahēsh?"

He smirked down at me. "You do not understand. He is First House. I am Twelfth House. The best I have killed before is Fifth House."

"Is that what demons do all day? Plot how to kill each other?"

His nose scrunched in thought. "*Hnn*. Yes, mostly. Males do."

"What do female demons do?"

"They eat and drink and lounge and raise young. And kill males."

I laughed and shook my head, unsure how to react. "The females kill males? Do males kill them too?"

"No." He widened his eyes. "I have never tried to kill a female. I would die."

I blinked. "You would?"

"Females are stronger," he said bluntly. "Their magic is …" He spread his hands wide as though measuring the size of something. "Much greater. We do not fight them. We fight each other."

"Wait. Female demons are stronger than male demons?"

"In *vīsh*. We are bigger, though."

"Even you?"

His upper lip curled in a silent, offended snarl. "Now that Tahēsh is dead, you will find the way I can return home?"

"Yes," I agreed, disappointed by the change in subject. "I'll start first thing tomorrow. I already made a list of sources. But this won't be quick. I can't find answers in a few days."

"If you are searching, I will wait."

I nodded, understanding. As long as I was making progress, he could be patient. "I've been thinking. My mother had a special grimoire about demon summoning—or I think it's about Demonica. She protected it for years, but now Uncle Jack has it. I'm pretty sure he used it to summon you and Tahēsh."

"*Na?*" He walked in silence for a moment. "All *Dīnen* fear being taken by the *hh'ainun*. Any moment they can turn to light and vanish. Some come back after a short time, some after a long time. Many never return. All Houses fear this ... except the First House and the Twelfth House."

My steps slowed. "What do you mean?"

"In some Houses, each *Dīnen* is taken almost as soon as he claims his title. In others, not as fast. In the First House, almost never. In my House, we are never taken. The others hate us because we are safe from *hh'ainun*." He slowed to a stop, his crimson eyes unreadable. "Until me. I was taken, but I do not know why."

"It's not your fault. It's because Uncle Jack got my mother's grimoire. It had your House name in it. Humans can't summon demons from a House without its name."

His brow furrowed. "Why did your mother have my House name?"

"I don't know." My nerves prickled and I hurriedly resumed walking. The Grand Grimoire building was just around the corner.

Why had my mother protected that grimoire? Had she concealed it *because* it had Zylas's House name? Or because it had the name of the First House? Or some other reason?

"Anyway," I muttered, "I think the grimoire has important information about summoning that could help send you home. We need to get it back from my uncle."

He trailed after me. "Is it something you need? Or do you want it because it is yours and not his?"

I inhaled sharply. Zylas was easy to underestimate, but he saw and understood more than I cared to guess—including this.

"I want it because it's mine," I said, staring at the ground. "But it might also help with my research."

He walked beside me, his tail swishing against the sidewalk. "I will help you."

My head snapped up. "You will?"

"If he used this grimoire to take me, I will help you get it back—and you will purge my name from it so my House cannot be taken again."

"Oh." I sighed. "I thought you were offering just to be nice."

"Nice? *Ch.* 'Nice' is for stupid *hh'ainun.*"

Annoyed, I marched toward the corner. "There are benefits to doing nice things for people, you know."

"*Zh'ūltis.*"

"There are! They'll do nice things for you in return, things you might not think to ask for. It builds trust and comradery and—"

"How is that useful?"

As we turned the corner, I glared at him. "You, selfish demon, are completely ignorant about a whole lot of 'stupid human' things."

"If they're *stupid* things," he mocked, "why do I need to know them?"

"I mean you think they're stupid when they're actually—"

He planted his hand on top of my head and pushed downward as though trying to shrink me. "Small and weak *and* stupid, *payilas*."

"Stop calling me stupid!" I whacked his hand. "And let me go!"

"I will if you—" Jolting in surprise, he dragged me to a halt beside him.

Two dozen yards down the sloping sidewalk, a streetlamp dimly lit the Grand Grimoire's green awning, and standing in front of the door was Burly—or rather, Todd, the guild member who'd greeted me and Amalia.

He stared at me and Zylas, his mouth gaping in silent horror.

He'd seen Zylas talking—something a contracted demon couldn't do. He'd seen me trying in vain to push Zylas's hand off my head—further damning evidence that I couldn't control him.

I opened my mouth but my brain had ground to a standstill. This was exactly what we'd needed to prevent. This was the worst-case scenario. My secret was out. The MPD would brand me a rogue and bounty hunters would kill me.

Todd's shock broke before mine. He whipped his infernus out of his jacket and red light blazed over it. His demon appeared in a swirl of crimson, towering seven and a half feet tall.

Zylas leaped forward.

I watched him dash down the slope, silent and lethal. Todd's spiky demon swung its huge fist. Zylas ducked the lethargic blow and sprang past the demon. His fingers were curled, red magic streaking down his hands to form six-inch talons.

He didn't turn on the spiky demon's back. He kept going.

And I realized his intention.

"No!" My shriek echoed through the silent night—but it was too late. A rasping tear. The splatter of liquid hitting the ground. The thud of a falling body.

Todd's demon, frozen in mid-swing, straightened. The blankness in its face melted away, and a mixture of rage and triumph twisted its bestial features. It turned around, the shift of its huge body revealing what lay behind it.

Zylas stood beside Todd, his crimson talons dripping. The man lay prone, blood spreading under him and trickling down the sloping concrete.

"*Gh'athirilnā nul thē,*" the spiky demon rumbled.

Zylas sneered at his kin. "*Ait eshilthē adahk Ivaknen īn idintav et Vh'alyir.*"

Crimson magic bloomed across the spiky demon. Its form dissolved into a cloud of light that shot at Todd. Glowing power hit his body, illuminating it from within like a scarlet light bulb. Then the radiance faded and the demon was gone.

The Banishment Clause, I realized numbly. Todd's death had freed the demon from its contract. It had possessed him, taken his soul, and escaped back to its world.

Todd's death.

Todd was dead.

Zylas had killed him.

I stumbled forward on weak legs. Zylas watched me approach, his eyes wary. Stopping a few feet from the body, I stared at the rivulets of blood running down the slanted sidewalk.

"You killed him."

Zylas silently regarded me.

"You killed him!" The words burst out, edged in hysteria. "He didn't do anything wrong! He was scared and—and he was only—*you killed him!*"

Zylas's tail snapped side to side. "You said no one can know I am not enslaved. I am protecting you."

"No!" I grabbed the sides of my head, holding my skull together against the boiling panic and horror. "No, this is wrong! You killed an innocent man!"

"You said—"

"I didn't say to kill people!" I shrieked. "Get back in the infernus! Right now!"

He snarled at the command, then a crimson glow swept over him. The pendant buzzed against my chest as his essence filled it.

Alone, I hugged myself and stared down at the dead man. An innocent man. He'd seen an out-of-control demon and called his own for protection. He'd been afraid. He'd been defending himself.

He was dead now. Because of me. Because I couldn't control Zylas.

Tears ran down my cheeks. My fault. All my fault. Tahēsh had killed people and I felt horrible guilt over that already, but I'd had no idea Zylas could or would free the other demon. The blame wasn't entirely mine. However, I'd known full well that Zylas was a risk to everyone around me.

I'd known, and I'd ignored the danger. Now an innocent man was dead. Why had he even been here? So late at night? Standing outside?

An electronic trill made me leap backward. The tune blared from Todd's body. His wife, calling to ask when he'd be home? Friends he was supposed to meet, calling to find out why he was late? His champion, who was supposed to protect him while he commanded his demon, concerned about where he'd gone?

My demon had murdered a guild member—on our guild's literal doorstep.

Before I knew what I was doing, I'd turned and bolted. I dashed up the street, cut west, and ran until I couldn't breathe. Then I kept on running, fleeing Todd's death and my own selfish decisions. I ran until my legs threatened to give out, then I walked.

I walked and walked until I found myself at our motel room. With unsteady fingers, I dug out my key card and unlocked the door. Inside, our beds were unmade—we couldn't let housekeeping in because Zylas had destroyed the TV—and our suitcases lay untouched.

Amalia wasn't in the room. I didn't know where she'd gone and I didn't care. I couldn't face her right now.

I stumbled to my bed and stopped. Carefully, as though it were a live bomb, I lifted the infernus off my neck, opened the nightstand's drawer, and set it beside the standard motel Bible. I closed the drawer and toed off my shoes, then collapsed onto the mattress.

Burying my face in the pillow, I cried silently, my voice muted by guilt, horror, and the petrifying dread of what awaited me in the morning.

25

I WOKE AT A QUARTER AFTER SIX, groggy, unrested, and sick with guilt. The room was dark, the sun yet to rise, and I sat up clumsily, my nose stuffed and eyes dry. My glasses lay beside the pillow. I'd slept in my clothes, sprawled on top of the unmade bed.

My gaze darted to the bedside drawer. Zylas was still inside the infernus. Maybe, with the access to my thoughts that our contract had awarded him, he knew I couldn't stand to see him right now.

Maybe he knew I loathed everything about him.

He was a remorseless killer. He didn't care that he'd slaughtered an innocent man. He felt no guilt and would never apologize. But he'd acted to protect me. He'd responded based on his understanding of the situation—based on the information *I* had given him.

Zylas had killed Todd, but the responsibility was mine. All mine.

My phone had fallen off the bed. Retrieving it, I slid on my glasses and pressed the power button to wake the screen. Twenty-six texts, eight missed calls, and three voicemails demanded my attention.

Stomach churning, I flipped open the texts. The first dozen were from Amalia, asking what was going on, but those had stopped at eleven. The rest were from Tae-min and spanned the better part of the night—informing me that I should come in immediately to see the GM. They grew progressively more urgent every time I failed to respond.

His last text told me he was heading home, but the GM was waiting at their headquarters and I should get my butt over there ASAP if I wanted to remain in the guild.

I called my voicemail and listened to the messages—all from Tae-min and saying the same things as his texts. He sounded annoyed and harried, but not panicky, horrified, or furious. That meant he either didn't know about Todd or didn't suspect me.

The last thing I wanted to do was return to the scene of last night's murder, but I couldn't avoid the GM any longer without arousing suspicion. Sighing, I pushed off the mattress and stretched. The sight of Amalia's empty bed triggered a cold prickle in my gut. Where was she? Why hadn't she come back last night?

I reclaimed my phone and called her number. It clicked straight to voicemail.

"Hey, it's Robin," I said. "Where are you? Please call or text me right away so I know you're all right. I'm heading over to the guild, but I'll have my phone."

I ended the call, then sent her a text saying the same thing. Worrying my bottom lip, I used the bathroom, brushed my hair, and mourned my wrinkled outfit. But without a change of clothes, my bookworm look would have to do.

As ready as I would get, I stared at the bedside table. Creeping over as though I might disturb a sleeping beast, I slid the drawer open and peeked inside. The infernus lay where I had left it. If I didn't wear it, could Zylas still hear my thoughts? Was he waiting for me to call him out?

My throat worked, my innards twisting. I slowly closed the drawer again. With a final glance back, I left the motel room.

I couldn't control Zylas. If I brought him with me, he could kill again. For all I knew, I might be heading toward my own arrest—and I would not let him kill the MPD agents who were rightfully protecting people from out-of-control demons and their selfish contractors.

Achingly aware of how alone I was, I walked away from the motel and the infernus.

THE CAB DROPPED ME OFF a block from the guild. I could've walked the entire distance, but that would've meant thirty minutes alone with my thoughts.

As I turned the corner and faced the guild's green awning, I cringed in anxious anticipation—but the street looked exactly as it had three days ago. I cautiously approached the door, unsure what I'd expected. Lines of police tape? A white outline of Todd's body on the sidewalk? The only sign that a man had died here last night was a dark patch on the dirty concrete. Had it rained, or had someone washed the blood away?

My nerves prickled again. I circled the building and used the side entrance as Tae-min had instructed, punching a six-digit code into the panel beside the door. Ascending to the second level, I peeked into the common room. It was empty. Like Tae-min, the guild's exhausted members had gone home to sleep and recuperate after spending three straight days hunting Tahēsh.

I continued to the third floor. Tae-min had said the GM's office was at the end of the hallway. Six doors lined the bland corridor, all closed, but the one directly ahead was open, revealing the corner of a steel desk.

Deep breaths. I tried to remember the advice of my current self-help book, but it felt like months, rather than a week, since I'd last picked it up. I couldn't even think of a famous mythic from history to inspire me, my mind stubbornly blank.

Raising my chin, I strode to the open door and peered inside. A man sat at the desk, his attention on his computer monitor and his back to a large window with a drab view of the street below. He looked like a Viking in a business suit— bulky, blond, thick beard, deep-set eyes, and a hooked nose.

I raised my hand to knock on the open door, but he looked up first. Surprise splashed over his face, then vanished so quickly I wondered if I'd imagined it.

"Robin Page, I assume," he barked in a deep, gravelly voice. "About time. You were supposed to come last night."

"I'm sorry, sir," I muttered, racking my brain in panic. What was his name? Tae-min had mentioned it, but I couldn't remember. Crap crap crap.

"Sit down," he ordered, thrusting his beard toward the plain office chair waiting in front of his desk. As I sank into the seat, he picked up the cellphone beside his elbow, tapped at the screen, then set it down. He returned to squinting at his monitor.

I waited another few seconds, then cleared my throat. "Um, sir?"

"Impressive work last night, Page," he grunted. "The MPD just issued the paperwork for your bonus."

"My bonus?"

"For the demon kill. Two hundred grand, split seventy-thirty between you and the guild." He drummed his fingers on the desktop. "They're generous with bonuses for unbound demons. Want to ensure everyone is as motivated as possible to take it out fast."

"Oh," I said faintly, struggling to appear calm. Any minute now, he would ask about Todd. Someone had found the body and moved it. The GM must know Todd had been murdered. The MPD had to know. The investigation would've begun hours ago. "Is ... is that what you wanted to see me about?"

He glanced at his phone, its screen black. "Your demon is a new House, is that correct?"

"Um ... well, it's rare," I hedged.

"Who's the summoner?"

I kept my expression as neutral as I could. "I'm sorry, but that's confidential."

"What about the unbound demon? What do you know about it?"

Fresh alarm blared through me. "What do you mean?"

His cold eyes fixed on me. "I've done a lot of research into the Houses. The unbound demon matched the descriptions I've found of the First House, but that lineage has been lost since the Athanas summoners disappeared at the turn of the last century."

I froze, unable to breathe.

"They're said to be the only summoner line to have possessed all twelve names. And your demon matches no description I've ever read." He leaned forward. "Didn't your champion mention family secrets?"

My mouth hung open, horror rooting me to the spot. *The Athanas summoners.* I knew that name, but not because I'd ever read about famous Demonica mythics of the past. Athanas was my grandmother's maiden name. My mother once told me how all the women in our family had kept the Athanas name until my great-grandmother, who'd abandoned it before emigrating from Albania. I'd never thought to question my mom about the story.

Suddenly desperate to leave, I stammered, "I got my demon from a summoner. I don't know anything about him or where he learned his demon names."

"Who is he?" the GM asked again, leaning forward. "Tell me now, Page, and I can protect you."

Protect me from *what*? Eyes wide, I shook my head mutely.

"I'm offering to help you, Page."

"I don't—"

An electronic chime sent my hand flying to my hip, but the sound had come from his cell. As he checked the message, I slipped my phone out of my pocket. Amalia hadn't responded to my plea for contact.

"It's a shame you won't be more forthcoming, Page," the GM grunted as he sat back. He tapped his phone on his desk. "You have to understand that building a powerful guild is expensive. When lucrative opportunities present themselves, I can't pass them by. It's simple business."

I stared at him, confused.

"I'm sure you would've made a decent asset to the guild, but I'm afraid you aren't worth that much as a contractor."

My confusion deepened. "I'm sorry, what—"

He waved a hand, but his gesture didn't make sense. I squinted uncertainly.

Behind me, a foot scuffed against the carpet. As I leaped from my chair, a hand seized my shoulder and something cold pressed against the back of my neck.

"*Ori somno sepultus esto.*"

Tingling magic swept over me, followed by suffocating numbness. My limbs collapsed. As I crumpled to the floor, my vision dimmed and my ears filled with buzzing.

A chair dragged across the carpet, then footsteps vibrated closer.

"I didn't expect her to show," the GM rumbled, his voice close yet impossibly distant. "Not after she killed Todd."

"We warned you her demon is lethal. You shouldn't have sent a lone contractor to take her."

I knew that voice. Who … who was it …

"Well, at least I don't have to pay him now," the GM muttered. "I have two missing members to cover up instead of one. I expect a commensurate increase in my compensation."

"It's your fault your man died. We're paying only for her."

A harsh laugh. "I hope you know what you're doing, kid. Once Red Rum pays you, they own you."

The crackling noise overtook my ears. My head spun, awareness fading, then I was gone.

26

"YOU'RE A TRAITOROUS COWARD, you know that?"

My head crackled and buzzed like a mistuned radio. I struggled toward consciousness, drowning in noise.

"I was already aware that you're a putrid vat of slime," the speaker continued, her acid voice echoing strangely, "but I didn't realize you were also a self-important yak with no clue how pathetic you really are."

I knew that angry female voice.

"You're the one with no clue," a man retorted.

I knew him as well. With a horrendous effort, I cracked my eyes open.

My vision blurred in and out, then steadied. I was sitting on a flimsy folding chair in a narrow, rectangular room with metal walls and no windows. I couldn't see a door. The only light came from a battery-powered lantern on the floor beside Amalia, who sat on a chair a few feet away.

When I saw the white zip ties binding her wrists to the chair's sides, I reflexively jerked my arms. Pain cut into my wrists. I was zip-tied to my chair too.

At my spasming movement, Amalia glanced at me. So did the second person: Travis. Stubble coated his jaw and the lantern light cast harsh shadows over his face, darkening the exhausted circles under his eyes. He regarded me for a moment, then turned back to Amalia.

"Look, I'm sorry, okay? I only brought you here so you couldn't tip off Robin that I'd found her. I'll let you go once we're done with—"

"No one is going to let me go, you brainless ballsack!" Amalia snapped. "Red Rum will kill me, kill Robin, and probably kill you too. I can't believe you're this stupid."

"They won't kill anyone. They just want her demon."

I gasped and almost choked. My mouth was duct-taped shut. Terror burned across my nerves but it was so hard to focus. My mind was spinning and the hissing racket in my ears was deafening. I couldn't hear myself think.

Amalia closed her eyes as though praying for patience. "Travis, Red Rum is the biggest, meanest, most murderous rogue guild on the west coast. Criminals like them don't let loose ends like us walk away."

"Dad can handle them. So can I."

"Dad couldn't handle them! He was terrified of them!"

Fighting for every second of clarity, I focused through the unnatural buzzing in my head, struggling to get a better hold on the conversation.

Amalia breathed harshly through her nose. "Untie us and we'll run for it together—before it's too late. I already explained that Robin's demon is—"

"*No*." Hands jammed in his pockets, he paced the length of the room, his footsteps echoing off the metal floor. "Dad won't give me a demon name. He never will. I'm not his real son." Bitterness hoarsened his voice. "This is my only chance."

"You're making the biggest mistake of what will be your very *short* life."

"Red Rum will either give me a name or pay me enough to buy one." He checked his phone. "I'm sorry, Robin. I never meant for you to get hurt or any of this shit. Just give up the demon and you'll be fine."

I widened my eyes in answer, a high-pitched noise screeching from my throat.

"She's laughing at how stupid you are," Amalia interpreted. "A few days ago, they were ready to feed her to that damn demon. They won't let her waltz off into the sunset so she can report them to MagiPol."

I hadn't been laughing—more like squealing in horror—but I liked Amalia's interpretation better.

"Besides," Amalia went on harshly, "demon contracts are for life. You can't just give away your—"

"Actually, you can," Travis interrupted. "MPD has it all hushed up, but Red Rum has a special ritual where the contractor and demon can surrender their existing contract and negotiate a new one."

"That's bullshit and you know it. If it were that easy, contractors would be swapping demons like—"

"Just shut up, Amalia."

He nervously paced a circle around us, then halted when metal clanged loudly. The far wall swung open, letting in a blaze of sunlight, and I realized the room was an empty shipping container.

A cold breeze smelling of sea water wafted inside as a small group entered. Karlson, Uncle Jack's client and the man who'd overseen my near death in the library, stopped to study me. New cronies flanked him, one with a sword sheathed at his hip and the other with an infernus resting on his chest.

"You're here," Travis said nervously. "I have the girl, so—"

Karlson flipped his hand toward Travis in a silencing gesture. "Where's the demon?"

"In the infernus. I put the confusion spell on her, like you said. She can't call the demon."

A spell? That was the reason for the noise in my head? I vaguely recalled reading about thought-inhibiting Arcana at some point, but I couldn't dredge up any details.

"And where is the infernus?" Karlson demanded.

"Uh …" Travis strode over to me and felt around my neck, his fingers cold and rough. "It's … right …"

Realizing my neck was devoid of an infernus chain, he pawed urgently at my chest and stomach, then yanked my shirt up, flashing my mauve bra to the room. When he didn't find the pendant, he grabbed at the front and back pockets of my jeans.

"Where—where—" he panted desperately.

Karlson's expression was colder than a subzero storm. "At no point in the last four hours did you confirm she had her infernus?"

"What contractor would go anywhere without it?" Travis muttered frantically. He grabbed the duct tape and ripped it off my face. "Where's your infernus, Robin?"

I gasped, tears stinging my eyes.

"Where's your infernus?" His shout blared through the metal room.

Cowering back, I stammered confusedly, but I couldn't string together a coherent sentence.

"*Where is it?*"

Karlson folded his arms. "You put a confusion spell on her. She can't answer."

Travis stumblingly faced his employer. "If she didn't bring it to the guild, then she left it at the motel. I know where their room is. I can—"

"You have proven yourself exceptionally incompetent," Karlson cut in. "I lent you two good men to capture her and her demon off the streets, and you couldn't even manage that."

My head buzzed. Capture us off the streets. The voices Zylas and I had heard. The sorcerer who'd shot a spell at me.

"Send Bartoli to her motel room to get the infernus," Karlson told the man with the sword. "We're heading back. The girls come with us."

The swordsman nodded, and the room brightened as he opened the door. My head spun and crackled, and the next thing I knew, a stranger was cutting the zip ties on my wrists. He seized the back of my sweater and hauled me out of the shipping container.

I squinted painfully. Heavy clouds shrouded the sun and I couldn't guess the time—anywhere from mid-morning to mid-afternoon.

The man holding my sweater shoved me forward. Behind us, Amalia swore at someone. Nearly a dozen men were waiting—Karlson, plus an assortment of contractors and champions. So many. Hopelessness dragged at my distorted thoughts but Travis's confusion spell drowned out my fear.

"We're not fighting this demon after all?" a contractor grumbled. "Damn, I was looking forward to it."

"Young Travis failed to ensure the girl had the infernus with her." Karlson checked his phone, then slipped it into the pocket of his suit jacket. "It isn't a complete loss, however."

My captor steered me across the uneven pavement of a wide lot that bordered the ocean. A concrete pier stuck into the dark gray waves, and across the harbor, gargantuan cargo ships were docked along the coast. Abandoned shipping containers, truck beds, and old tractor-trailers edged the lot, and to our left rose a huge gray building—a factory or manufacturing plant.

Moored at the short pier was a shiny white boat large enough to transport fifteen people. Panic cut through the noise in my head, and I could see my fate clearly: kidnapped by the worst and most powerful criminal guild on the west coast, put on a boat, carried into international waters ... and never seen again.

If I'd kept the infernus, would this have happened? Would Zylas have saved me back at the Grand Grimoire? Would he have rescued me while Travis held me and Amalia captive in the shipping container? But I'd left him behind, afraid to take responsibility for the creature I had unleashed.

"Hurry up and get them on the boat," Karlson barked. "I want to—"

A flicker of red—and the boat exploded.

The boom hit my eardrums like stabbing knives. A crimson-laced fireball roared upward, belching black smoke. The men staggered in shock, then one yelled in terrified agony. As the rogues whirled toward the sound, another man screamed. Blood misted the air and a mythic collapsed.

A dark blur shot away from him, red magic streaking from phantom claws.

"Demon!" someone roared.

Chaos erupted—contractors grabbing their pendants, champions drawing weapons. Zylas skidded on the concrete, tail snapping out, and he leaped onto the back of a contractor, snapped his neck, and sprang off the falling man. He landed on the next mythic's shoulders, his six-inch crimson talons disappearing into the man's throat.

Red magic blazed as demons materialized around us.

Zylas jumped off the collapsing man, slid aside from a swinging sword—which hit another demon instead—and launched straight at me.

He hit me and my captor. We went down in a tangle of limbs, then I was whirling through the air, a band of steel across my chest. The world came to a dizzying halt. Zylas held me against his torso as he angled toward the street.

"*Ori impello potissime!*" a sorcerer shouted.

An invisible force hit us like a battering ram. Everything spun wildly again, and I slammed into the concrete, the impact jarring through my back. I jolted up as two demons charged Zylas, who'd landed nearby.

He dove, skidding under a demon's long legs, and reappeared behind it. Another swift leap—and a man died beneath his talons. The contractor's demon dissolved into crimson light.

I shoved myself to my feet, trembling and weak but with my head miraculously clear. Getting hit by more Arcana had broken Travis's confusion spell. Or something. I whirled, searching for Amalia—

Charging in out of nowhere, Travis grabbed my hair and yanked my head back. A cold, sharp edge pressed against my throat.

"Stop or I'll kill her!" he yelled.

Zylas sprang off the shoulders of a heavyset man with an infernus on his chest, landed on the pavement in a crouch, and turned glowing crimson eyes on Travis. His final victim crumpled in a heap, head lolling on his broken neck. Another demon melted into a red haze, swept into the corpse, and faded.

Everything was suddenly still, the silence broken only by the choking gurgles of a man bleeding out a few yards away. Half the Red Rum mythics were dead. That fast, Zylas had killed half of them.

Travis held the knife to my throat, the edge slicing the first layers of my skin. A wet tickle ran down my neck. My pulse hammered desperately as I stared at Zylas, elated that he'd come, terrified that he was far too late.

His face, normally so humanlike, was hard and cold, his canines flashing, his hunger for violence rolling off him in waves.

"Why did the demon stop?" Karlson asked, his tone low and cautious.

"Her contract," Travis replied, breathing hard, "requires that the demon protect her. If it moves, I'll kill her, so it can't do anything."

Panic churned in my head. How did he know that? The only people who knew the details of our contract were me, Zylas, and—

My gaze darted to Amalia, several long steps away. A tall, lanky man had his arm locked around her throat. At Travis's declaration, horror widened her eyes and she shot me a guilt-stricken look. How much had she told him? Did he know Zylas and I had no Banishment Clause?

Pacing to my side, Karlson took in Zylas like an artist studying his latest painting—critical, assessing, appreciative.

And beneath that, lusty greed burned in the man's narrow face and dark eyes.

"Well," the man murmured, "this makes things easier. We can proceed immediately with the contract substitution."

Zylas didn't react, still crouched and motionless. He wouldn't move—the contract's magic didn't allow him to put my life in danger. As long as I was helpless, he was helpless too.

Karlson glanced across his remaining men, blind to the bodies. "Leonard, are you ready to take on this demon?"

Another mythic stepped forward—thickly muscled, a beard bristling over his jaw as he grinned. "I'm more than ready. This fiend may be small, but with speed like that, the possibilities are endless."

"A perfect assassin," Karlson agreed. "Demon, you will submit to a new contract with Leonard, and whatever terms we stipulate, or the girl will die."

Zylas's eyes flared with power, twin spots of churning lava. Rage deeper and more coldly vicious than anything I'd seen before twisted his face, and the breeze chilled. The temperature dropped below freezing, ice frosting the pavement around his feet.

I shuddered in horrified denial. Zylas had sworn to never submit to humans. He'd prefer to die than be enslaved, and he'd only agreed to a contract with me because he could retain his autonomy. But now he would lose it. Because of me, because he was bound to protect me, he would surrender his mind and body to Red Rum. The magic of the contract would force him to submit.

Karlson's murky stare found mine. "Robin Page, you will give up your contract with this demon."

I stared hard at Zylas, thinking loud and clear in my thoughts. *They won't kill me. They want you and they think I promised you my soul.*

His crimson eyes narrowed but he didn't move. My assurance must not be enough. As long as the knife was at my throat, our fates were solely in my hands. Terror flooded me, weakening my legs, but I forced a single whispered word past my numb lips.

"No."

Karlson rocked back on his heels. "What did you say?"

I swallowed painfully. "No. I won't give you my contract."

"You don't have a choice."

But I did. I couldn't surrender him to these men. I couldn't throw him into his worst nightmare, the fate he most feared.

"Robin," Travis whispered, moving the knife off my neck but keeping the blade close, "give up the demon. You didn't even want this contract. You can go back to your normal life."

I clenched my jaw and held my silence.

Karlson released a harsh, angry breath. "It won't take much to break her. Leonard?"

"Yeah, boss?"

"Start slow. Keep the blood to a minimum."

The man strolled over to me, and my heart sped up with each step he took. He grabbed my right hand. I flinched and Travis's fist tightened in my hair. Leonard stroked my fingers as though reassuring me, then took my pinky finger and started bending it backward. Pain tore through it. My breath whistled through my gritted teeth.

He bent it further. Then further still. My arm spasmed, trying to tear my hand free. He bent it past a right angle and the joint gave way with a pop.

I screamed.

Zylas bared his teeth and his tail lashed once, the motion swiftly stifled.

"Give up the demon," Karlson ordered.

"No," I panted.

"This is just a warmup, girl," Leonard warned. "It'll only get worse."

I knew that, but it changed nothing.

He grasped my ring finger. Bent it back. I was already screaming when it dislocated.

"Give up the demon," Karlson commanded again, "and we'll let you go."

"No."

When Leonard popped my middle finger out of joint, I couldn't hold back my shaking sobs. Travis shifted the knife further from my throat before I gouged myself.

"Give up the demon."

"*No!*" I shrieked, my breath catching on an agonized sob. I wouldn't. Zylas had been willing to die to escape enslavement. How could I give away his autonomy? I didn't know what would happen, what they would do to me, but I couldn't betray him.

Through tear-blurred vision, I found his glowing eyes and anchored myself as the torturer grasped my index finger.

Kill them all, I thought as clearly as I could. *The first chance you get.*

His tail twitched, his stare boring into mine. The connection between us burned hot, an invisible thread that bound our fates together. Crimson light glowed across his fingers and the semi-transparent talons that tipped them. His tail slid slowly across the pavement. The twenty yards between us yawned even wider.

My torturer wrenched my finger back and another scream tore from my throat.

Zylas launched off the concrete, a dark blur.

"Stop!" Travis bellowed. "Stop or—"

Karlson grabbed Travis's hand and shoved his knife toward me. Zylas flashed across the final yards, magic blazing up his arms.

He slammed into me and power ruptured the world around us.

As his spell hurled the mythics backward, his hands closed around me. He leaped clear of the humans, landed lightly, and sprinted away, the wind tearing at us. Shouts, outcries. Flashing magic. Racing steps, dizzying momentum, then the light dimmed. A metal door slammed and red power flared.

My back hit a hard floor. Zylas knelt over me, his face filling my vision. His hands were on my throat, squeezing.

"Hold on, *payilas*," he whispered.

I couldn't move. My limbs had gone weak, my head was spinning, and my heart thundered louder than I'd ever heard it.

Scarlet magic reflected off the metal walls. Hot power suffused my skin beneath his hands. It veined his arms in shifting lines, and concentration tightened his jaw. His gaze darted across my throat and his lips moved with words I couldn't hear.

All I could hear was my racing, booming heart. My stuttering, faltering pulse.

Red light flared. Agony lanced my throat, the torment building into an inferno. I convulsed, limbs flailing violently, and Zylas dropped down, pinning my body to the floor with his, still crushing my throat in his powerful hands. The excruciating burn rushed down my neck and into my chest where it lit a new fire. I screamed as my bones turned to magma inside me, scorching my innards.

Then it was over. I lay panting, hurting everywhere as my nerves gradually reset. The only agony that persisted was my throbbing right hand. I swallowed, my throat flexing against his fingers.

Lying on top of me, his weight heavy and warm, he cautiously released my neck. Blood coated his fingers and drenched his palms, drips plopping steadily onto the metal floor. My hand crept up. Fingertips sliding across slick blood, I found the thin ridge, two inches long, where the knife had sliced my throat. Where Karlson had shoved the blade when Travis had failed to do it.

He'd thought killing me would stop Zylas. That my death, and the Banishment Clause, would save them from Zylas's wrath.

"They will not survive my wrath," Zylas growled quietly.

"I told you to stay out of my head."

A metallic boom reverberated through the dark space and I looked past him. We were back in the shipping container, the doors closed and glowing with a demonic rune-filled circle. Another powerful blow hit the steel.

"Why did you leave me, *payilas*?"

My attention snapped back to him, his face hovering above mine. He was braced on his elbows, his weight pressing me down, our noses inches apart. With those crimson eyes locked on mine, I couldn't hide the truth—not from him or myself.

I didn't know what to say, how to explain myself. Then again, there was only one explanation.

"Because I'm *zh'ūltis*," I muttered resignedly.

A corner of his mouth pulled up. "I have been telling you that."

"Yes."

"You keep disagreeing."

"I did, but you were right all along."

His gaze slid across my features as though reassessing them, then he pushed himself up, straddling my hips. He found my right wrist and lifted it. My gut clenched at the sight of my fingers. Bent backward. Contorted. Unmoving.

Tightening his grip on my hand, he took hold of my index finger. "Close your teeth, *payilas*, so you do not bite your tongue."

I snapped my jaw shut a second before he pulled my finger straight. I screeched through my gritted teeth. Another boom struck the container, shaking the floor, but Zylas ignored it as he straightened my fingers one by one.

Breathing fast, I waited for the pain to subside. He cradled my hand, lightly pressing on the joints to ensure my bones were properly aligned. I peeked at him, my vision blurred with fresh tears. The loudest bang yet shook the entire container. The spell Zylas had cast on the doors shuddered under the impact, and I clamped down on a new surge of fear.

"Now what?" I whispered.

"*Hnn.* I think you said … kill them all." He flashed his canines, savage voracity lining his face. "I will do that."

"But how? There are still so many of them." Two champions, four contractors, four demons, Karlson, and Travis. Twelve opponents, plus Amalia was in danger and needed help too.

Zylas eyed me sideways, then reached for his hip. With a twist, he freed the infernus's chain from his belt and dangled the pendant above my face.

"*Payilas*, can you make the spell of bright light again?"

"I need something to draw with. Something like—" I watched a drop of blood run down the side of his hand. I was lying in a pool of it. "Yes, but if you tell me what you have in mind, I might be able to do better than a light cantrip."

As he grinned, vicious and eager to deal death, I grasped the hanging infernus. This time, I wouldn't try to stop him. This time, I would help him protect us both.

27

BOOM. The shipping container jolted violently as the hammering continued. The doors, held together by Zylas's glowing spell, caved inward.

In front of the shaking doors, I'd drawn a three-foot-wide rune in my own blood. Yuck. Even knowing Zylas's super-speed healing magic had repaired my neck and replenished my blood, I was still freaked out that so much of what was supposed to be inside my body was all over the floor. Painful thirst constricted my throat.

I tightened my hands on his shoulders. He was crouched just behind the rune, and I clung to his back with my legs clamped around his waist. Crimson talons extended from his fingers, and he raised one hand toward the door as another powerful blow shook it.

"Are you ready, *payilas*?" he asked.

"Yes," I replied tersely. My pulse was racing, my throat was dry, and my limbs shivered with adrenaline. But Zylas knew what he was doing. He didn't start fights he couldn't win.

Power lit across his palm and crawled up his arm in twisting veins that glowed through his sleeve and armguard. A circle formed around his fingertips, runes flashing through its center.

"Now," he said, and a streak of red power leaped from his hand and hit the doors, blasting them open.

"*Luce!*" I cried, squeezing my eyes shut.

My rune blazed into an incandescent brilliance that shone through my eyelids. As the men outside, blinded by the spell, shouted in pain and alarm, Zylas leaped forward. He could still see; with his infrared vision, he was hindered by neither a lack of light nor an overabundance of it.

We flew out into the cold sea breeze, my arms wrapped desperately around his shoulders. He landed with a crunch on the concrete. I cracked my eyes open as he sprang between two demons, unmoving while their contractors were disoriented. Aiming at his first target, Zylas slashed his talons across the man holding Amalia.

As the rogue fell, I dropped off Zylas's back. Grabbing Amalia's arm, I hauled her away from the Red Rum mythics and their demons. They had recovered from the light spell and were turning on Zylas—four demons controlled by four contractors, and two armed champions protecting them.

The wall of lumbering muscles, horns, and spikes closed in on Zylas, the demons spreading out to encircle him.

I raised my arm. My sleeve was pushed up to my elbow, and I'd drawn three bloody cantrips on my skin. The most basic Arcana—draw the rune, speak the single-word incantation, and unleash a simple spell.

"*Surrige*," I declared.

An invisible force caught the nearest contractor and lifted him off his feet. As he flailed in confusion, his demon halted all movement.

Zylas dove under the immobile demon. Lunging for their adversary, the other three bowled over their ally, and Zylas wheeled toward the four contractors, his tail snapping out for balance. The two champions rushed forward to intercept him, one with a shining broadsword and the other with a pair of small but terrifying battle axes.

The swordsman slapped a hand to his blade and the earth trembled with his magic. The other pointed an axe and shouted an incantation.

I thrust my arm out. "*Ventos!*"

My second rune flashed and wind erupted, buffeting the champions and whipping grit in their faces. The gust scarcely made them stumble, but it created the distraction Zylas needed.

The sorcerer's spell missed him by inches. The spiral of burgundy power hit the pavement and exploded in a wave that covered everything nearby in a glistening layer of... something. Shouting furiously, the terramage whipped his sword out, and the earth split open in front of him—but Zylas had already leaped. He slammed into the mage, plowing him into the ground as his claws flashed.

The demons were moving again, all four barreling toward Zylas and the two—now one—champions.

I swung my hand toward them. "*Nebu—*"

Amalia grabbed my shirt and yanked me backward. A dart of searing hot magic grazed my shoulder as a spell whipped past me—launched by the axe-wielding champion.

"*Nebulam!*" I yelled as fast as I could get the word out.

ANNETTE MARIE

The largest cantrip on my arm flickered and a hazy mist rose off the ground, billowing around us. The last thing I saw was Zylas turning on the remaining champion as four demons charged him. Mythic and demon forms blurred in the fog.

A scream rang out. Metal clanged. Another cry of agony.

The fog cantrip was already fading, too small and weak to last against the sea breeze. Shadowy shapes reappeared—a pair of unmoving demon statues, and the two demons still in battle, controlled by the last survivors. Zylas was a lethal blur darting among them, glowing magic dancing over his hands.

Dh'ērrenith, he would've called this moment. Assured victory.

"Watch out!" Amalia yelled.

I whirled around. Karlson, the short Red Rum leader, came at me with a silver knife in his fist. I lurched backward, my hand flashing up, a bloody rune drawn on my palm.

"*Impello!*" I cried.

The invisible push spell hit him and he staggered, the blade knocked from his grasp. He paused, his eyes burning with fury, then extended his empty palm, concentration hardening his jaw.

A steel battle axe appeared in his hand.

He stepped forward, the blade gleaming. It was the champion's axe. Somehow, the fallen champion's weapon was now in Karlson's hands—and he was almost on top of me, the deadly edge angled toward my body.

"Stop your demon," he spat. "*Now!*"

Another scream split the air—the last contractor dying. Karlson's gaze darted to the bloody battlefield, and I saw the decision in his eyes. No demon was worth his life. He was going to kill me to stop Zylas.

His other hand opened and a second battle axe appeared in his grip. He swung the weapons up and I stumbled back, too close, too clumsy—

He jerked convulsively. His face went slack, then he pitched forward. His weapons hit the ground with clangs that echoed in the sudden quiet. Travis stood behind the collapsed man, holding a blood-splattered rock. He stared at Karlson, his face white.

Ten yards away, Zylas stood alone, surrounded by his fallen enemies. All the demons had disappeared, their contractors dead, and blood had turned the musty concrete into a macabre painting. Zylas was splattered all over.

My stomach squirmed and I looked away. So much death. So many lives ended. Numbness spread through me, and I didn't know what to feel. Should I have felt anything else besides the relief coursing through me?

Tail swishing, Zylas hopped across the battlefield. When he'd cleared the bodies, his gait shifted to a dangerous prowl, gaze fixed on Travis.

"Well, *payilas*?" he crooned as Travis's expression slackened with terror. "Should I kill this one too?"

I studied Travis, who clutched his rock like it might save him. Amalia gave me a pleading, desperate look.

Briefly closing my eyes, I took a deep breath. "Zylas, I think enough people have died already."

"Mercy is for the weak, *payilas*."

"The weak can't afford mercy." I met his eyes. "I think we can."

He stared at me, then grimaced—his favorite "you're so dumb you don't even make sense" grimace. I rolled my eyes. Looking like he could hardly believe his luck, Travis cleared his throat to speak, then changed his mind. We stood mutely, silenced by the trauma and violence we'd survived.

"We should leave," Amalia suggested.

Travis nodded eagerly. "I have a car parked on the street. This way."

Together, the three of us started across the lot, leaving the massacre and Red Rum's burning boat behind. Zylas trailed after us, rubbing at the blood on his hands with his nose wrinkled in disgust. As we passed the bumper of an abandoned tractor-trailer, the three of us stopped abruptly. A road ran alongside the concrete lot, and directly ahead, a black car with tinted windows idled at the curb.

The driver's door opened. A man stepped out, large sunglasses obscuring his face, but a distinct scar ran up his chin and distorted his lower lip.

"Claude?" Amalia and Travis exclaimed.

Uncle Jack's partner and fellow summoner smiled with warm relief. "Amalia, Travis—and Robin—I'm so glad you're safe."

"How did you find us?" Amalia demanded.

"I have many contacts in various circles." He lifted his sunglasses to peer at Zylas in appreciation, strangely unalarmed. "So that's the demon from the library, is it?"

"What are you doing here?" Travis asked sharply.

I wasn't the only one wondering what was really going on.

"I came to fetch you—to get you all away from Red Rum." Claude waved at his car. "Come along, kids."

Part of me, the part that was exhausted and terrified and heartsick, wanted nothing more than to climb into that car and let a smart, experienced adult take over. But I wasn't desperate enough to ignore the warning in my gut, and judging by the tense look Amalia and Travis shared, they felt it too.

Claude's faint smile didn't falter, but his eyes cooled. A slight shift in his expression, as though his attention had turned elsewhere. Turned *inward*—

Zylas sprang.

He crashed into me and I hurtled backward. I hit the ground as a reddish shadow plummeted out of the sky. It slammed down on the spot where I'd been standing—where Zylas was now crouched, having thrown me clear.

Monstrous wings flared as the demon smashed Zylas into the concrete. Crimson power burst off Zylas and he twisted free, whirling away in a blur—and the other demon followed, almost as fast, its long arms reaching. The demon and Zylas tangled, claws flashing, then Zylas broke away with an unsteady stagger.

I scrambled onto my feet as Zylas backed toward me. He turned, forgetting his adversary entirely. His eyes were dark, unfocused, blankly staring.

He dropped, his metal greaves clanging against the pavement. I leaped and caught him as he pitched forward. On his knees, he sagged against me, face against my stomach, his weight pushing me backward.

"Zylas?" I gasped, gripping his shoulders.

The attacking demon watched us, its eyes burning like magma. I'd almost thought it was Tahēsh, somehow returned to life, but at six and a half feet tall, this demon wasn't as large. Its wings were more delicate, its tail ending in barbs similar to Zylas's. Long black hair was pulled away from its sharp features and tied in place with a strip of leather.

The unfamiliar demon tossed a small object to Claude. The summoner caught it—a steel syringe with a thick, sturdy needle. Dark blood coated the sharp point.

"A good summoner," Claude commented as he slipped the syringe into his pocket, "knows how to neutralize a demon safely. Neutralizing humans is far simpler, though."

The demon turned and grabbed Amalia and Travis by their necks. It lifted them off the ground. They writhed, grabbing at the demon's wrists, mouths gaping silently.

"No!" I cried, clinging to Zylas's head and shoulders. He weakly grasped my legs and I lost my balance. I fell, landing on my butt, and he sprawled across my lap, twitching feebly as though struggling to move.

The demon continued to strangle the step-siblings, Travis hanging limply and Amalia's legs spasming.

"Don't kill them! Please don't!" I begged, tears spilling down my cheeks.

Claude considered my plea, then nodded at the demon. It opened its huge hands. Amalia and Travis hit the ground and crumpled, unconscious. Were they breathing? Did they need CPR?

"Why are you doing this?" My fingers twisted in Zylas's hair as I mentally implored him to get up. I needed help. I couldn't do this alone.

"Why?" Claude repeated. "It's quite simple, Robin. I've invested years into acquiring the demon you stole from under my nose."

"What ..."

He crouched so we were at eye level. His demon towered beside him, wings folded and tail lashing idly.

"With the acquisition of the First and Twelfth Houses, I'm the first to possess all twelve names since the Athanas summoners. The First House is the most powerful, but the Twelfth House …" His gaze swept over Zylas, collapsed across my lap. "The Twelfth House is truly special."

"Special how?" I whispered.

"I'm not entirely sure. The answers lie in your mother's invaluable grimoire."

My hands tightened on Zylas. "The grimoire belongs to me."

"Indeed it does, which is why I have a proposal for you, Miss Page." He smiled invitingly. "Come with me. I'll teach you how to survive, how to build a relationship of true power with your demon, and together, we can translate your family's grimoire and discover all the secrets your mother kept from you."

28

CLAUDE'S OFFER echoed in my head.

A relationship of true power ... The summoner's demon stood patiently beside him. Watching. Listening. Its tail twitched just like Zylas's—an idle movement no legally contracted demon could make.

"You'll be safe with me, Robin," Claude added gently.

My throat had gone dry, my pulse hammering. Everything I wanted: safety, my mother's grimoire, and someone else in charge. All I had to do was trust a man who'd just sicced his demon on his former partner's family.

I swallowed. If I refused his offer, he might kill us. I would agree for now, and find a way out later, when Zylas had recovered—assuming he recovered before we were in too deep. Assuming he recovered at all.

"You have to leave Amalia and Travis alive. Don't hurt them anymore."

"If you prefer." He held out his hand. "So you're with me, then?"

"Yes," I lied, cautiously reaching for his hand.

He closed cool fingers over mine. "Hmm. I'm disappointed, Robin. Haven't you realized yet that demons can detect lies?"

My eyes, widening with horror, shot to his demon, and I tried to yank my hand away. A silver ring on his index finger bit into my skin.

"*Ori profundior decidas.*"

Hot magic rushed into my hand and swept down my arm. Every muscle in my body clenched, then went limp. I collapsed sideways, unable to move, Zylas's dead weight pinning my numb legs.

Claude rose to his full height. "Kill the Harper brats, then bring those two. The extract will wear off soon, so I need to dose the demon again."

His demon chuckled nastily. I couldn't move, my head canted at an awkward angle, jaw slack, glasses askew. The demon's blurred shape loomed over the unconscious siblings as it reached down.

Reddish light erupted—but not demon magic.

A burning orb struck the demon between its wings. The fire burst like a water balloon, liquid flames splattering the demon's skin. As it reared back with an agonized bellow, the ground trembled. The concrete between the demon's feet split and the beast staggered sideways.

Three men appeared—literally out of thin air. A trio of mythics in black combat gear, weapons in their hands, formed a triangle around the demon. The nearest—salt-and-pepper hair, close-cropped beard. Recognition punched me in the gut.

Darius King, the guild master of the Crow and Hammer.

A pair of silver daggers in his hands, he pointed a blade at Claude from a dozen paces away. The summoner stumbled backward, grabbing at his face.

"What's happening?" he yelped. "I can't see!"

His demon snapped its wings, flinging the liquid flames off its back, and lunged for Darius. The mythic vanished, but the demon whirled as though tracking an invisible target.

Darius's teammate leaped in behind the demon, a heavy staff spinning in his hands. He slammed the end into the concrete. A fissure opened under the demon, spewing a geyser of lava over its legs. Snarling, the demon leaped away from the bubbling lava.

Darius reappeared, arm cocked back, and he hurled a small object at the demon. It exploded, throwing the beast forward.

The third teammate pulled a pistol from the holster on his belt. His lips moved in an incantation, then he fired. Each bullet hit the demon with a burst of displaced air, the force hammering it backward. It crashed down.

But a demon wasn't so easily defeated.

It lunged up, slowed by neither pain nor injuries. Red magic swirled along its arms. The air turned arctic and frost swept over the lava, hardening it into black lumps. A six-foot-wide rune circle appeared beneath its feet.

Zylas pushed up on shaking arms and dragged himself on top of me.

The demon's spell exploded and the impact hit us like a speeding car. Zylas shielded me with his body, his arms wrapped around my head. The ground shook and crimson light flared wildly.

The fierce glow faded and quiet settled over the concrete lot. Zylas laboriously lifted his head. I still couldn't move but I could see the winged demon. It carried Claude under one arm, its wings beating hard as it flew out of range.

"Damn," a voice muttered.

Footsteps crunched, coming nearer. Scooping my limp body against him, Zylas lurched onto unsteady feet. He got a few steps before dropping to one knee, unable to stand.

Darius and his two teammates—Girard, the guild officer I'd spoken to last night, and a volcanomage—formed a half-circle around us. Girard was unscathed, but the other two were banged up, their clothes singed and scuffed with dirt; they hadn't escaped that magical explosion.

Zylas snarled, his arm tightening around my chest. All I could do was hang there, limp as a doll under Claude's spell.

"Is it just me," the volcanomage began in a deep voice, "or is that demon acting independently?"

"She could be controlling it even if she can't move," Girard suggested.

Darius stroked his beard. "Robin? If your demon stands down, we can remove that spell."

Zylas, I thought at him, *I think they'll help us.*

He bared his teeth. "One of you may approach."

Identical expressions of disbelief washed over their faces. Why was he talking to them? He'd just blown our secret!

"Well, I'll be damned," Girard muttered. "I've never heard a demon talk before."

Zylas snapped his tail against the concrete. "Stupid as every *hh'ainun*. Why would I not talk?"

Because you're supposed to be contracted, I silently yelled.

"I bet you've never been insulted by a demon, either," the volcanomage remarked dryly. "This is clearly an illegal contract, Darius."

The GM studied Zylas, his gaze lingering on the demon's arm around my chest. He sheathed his daggers. "Girard, a dispelling artifact, please."

"You can't approach it. That demon is out of control."

He extended his palm expectantly.

Frowning in disapproval, Girard withdrew a silver marble from a pouch on his belt and dropped it in Darius's hand. Holding the artifact, the guild master walked slowly toward us. Zylas's fingers twisted in my sweater as the mythic knelt. With a lethal demon breathing down his neck, Darius touched the marble to my forehead and murmured an incantation too quiet for me to hear.

Cool magic swept over me and the numbness in my limbs faded. I gasped in my first deep breath since the spell had hit me.

Zylas shoved Darius's arm away from me. "Get back."

Instead, Darius sat on his heels. "You're very protective of your contractor."

Zylas's lips peeled back. Because I knew him pretty well now, I was already lunging up. Before his slashing claws could find Darius's flesh, I yanked Zylas's face into my chest and clamped my arms around his head as tightly as I could.

He grabbed my shoulders to shove me off, but he was still weak from Claude's mysterious injection—and I was holding on like my life depended on it. To make me let go, he'd have to hurt me.

He yanked furiously at my sleeves. "*Payilas!*"

"You can't kill people whenever you want," I told him breathlessly, bracing my knees against the concrete so he didn't tip me over. "And you're not killing someone who just saved us."

Unable to free his head, he snarled into my shirt like a rabid wolf.

Tightening my hold, I peeked at Darius through my crooked glasses. "Um, so … I can explain."

"Can you?" Darius muttered, crouched two feet away and staring at the demon whose face I was mashing into my boobs. Okay, it was a weird situation, but I didn't have any better ideas on keeping Zylas under control for a few minutes.

He sank his claws into my sleeves and shredded the fabric to ribbons. Or … not so under control.

Darius rose to his feet and backed up until he'd rejoined his two teammates—who couldn't decide what expression to wear and looked a bit dumbfounded as they gawked at me.

"Maybe you should let him go," the GM suggested.

I relaxed my arms and Zylas jerked away from me, his eyes blazing with fury and returning power. "*Kanish zh'ūltis! Eshathē dilēran!*"

"Don't call me stupid," I growled back at him as I straightened my glasses. "You're the stupid one! All you had to do was keep your big mouth shut so they wouldn't know you aren't properly contracted."

"He already knew because he used his blindness *vīsh* on me!"

I faltered. "That wouldn't work on a de—oh."

He glowered at me. I grimaced.

"Ah," Darius interrupted delicately. "I was wondering about that—why blindness doesn't affect demons."

"They have infrared vision as well as—"

"Why are you answering?" Zylas cut in. "*Zh'ūltis!*"

"Stop calling me stupid!"

He grabbed the front of my sweater. The three men took urgent steps closer, but Zylas merely yanked me to my feet. As he wobbled unsteadily, I put my arm around his waist, bracing him. He growled at me.

"I don't believe what I'm seeing," the volcanomage rumbled.

"Me neither," Girard muttered.

Darius nodded slowly. "This is quite the conundrum, isn't it?"

This man was a guild master. He had influence and authority in the mythic community, and I had no idea what to do now that he and his two powerful teammates knew my secret. Not only was I loath to kill anyone else, let alone the men who'd saved us, but I wasn't sure Zylas could win against them. Not in his current condition.

The GM studied me for a long minute, then sighed heavily. His hands closed around the hilts of his silver daggers.

"I'm sorry, Robin, but your demon is clearly a danger. We have no choice but to exterminate it for the safety of—"

"No!" I leaped in front of Zylas, my arms outspread. "You can't!"

Darius frowned. "Robin—"

"You'll have to kill me too!" I raised my chin defiantly even as my stomach shriveled with despair. "He saved my life. He's not enslaved to me, but he—he's my partner. And I won't—"

Zylas grabbed my sweater and swung me behind him. "Stupid *payilas*. I will protect you."

"You can barely stand straight!" I protested as I ducked around him. He shoved me back again. "I'll—"

"You will what? Yell at them until they die?"

I gritted my teeth. "You're such a jerk."

"*You* are *mailēshta* and *nailis* and *taridis*—"

"Stop insulting me!"

Darius coughed pointedly. I peered around Zylas's arm as the GM rubbed his mouth to erase the expression off his face. "Perhaps exterminating your demon is too hasty a decision."

Girard looked at his superior in alarm. "Darius, the law is clear that—"

"Second rule, my friend. Let's not destroy something before we understand it." He regarded me. "Robin, you said you can explain, and I'd very much like to hear your explanation—but now is not an ideal time. If you agree to meet with me as soon as possible, we'll get you out of here before I call this in."

"All right," I agreed cautiously.

"Excellent. Girard will escort you and your companions to a healer while Alistair and I bring the MPD's attention to the large number of Red Rum casualties."

"How did you know about the Red Rum …" My forehead scrunched. "Actually, how did you know to be here at all?"

He smiled and tapped his nose. "Our first encounter on Halloween, and that misbehaving sorcerer, set us on the hunt. It was abundantly clear that something larger than a single loose demon was developing—and I think your explanation will fill in the final pieces of the puzzle."

As Girard leaned over Amalia, I murmured to Zylas, "You should return to the infernus for now." *And recover your strength in case we need it later.*

He heard my silent warning. With a glower toward the Crow and Hammer mythics, he dissolved into red light and swept into the infernus. I sagged in relief.

Darius stepped to my side, watching as Girard and the volcanomage carried the unconscious siblings to the road.

"By the way, Robin," he murmured. "The expression on your demon's face when you called him your partner was fascinating."

My mouth dropped open.

He smiled. "I'm looking forward to hearing the whole story."

With that, he strode after his teammates. Pulling myself together, I wondered whether trusting this man was the right call—or my worst mistake yet.

29

I STARED AT THE FLOOR between my brand-new running shoes. My old ones had been so stained with blood I'd thrown them away. I'd also bought new jeans, a sweater, and a nice coat. Resisting the pink one had been difficult, but in keeping with my new contractor title, I'd purchased a sleek black one instead.

Breathing deeply to control my nerves, I peeked up through my bangs.

Darius, guild master of the Crow and Hammer, leaned back in his chair, the width of his desk between us. He studied me with somber gray eyes, then turned his gaze to the chair beside mine.

Zylas crouched on the seat, arms braced on his knees, chin resting on one hand as he stared back at the GM. The demon's tail hung off the chair, its barbed end swishing back and forth. The office's fluorescent lights washed out his reddish-toffee skin, giving him a bronzy-amber tone instead. His tangled black hair teased his crimson eyes, and small horns poked through the locks.

If his unusual guests had thrown Darius off balance, he didn't show it as he pondered the story I'd delivered—most of it a jumbled, emotional mess.

I'd told him *almost* everything. How I'd moved in with my uncle to get my inheritance, how I'd discovered his illegal summoning activities, and how I'd ended up contracted with Zylas. How I'd filed forged paperwork and joined the Grand Grimoire to hide, only for the GM to sell me out to Red Rum. I'd glossed over Amalia's and Travis's roles as apprentice summoners, but I didn't think Darius was buying my suggestion that Amalia knew nothing of her father's illegal activities.

"Well, Robin," he finally said, "you've certainly had an adventure to rival all others."

Couldn't disagree there. I nudged my glasses up my nose.

He laced his fingers together, elbows propped on the desktop. "You've broken some of the strictest MPD laws, but by their very nature, laws don't take individual circumstances into account."

"If you're suggesting my actions were lawfully wrong but morally right," I mumbled, "I disagree. I put people in danger. A lot of mythics died because of me."

"They died as a result of their own actions," Darius corrected sharply. "If you knowingly walk in front of an oncoming car, whose fault is it when the vehicle hits you? Those rogues were fully aware of what they were doing."

I hunched my shoulders. "But Todd from the Grand Grimoire—"

"Intended to kidnap you," Darius interrupted. "I'm certain he knew that whatever his GM planned, it was nefarious. Like the Red Rum rogues, he knew he was stepping into danger's path—or rather, your demon's path."

He appraised Zylas, then refocused on me. "Instead of putting others in danger, you risked your life to kill the unbound demon. I'm confident in your moral integrity. Your demon, however ..."

Zylas snapped his tail in annoyance.

"The MPD," Darius continued after a beat, "with a little encouragement, has determined the Red Rum squad found dead at the pier was behind the unbound demon. Agents have posted a bounty for information on the men's deaths, but for better or worse, the case can be considered closed.

"Your involvement, Robin, has gone unnoticed. The only ones who can tie you to Red Rum are your cousin Travis, the Grand Grimoire guild master, and the summoner Claude Mercier. I think your GM will keep silent rather than risk exposing his own transgressions. Travis, you said, has gone into hiding to avoid Red Rum's retribution."

I nodded. As soon as a healer had deemed him fit, Travis had fled the city—though he'd promised to keep in touch and, if he found Uncle Jack, to let Amalia know where their father was hiding. He'd chosen greed over his family once, but nearly losing everything had sparked a change of heart. I hoped it would last.

"That leaves Claude," Darius concluded. "My impression is that he's a lone wolf. Dangerous, but not one who would report you to the MPD."

"Actually," I interjected with hesitant determination, "you forgot someone."

"Who is that?"

I met his eyes. "You."

"Ah." Darius smiled faintly. "I'll be frank, Robin. I don't believe you or Zylas deserve execution—not for anything you've done yet. However, knowing the nature of your contract, I can't disregard my moral responsibility. Allowing you to disappear, and potentially wreak the havoc and destruction only an unbound demon can inflict, would be unconscionably irresponsible."

I shifted nervously in my chair. "So, if you aren't turning us in but can't ignore us, what do you plan to do?"

"My first inclination is to induct you into my guild. You can't stay at the Grand Grimoire, and any other Demonica-licensed guild presents its own dangers. Here, I can keep watch over you two."

Zylas hissed at the last part.

"However"—Darius's face hardened—"I'm also responsible for the safety of my guild."

And Zylas was dangerous. Powerful, unpredictable, and uncontrollable.

My shoulders wilted. "I understand. I don't want to put your guild members in danger either."

"Since inducting you isn't an option, the best alternative would be—"

"*Na?*" Zylas cut in, his husky voice sharp with annoyance. "Why are you not asking me?"

Darius started as though he'd forgotten Zylas was an equal participant in the conversation—probably because the demon hadn't spoken until now.

"Asking you what?" the GM inquired politely.

"*Are you dangerous? Will you kill my guild members?*" His imitation of Darius's accent and inflection was so good I did a double take. Zylas planted his hands on the seat of his chair and leaned forward. "Or do you think I am a stupid beast and cannot answer?"

Darius blinked in renewed surprise. "My apologies, Zylas. However, I don't see how I can trust your answers."

"Because you did not ask."

The GM placed his hands on the desktop. "All right. Are you dangerous?"

Zylas flashed his canines. "Yes."

"Will you kill my guild members?"

"Yes."

As silence settled over the office, I put a hand over my eyes and suppressed an embarrassed groan.

"Enlightening," Darius commented dryly.

"*Ch.* You are as stupid as the rest."

This time, I didn't hold back my groan. "Zylas, would you just—"

"Ask me now: Will I kill Robin's allies?"

Behind my hand, my eyes flew open. Zylas hadn't used my name since I'd told it to him.

Darius was quiet for a moment. "Will you kill Robin's allies?"

"No."

"Why not?"

"Because she needs them." As Zylas spoke, I peeked over my hand. He gazed steadily at Darius. "If your guild members are her allies, I will not harm them. If they betray her, like the last ones, I will kill them."

Studying the demon, Darius sat back. "I see. And I have your word on that? Your promise?"

His mouth twisted with distaste. "I will not promise you anything, *hh'ainun*."

"Then—"

Zylas spun on his chair to face me. "*Payilas*. I will not harm your allies."

I resisted an unexpected sting of tears. "Thank you, Zylas."

"If you were not so weak, you would not need any allies but me."

My sappy gratitude evaporated. "Every time you say something nice, you ruin it."

"We talked about *nice*."

"And I told you being nice has benefits, but you're too stubborn to—"

Darius cleared his throat. "In lieu of a promise to me, I'll accept his promise to you, but your abnormal contract must remain a secret, even here, Robin. I won't implicate my entire guild in a coverup. If you're discovered, I will have to turn you in."

That had been a risk all along, and in his place, I would do the same. "I understand. Zylas is good at pretending to be properly contracted—"

"Enslaved," the demon corrected.

"—as long as he can keep his mouth shut."

"Do you accept my offer, then, Robin? And … you as well, Zylas?"

"We accept." I shot Zylas a glare before he could speak. "Just be quiet for once."

"Very well," Darius said. "There are more details to arrange, but for now, let's adjourn this meeting. I'll have my AGM start your paperwork. If all goes well, we can formally induct you within a week."

I nodded. "Thank you, Darius. This is … we really appreciate it."

Zylas growled at the "we." I ignored him.

Darius smiled and my anxieties quieted as a feeling of safety spread through me. He was taking a big risk—and saving my life. Without him, without this guild, I had no idea what I would do.

"Welcome to the Crow and Hammer, Robin."

I tried to smile and my lips quivered with emotion. A true welcome. A safe haven. If I didn't screw it up, this guild could be the sanctuary I needed. I wouldn't let Darius down.

With that in mind, I thanked him again, bid him farewell, and hauled Zylas out of the office and into a larger work area filled with three unmanned desks.

"Zylas, we have to do this right," I whispered ferociously. "This guild will keep me safe, and if I'm safe, I can focus on researching a way to get you home."

The demon speared me with a disparaging look. "I *know* that, *payilas*. Why do you think I convinced him to accept you?"

I hadn't explained to Zylas how important it was to win Darius's approval—though in retrospect, I really should have. Zylas was disconcertingly observant; he could figure out far more than I ever anticipated without needing any explanation.

"Thank you," I mumbled, "for convincing him."

I could feel the demon's attention on me as I stared at the floor.

"Find me a way home, *payilas*."

"I will. I promise." With a deep breath, I pushed my shoulders back. "You'll have to pretend to be enslaved when you're outside the infernus. No more talking."

"I know," he said, annoyed. "You will have to be smart when I am not with you—if you can."

A scowl pulled at my mouth. "I can handle it. And Zylas, if someone does find out this time, don't kill them immediately. Darius knows about you now, so you can't go around murdering people."

He glanced thoughtfully at the closed office door. "You did not tell him about the grimoire."

Though I'd explained almost everything to Darius, I hadn't told him about my mother's grimoire or Claude's insinuation that Zylas was special compared to other demons.

"No one can know about it," I whispered. "It's too valuable and too dangerous. As soon as we're set up with this guild, we'll find Uncle Jack and make him give up the grimoire."

Zylas grinned viciously.

"You can't kill him," I added.

His grin faltered into a growl. "Why not?"

"Because he's my uncle!" I paused. "You can scare him, though. I think I'd like to see that."

Zylas laughed huskily. "Closer, *payilas*."

"Closer to what?"

"To not being a weak *hh'ainun*."

Scowl returning, I marched to the stairs that would take me down two stories and out of the guild. As Zylas's laugh followed my retreat, red light flared. Streaks of power swirled around me as he returned to the infernus.

I WIPED MY HANDS on my apron, let out a weary breath, and picked up the platter. Balancing it carefully, I set it on the counter.

Zylas, perched on the stool across from me, stared at the dish.

"My best recipes," I told him, gesturing at its contents. "Chocolate-dipped toffee butter cookies, salted caramel pretzel pecan cookies, red velvet and white chocolate cookies, raspberry almond shortbread cookies, and my personal favorite, marshmallow-stuffed s'more cookies."

He blinked slowly at the heaps of fresh-from-the-oven deliciousness. Behind me, the tiny apartment kitchen was a disaster of batter-coated dishes. Flour dusted my apron and a chocolate smear had dried on my arm.

Amalia and I had moved into the small two-bedroom apartment yesterday, and my first act as a renter had been to buy all the baking ingredients I needed, plus an entire bakery's worth of bowls, trays, utensils, and measuring cups. Our cramped kitchen could barely hold it all.

"Don't you want to try them?" I asked Zylas, uncertain why he was just sitting there. "This is part of our contract. You don't need to trade for them."

"This is … a lot," he muttered. "Why did you make so much?"

"Because you've been protecting me this whole time, and I wasn't holding up my end of the deal. It wasn't fair." I twisted my hands. "I also wasn't sure what you'd like."

Head canting, he picked up a shortbread cookie, its center packed with sugary raspberry filling and the top drizzled with sweet vanilla icing. He lifted it to his mouth, nostrils flaring to take in the aroma, then bit into it.

I waited hopefully. Squinting at me, he held it in his mouth—then swallowed it whole.

"*Chew*," I told him in exasperation.

"*Ch.*" He shoved the rest in his mouth, then picked up a s'more cookie with a crumbly chocolate-and-graham topping. He chomped it in half and gooey marshmallow stretched between the cookie and his teeth. He mashed the whole thing in his mouth.

"Do you like them?" I asked anxiously.

He selected a red velvet cookie. Ate it. Said nothing.

"You were so quick to tell me my blood tasted gross, but you can't come up with a single observation about my baking?"

Smirking, he ate a fourth cookie without comment.

"You're infuriating."

His tail swished. He sampled the final cookie option, then licked a smear of sticky caramel off his finger. Grumbling under my breath, I turned to the sink heaped with dirty dishes.

"In my world," he said unexpectedly, "there is a type of … tree."

I faced him again, my brow furrowed in puzzlement.

"On the tree, it grows small …" He cupped his hands as though holding something. "… small fruits. The outside is poisonous, deadly, but inside is juicy and sweet. We fight over these trees. I have killed to take the fruit when it is ripe."

He picked up another s'more cookie. "These are better."

My heart swelled, but I waited warily. Whenever he said something nice, he always ruined it.

Shoving the cookie in his mouth, he crunched it twice between his teeth, swallowed, then chose a pretzel cookie and bit it in half. No further comments. No insults or disparaging smirks. I quashed my wobbly smile and hurriedly started washing the dishes, afraid if I thanked him, he'd say something mean and ruin the moment.

He thought my cookies were better than a fruit he'd killed to eat.

My hands, submerged in soapy water, paused. I'd have to make sure no one ever tried to take food from him. It sounded dangerous.

While I washed dishes, he devoured every last cookie, then wandered into the empty living room. A blanket was folded on the floor where I'd been reading earlier. Zylas stared around in a dazed sort of way, then sank down on the blanket.

Hmm. That might have been too much sugar for him.

Grinning goofily, I continued cleaning, periodically glancing over at the demon rapidly slipping into a sugar coma. He liked my cookies. I didn't know why that revelation had sent me into a state of complete elation. Maybe it was because I hadn't been able to share my passion for baking with anyone since my parents had died.

Or maybe it was because I'd gotten another glimpse of the complex being hidden beneath Zylas's demonic exterior. There was still so much to uncover—so much I didn't understand and wanted to learn. The workings of his agile mind were a mystery. His wants, his needs, were an unknown. He revealed so little.

He wasn't safe and never would be. I hadn't tamed him—I doubted that was possible—but this strange trust we had stumbled into was far better. We were allies. Partners in this battle of survival.

Lost in thought, I finished cleaning, then showered, dressed, and did my hair as best I could with no straightening iron. I'd have to visit my storage unit and stock the apartment with household supplies.

Zylas catnapped as the evening grew later. Half reading a book, I checked my phone every twenty minutes. Finally, at almost ten, the door opened. Amalia breezed in, her arms loaded with shopping bags.

"You're late!" I exclaimed, leaping off my stool. "I sent you a dozen texts!"

"Sorry," she replied carelessly. "The cab took forever to pick me up."

"We were supposed to be there three hours ago."

"It's a party, Robin. You're supposed to be late to parties." She unloaded her bags on the counter. "I lost all my clothes when the demon burned my house down. I needed a new wardrobe."

"This isn't *just* a party," I complained, wringing my hands. "Darius wants to introduce us to the guild."

"Keep your panties on. I'll get ready."

I paced as she bustled around her bedroom, spending a ridiculous forty-five minutes on her hair and makeup. Finally, I ushered Zylas into the infernus, pulled on my jacket, and all but shoved Amalia out the door.

"We're so late," I fretted as we exited the drab apartment building. It was a dump, but it was cheap, close to the Crow and Hammer, and had immediate availability. We'd been able to move out of our horrible motel room the same day.

Maybe the place was too cheap, though. Along with completing my and Amalia's guild transfer paperwork in record time, Darius had somehow convinced the Grand Grimoire GM to hand over my portion of the bounty for killing Tahēsh. I was reasonably flush, but without knowing how long I'd be surviving off the bonus, I was keeping my spending low.

Tomorrow, I'd begin the search for Uncle Jack—and when I found him, I'd walk away with every penny and every page of my rightful inheritance. First, I needed to survive *this* hurdle—officially joining the Crow and Hammer. During a *party*.

Social interaction. Public spotlight. A thousand opportunities to embarrass myself. At least Zylas had agreed to stay in the infernus unless I called him. One less anxiety to add to the pile.

"Calm down, Robin." Amalia rolled her dark-lined eyes, the chilly November air frosting white with her words. "It'll be fine."

"But meeting the whole guild … what if they all laugh at me like the Grand Grimoire?"

"Considering it's after eleven, it won't be the whole guild. I wouldn't be surprised if the crowd has thinned out." She shrugged. "Besides, a belated Halloween party? What kind of dork guild is this?"

"Darius said their original party was canceled because of the demon hunt," I told her. "And don't be like that. He was extremely generous in offering you a spot at the guild too."

"I don't trust him. He must have an ulterior motive. Otherwise, why would he let you into his guild knowing your demon is out of control?"

I didn't let her pessimism dampen my hope that the Crow and Hammer would be everything the Grand Grimoire hadn't been. "Zylas has been behaving himself really well."

"Yeah, but for how long?" She pointed. "Is that the place?"

Across the street, a square building with a brick façade rose three stories, its dark front door hiding in the shadows of a recessed entrance. We crossed the quiet road and stopped in the alcove. Painted on the old wooden door was a crow, wings flared aggressively, perched on a war hammer.

My nerves ratcheted at the faint music leaking through the door. "Amalia …"

"Yeah?"

"Thanks for sticking with me."

She grimaced at the door, struggling internally with something. "Thanks for saving me."

"Huh?"

"When Red Rum had us. You and that speedy demon of yours could've run for it, but you saved me instead. You two came right for me when you burst out of that shipping container." She blinked at the ground, avoiding my eyes. "My own dad ditched me to protect himself and my lousy stepbrother straight up betrayed me. But even though I've been a bitch to you, you still saved me."

Her gray eyes met mine. "I think I'd rather stick with you than go back to those worthless cowards."

An amazed smile spread across my face, and she returned it.

"Though," she added, "Zylas makes me damn nervous. Have you figured it out yet?"

"Figured what out?"

"How he's interpreting the protection clause of your contract."

I lowered my voice to a whisper. "We already know that. Protecting me means he can't hurt me or put me in danger, which is why he mostly does what I ask."

She'd started shaking her head before I'd finished. "Robin, didn't you notice?"

"Notice what?"

"When Red Rum was forcing you to give up your contract," she said, "Zylas caused them to cut your throat. If the contract prevented him from endangering you, he wouldn't have been able to move while that knife was anywhere near your neck."

"Wait … what?" I suddenly felt dizzy. "I don't understand."

"It means we have no idea what he can and can't do under the contract." Her stare pierced me warningly. "But you need to figure it out."

I was still gaping at her when she knocked on the guild door.

Wild questions spun through my mind and I almost missed the door opening, but the shocking sight of Darius with a long beard derailed me. As he invited us in, I realized he was in costume, along with the dozen or more people gathering around the entrance. A Halloween party. Were Amalia and I supposed to be in costume too?

The thought scarcely registered, my mind consumed with bigger worries than whether I was dressed correctly.

Zylas had put me in danger. Did that mean the contract wasn't stopping him from letting harm befall me? No coercive magic was forcing him to behave like an enslaved demon, to obey me, to promise not to harm my allies?

Girard, the volcanomage Alistair, and a woman in a scarecrow costume—the assistant guild master, I remembered—were welcoming me and Amalia to the guild. I barely heard them.

Was Zylas choosing to do all those things of his own free will? How did the contract bind us, then?

Darius faced the gathered mythics. He was speaking to the small crowd.

Where was the line between contract and choice?

Gesturing to Amalia, Darius proudly introduced her as an apprentice sorceress.

Why would Zylas go to such lengths to keep me safe from *all* danger if the contract wasn't forcing him?

Darius reached around Amalia.

Why?

His hand closed on my shoulder and he pulled me to the front. All eyes fixed on me and I froze as a surprised murmur rippled through the assembled guild members.

"And this," Darius announced, "is Robin Page, our very first demon contractor."

Gasps whispered through the mythics. Quaking where I stood, I forced myself to look up into the shocked faces of my new guild mates, and my gaze caught on a pair of wide hazel eyes. The redhaired woman stared at me, her lips parted in what might have been horror.

I recognized her.

Three handsome men surrounded the woman, and I recognized them too—one with copper hair and blue eyes, one with black hair and dark eyes, and a third with curly brown hair and a bold scar that cut down the left side of his face.

Those four were the mysterious bystanders who'd witnessed Zylas's defeat of Tahēsh. The ones who'd fled the scene immediately afterward, racing away in a red sports car. The ones who Zylas had said carried the scent of a third demon—the unknown, unseen, powerful demon that had wounded Tahēsh when Zylas couldn't land a single blow.

I stared at the four mythics, and they stared back at me.

This guild had far more secrets than I'd realized, and keeping my own safe and hidden had just gotten perilously complicated.

ROBIN'S STORY CONTINUES IN

SLAYING MONSTERS FOR THE FEEBLE

THE GUILD CODEX: DEMONIZED / TWO

I'm bound to a demon.

For my entire life, I avoided magic at all costs. Now, I'm responsible for a demon who wields magic more powerful than the toughest mage or sorcerer.

Demons are evil.

That's what my textbooks say. That's what I see. He's ruthless, he's temperamental, he's cold. But he protects me without fail. I wonder if he's hiding a heart behind his hostility.

My demon is a monster.

Whether he's heartless or not, my contract with him is illegal and beyond dangerous. Together, we must find a way to return him to his own world before anyone discovers our secret. If that wasn't bad enough, I've come to realize something else:

My demon isn't the only monster I should be worried about.

——— KEEP READING FOR THE FIRST CHAPTER ———

SLAYING MONSTERS FOR THE FEEBLE

I

I WAS IN HEAVEN.

The musty scent of paper and old leather filled my nose, and my fingers tingled with the urge to touch the embossed spines surrounding me. I ambled between the tall bookshelves, my gaze caressing the tomes. Giving in, I slid my fingertips across a set of encyclopedias.

Not just any encyclopedias. The complete *Encyclopaedia Alchemia*—sixteen thick leather spines detailing every alchemic ingredient known to mythics.

Elation bubbled through me and I allowed myself one happy bounce before focusing. As much as I wanted to peek inside *One Hundred Transmutations for Everyday Life* or slip *Defensive Alchemy: An Apprentice's Compendium* off its shelf, I wasn't here to sate my endless curiosity. I was on a mission. Leaving the alchemy section, I checked the signs hanging above the entrance to each aisle.

I walked past *Arcana – Language Studies*, *Arcana – Spells & Casting*, *Arcana – Artifacts & Artifact Engineering*, and *Arcana – History*. That last section occupied three aisles on its own.

Elementaria came next. I skipped over Psychica, then turned down a Spiritalis aisle. I couldn't help but pause to read a few titles, including *A Young Witch's Guide to Familiars*, *Power Corrupts: A Case Study of Darkfae Subversion*, and *Is Druidry an Aberration? A Dissertation by the North American Partnership of Covens*. I shook my head at the third one. The fervent loathing between witches and druids was legendary among mythics.

I emerged into another corridor, the butt ends of the shelving units marching on either side like wooden soldiers. Deeper into the library, I found the sign I was looking for: Demonica.

Was it my imagination, or did a cool shadow fall across me when I stepped into the aisle?

I squinted back the way I'd come. Ah, a privacy wall around a study area blocked the windows at the library's front end. I *had* walked into shadow. Had the librarians deliberately picked this dim corner for the section on hellish fiends and soul-binding contracts?

Nudging my glasses up my nose, I skimmed titles. The first shelf held a row of identical, and familiar, copies of *Legal Demonica: The Summoner's Handbook*. Useful, but not what I needed. I continued scanning. *Contractor Control – Advanced Demon Wielding*, *The Ultimate Weapon: Demonica Guilds in Modern Society*, *A History of Summoning*, *The Casual Contractor's Guide to Self-Defense*.

A book for casual contractors? What person would *casually* give up their soul to a demon? I slid it off the shelf and examined the glossy, modern cover with bold red typography and a cartoon demon on the front. Eyebrows climbing higher, I flipped the cover open and read the introduction. As promised, it was a how-to book for contractors who wanted to learn the bare basics and nothing more.

I turned the page. Chapter One, "Getting Started." Large, jaunty text with colorful headings in a sans serif font filled the page beside another cartoon demon, this one making a ghoulish "boo" face.

Congratulations! You're a contractor!

You now belong to the small community of mythics who command demons. Never fear for your safety again. Never take second place to a flashy mage or cocky combat sorcerer. You're a member of the most powerful class now!

But first, you need to learn the basics of controlling your demon.

Wondering where to start? Let's begin with *calling out your demon*.

All contractors have an "infernus"—the artifact that holds your demon's power. Don't lose it! Without it, you can't control your demon. Wear it around your neck on a chain, keep it in your pocket or purse, or leave it in an easy-to-access spot at home. The farther the infernus is from you, the weaker the connection to your demon.

I blinked bemusedly. The way this book was written, you'd think literally anyone could pick up an infernus at the local Demon Mart. I didn't know how much demon contracts cost, but I was pretty sure they *started* at six figures. Most people didn't drop that kind of cash, then learn control techniques from a gimmicky book.

Now let's practice the first step in wielding your demon. There are only two magical command words tied to your infernus, and you'll need to memorize both.

RISE calls your demon out of the infernus
Command: **Δαῖμον, ἀναστῆθι**
Daimon, anastethi! (DHEH-mon, ah-nah-STEE-thee)

REST returns your demon to the infernus
Command: **Δαῖμον, ἡσύχαζε**
Daimon, hesychaze! (DHEH-mon, ee-SEE-cha-zeh)

Practice saying both commands. When you're ready, hold your infernus and concentrate on where you want your demon to manifest—not too close to you! Now speak the *Rise* command. Did your demon appear? Perfect!

Remember, *focus is important*. Repeat the *Rise* and *Rest* commands as needed. Once you're comfortable with the process, you can transition to thinking the commands silently.

(Commands not working? Turn to pg. 12 for trouble-shooting help.)

I snorted at the thought of a "troubleshooting" page, imagining their suggestions. *Demon won't boot properly? Try turning your infernus off and on again.*

Under normal circumstances, a contractor controlled their demon like a puppet, manipulating its every movement through a telepathic connection. I didn't have to worry about that. In fact, I had zero control over my demon.

Which, all in all, was a terrifying problem to have.

I tapped the page. "'There are only two magical command words tied to your infernus.' Hmm."

Command words tied *to the infernus*. That could mean they were built into the contract *or* built into the magic of the infernus. Since I didn't have a real contract, I suspected the commands wouldn't work, but only one way to know for sure.

Balancing the book on one hand, I tugged my infernus from under my jacket and tilted it toward the light, the chain jingling. I examined the palm-sized silver pendant. Perfectly round, flat, and thin, with a spiky emblem etched in the center. Arcane runes marked the outer edge.

Focusing on the empty aisle a yard away, I muttered dubiously, "*Daimon, anastethi.*"

Red light flared across the infernus and I almost dropped it. Arcing out of the pendant, the bright blaze hit the dusty tiles and pooled upward, as though filling an invisible mold. At almost six feet, the light solidified into the familiar shape of my demon.

My extremely displeased demon.

Crimson eyes stared down at me, their eerie glow obscuring dark pupils that had contracted to slits against the overhead fluorescent lights. Four small horns, two above each temple, hid in his tangled black hair, and a mixture of dark fabric, sturdy leather, and gleaming metal armor partially covered smooth skin the color of toffee with a burgundy undertone.

His dusky lips pulled back from his teeth, revealing pointed canines. "What did you do, *payilas?*"

Demons inspired panic in everyone and I was no exception—but my sharp alarm was for a different reason. I frantically checked if anyone had noticed that flare of light.

When no one started screaming about the demon in the library, I glanced from the book to Zylas. I had … I had called him out of the infernus?

"*Payilas*," he growled.

"Um." I hesitantly lifted the book. "I found the commands for the infernus?"

Those lava-like eyes narrowed, then swept away from me to take in our surroundings. His nostrils flared with a silent inhalation and his nose wrinkled in distaste.

"What is this place?" he asked, an alien accent swirling through his husky voice.

"It's a library … part of the Arcana Historia guild. Which, uh, means you should go back into the infernus before someone sees you."

His long, thin tail swished, the two curved barbs on the end just missing a shelf of invaluable texts. He canted his head as though listening.

"There is no one close." He waved a hand around us. "What you need, is it here?"

"I don't know. I only just started looking. Will you get back in the infernus now?"

His upper lip curled, flashing his canines again.

Nerves tightened my stomach. My demon was standing in the middle of a mythic library. If anyone saw him, at best, I would get kicked out. At worst, I would be discovered as an illegal contractor and put to death.

Time to test the "rest" command. I concentrated on my infernus. *Daimon, hechaze!*

Nothing happened. Crap. Was I messing up the Ancient Greek? I was better at Latin. I looked down at the open book.

It vanished from my grasp. Zylas held the book up as though debating whether to burn it to ash on the spot. Turning, he stretched onto his toes, reached for the highest shelf, and shoved the book into the back.

He dropped onto his heels and faced me. Barely topping five feet, I had no chance of reaching the book without a ladder. Which he knew. Jaw clenched, I turned my back on him and glowered at the nearest shelf. What was that command? *Hecheze … hesachaze … hesychaza …*

Warm breath brushed across the top of my head, stirring my hair.

I shot a glare over my shoulder at Zylas, who was standing obnoxiously close. "Back up. I can't concentrate."

"Concentrate on what? You are not doing anything."

I gritted my teeth. The only thing worse than a disobedient demon was a *grumpy* disobedient demon.

"You have not done anything for *weeks*," he complained. "Days and days of nothing but sleep and lounge and sleep—"

"I wasn't sleeping because I'm lazy," I snapped. "I was sick. I had the flu."

"You promised to search for a way I can return home."

"And I am. Right now. Or I would be if you'd stop bothering me." I grabbed a book at random. "The more you distract me, the longer this will take."

He finally stepped back, taking the scent of hickory and leather with him, and drifted away in moody silence. I unclenched my jaw, resisting the urge to order him back into the infernus. The harder I pushed, the more he would resist.

I briefly closed my eyes. If I'd learned anything in the five weeks since we'd been bound together in a contract, it was that

Zylas was infuriatingly stubborn. And deliberately contrary. Defiant. Ornery. Contentious to the point of—

"Should I describe *you*, *payilas*?"

His hiss floated back to me and I flushed. Thanks to that telepathic connection that was supposed to allow *me* to control *him*, he could hear my thoughts. Not always—it depended on how forcefully I was thinking them—but often enough that it was completely unfair.

Pretending I hadn't been insulting him in my head, I opened the book and blinked at the title page. *Demon Psychology: Monsters Born or Made?*

Hmm. I flipped the page and scanned the introduction.

The debate of nature versus nurture has dominated discussions on psychology for centuries. Are humans inherently good or is morality a learned behavior?

In the coming pages, we will examine how this concept applies to the preternatural creatures known as demons. Though psychology is, in theory and in practice, applicable only to humans, we now apply our well-practiced diagnostic methods to the demon psyche.

The symptoms most often displayed by demonkind (aggression, violence, lack of empathy, lack of remorse, inability to form emotional bonds, narcissism, manipulativeness) would earn most humans a swift diagnosis of antisocial personality disorder, more commonly known as psychopathy.

However, the question remains: Is demonic violence a product of the demons' mysterious home environment, or, as long believed to be the case, are they born monsters?

I peeked over the top of the book. At the end of the aisle, Zylas was crouched low as he peered around the corner.

Aggressive, violent, manipulative—check, check, and check. Unempathetic, remorseless, selfish—three more checkmarks. My brow wrinkled as I turned the page and skimmed the table of contents to see if there was a nice, neat "Conclusions" chapter I could read. Biting my lip, I glanced up again.

The aisle was empty.

With a horrified gasp, I shoved the book onto the nearest shelf and sprinted to the end of the aisle. It opened into a wider path with tables lined up against the wall. Halfway along, my demon, in all his horned, tailed, leather-and-armor glory, was prowling past the third table.

I dashed to him so fast I smacked into his back and bounced off, almost dislodging my glasses. Grabbing his arm, I hauled him backward—or I tried. I could've been an ant for all the notice he took of my attempt.

"What are you doing?" I whispered in a panic. "Get back in the infernus before someone sees you!"

"Be quiet," he hissed.

I yanked on his elbow. "You need to—get—back—over—*here*."

I gave his arm a final heave and my hands slipped. Lurching back, I bumped hard into a chair, which clattered loudly against the table, then tipped sideways. I caught it and shoved it upright. Its feet banged down on the floor.

"*Dahganul*," he snarled.

I had a moment to be irritated by the new insult—it was most definitely an insult, even if I didn't know what it meant—before I heard the distinct sound of high heels clacking against tiles. I lunged for him as though I could forcefully mash him back into the infernus—except the bright glow of his power would be a beacon for the approaching librarian.

He shot me a withering stare, then dropped into a crouch and slipped between two chairs. He disappeared under the table.

As the authoritative snap of heels grew louder, I lost my head entirely and dove after him. With the chairs jutting under the table and the wall behind it, only a narrow rectangle was free, and Zylas took up most of it. Too late to go back, I squeezed in beside him.

The librarian's steps drew closer, then hesitated a few tables away. I held my breath and waited for her to keep walking.

Eyes gleaming in the shadows beneath the table, Zylas leaned toward me and whispered, "Move."

I shied away from the closeness of his face. "Huh?"

"Move, *payilas*."

"Why? We need to—"

"You're on my tail."

Belatedly, I realized the floor under my butt was uneven, and on my right, I spotted the rest of his tail coiled across the floor. My face heated.

"There's nowhere to move. Can you just wait?" When he glared in answer, I hissed, "This is your fault, you know. Why are you wandering around where anyone could see you?"

"I would not be seen. *You* made noise, not me."

The librarian clacked closer and I bit back my retort. A pair of black pumps and gray dress pants appeared. The woman walked past the table, and her footsteps grew muffled as she continued to the library's farthest corner.

"You are useless," he added ruthlessly. "You walk loud and talk loud and breathe loud—"

"I do not *breathe* loud." I sat forward, getting off his stupid tail, and crawled for the gap between chairs.

He seized the hem of my sweater and yanked. I flopped backward with a gasp and landed in his lap with a muffled thump. He clamped a warm hand over my mouth.

A pair of men's leather shoes appeared, near silent on the tile floor compared to the woman's clicking heels. The man strode past our hiding spot and disappeared into an aisle.

"Useless," Zylas repeated, his warm breath tickling my ear. "Can't you do anything?"

He exhaled against my cheek—then pushed his nose into the spot under my ear. I squealed into his hand and twisted away from his face. His husky laugh was more vibration than sound. He shoved me off his lap, crawled over my legs with more grace than should've been possible, and slipped between the chairs.

Muttering nasty things under my breath, I rushed out after him. As I wobbled to my feet, he was already ghosting down the aisle—not back into the Demonica corner, but toward the front of the library.

"Zylas!" I hurried to his side, quietly this time. "Where are you going?"

He paused, crimson gaze sweeping the aisles as he inhaled. "This way."

"Which way? What are you—"

Feet silent on the floor, he entered a short hall. A door marked with a bathroom sign waited at the end, but Zylas was interested in a door with a *Guild Members Only* plaque on it.

"We're not allowed in there," I told him.

He grasped the handle. White light sparked across it—some kind of spell. A sizzle ran over his knuckles and up his wrist. He narrowed his eyes, then rammed his shoulder into the door.

The frame split and the door swung open, the arcane magic on the handle useless.

Crap, he'd broken the door. How would I explain *that?*

"Zylas, we can't—"

He ignored me and walked in. Why was I not surprised?

The interior was dark, the air heavy with dust. I felt along the wall, found a light switch, and pressed it. Fluorescent bulbs buzzed awake.

Familiarity hit me in the gut. A long table was stacked with books in various states of disassembly. Tools I'd seen my mother use daily lay across the work surface—blades and cutting tools, glue, string, leather presses, pens and ink. A large magnifying glass on an adjustable arm was positioned above the book restorer's current project.

Zylas glided toward the table, paused to inhale, then angled toward the cabinets along the wall. He homed in on the corner one, the metal doors secured with a heavy padlock.

I minced to his side. The lock had no keyhole and its face was marked with a set of runes. "What is it?"

He sniffed the air. "I smell blood."

My stomach performed an adrenaline-fueled flip. "Blood" wasn't even on the list of answers I'd expected.

"Old. Faint." His tail snapped sideways. "The scent of demon blood and magic."

He reached for the padlock but I grabbed his wrist. I didn't doubt he could break it with either pure strength or magic, but that was the problem.

"Don't," I whispered urgently.

His eyes glowed, his jaw set. I knew that look—the *"I'm about to do the opposite of what you want just to prove I can"* look.

If he broke that lock, I'd be in so much trouble.

I pulled on his arm, straining to bring up that page of commands in my mind's eye. His mouth twisted and he again reached for the padlock, dragging me across the floor.

With a shot of panic, the Ancient Greek popped back into my head. "*Daimon, hesychaze!*"

Crimson power lit up his extremities. I caught a glimpse of his glowing eyes, wide and furious, just before his body dissolved into light and streaked back into my infernus. I shoved the pendant back under my jacket, breathing faster than the situation warranted.

I'd forced Zylas into the infernus. It was the first time I'd ever forced him to do *anything*.

Heels clacked loudly in the hallway outside. I spun around, my elation shriveling into dread. The footsteps snapped loudly, then the librarian stepped into the open doorway, shock and anger stamped across her face.

Damn that demon.

www.guildcodex.ca

ABOUT THE AUTHOR

Annette Marie is the author of YA urban fantasy series *Steel & Stone*, its prequel trilogy *Spell Weaver*, romantic fantasy trilogy *Red Winter*, and sassy urban fantasy series *The Guild Codex*.

Her first love is fantasy, but fast-paced adventures, bold heroines, and tantalizing forbidden romances are her guilty pleasures. She proudly admits she has a thing for dragons, and her editor has politely inquired as to whether she intends to include them in every book.

Annette lives in the frozen winter wasteland of Alberta, Canada (okay, it's not quite that bad) and shares her life with her husband and their furry minion of darkness—sorry, cat—Caesar. When not writing, she can be found elbow-deep in one art project or another while blissfully ignoring all adult responsibilities.

www.annettemarie.ca

SPECIAL THANKS

My thanks to Erich Merkel for sharing your exceptional expertise in Latin and Ancient Greek. Any errors are mine.

THE
GUILD CODEX
DEMONIZED

Demons are evil. That's what Robin's textbooks say, but when it comes to Zylas, nothing is simple. He's cold, ruthless, and temperamental … but is he heartless? Robin needs to figure it out, or they'll destroy each other before the real monsters get a chance.

THE
GUILD CODEX
SPELLBOUND

Meet Tori. She's feisty. She's broke. She has a bit of an issue with running her mouth off. And she just landed a job at the local magic guild. Problem is, she's also 100% human. Oops.

Welcome to the Crow and Hammer.

DISCOVER MORE BOOKS AT
www.guildcodex.ca

The only thing more dangerous than the denizens of the Underworld ... is stealing from them.

As a daemon living in exile among humans, Clio has picked up some unique skills. But pilfering magic from the Underworld's deadliest spell weavers? Not so much. Unfortunately, that's exactly what she has to do to earn a ticket home.

A destiny written by the gods. A fate forged by lies.

If Emi is sure of anything, it's that *kami*—the gods—are good, and *yokai*—the earth spirits—are evil. But when she saves the life of a fox shapeshifter, the truths of her world start to crumble. And the treachery of the gods runs deep.

This stunning trilogy features 30 full-page illustrations.

Made in the USA
Coppell, TX
23 March 2020

17537562R00210